Collector's Library

OLIVER TWIST

OLIVER TWIST

Charles Dickens

With Illustrations by
GEORGE CRUICKSHANK
and an Afterword by
SAM GILPIN

BARNES & NOBLE BOOKS
NEW YORK

© CRW 2003
Text and Afterword copyright ©
CRW Publishing Limited 2003

M 10 9 8 7 6 5 4

ISBN 0 7607 4866 7

Typeset in Great Britain by Antony Gray
Printed and bound in China by Imago

Contents

Illustrations

9

OLIVER TWIST

CHAPTER I

Treats of the place where Oliver Twist was born,
and of the circumstances attending his birth

Among other public buildings in a certain town,
which for many reasons it will be prudent to refrain
from mentioning, and to which I will assign no
fictitious name, there is one anciently common to
most towns, great or small: to wit, a workhouse; and in
this workhouse was born; on a day and date which I
need not trouble myself to repeat, inasmuch as it can
be of no possible consequence to the reader, in this
stage of the business at all events; the item of mortality
whose name is prefixed to the head of this chapter.

For a long time after it was ushered into this world
of sorrow and trouble, by the parish surgeon, it
remained a matter of considerable doubt whether the
child would survive to bear any name at all; in which
case it is somewhat more than probable that these
memoirs would never have appeared; or, if they had,
that being comprised within a couple of pages, they
would have possessed the inestimable merit of being
the most concise and faithful specimen of biography,
extant in the literature of any age or country.

Although I am not disposed to maintain that the
being born in a workhouse, is in itself the most
fortunate and enviable circumstance that can possibly
befall a human being, I do mean to say that in this
particular instance, it was the best thing for Oliver
Twist that could by possibility have occurred. The fact

is, that there was considerable difficulty in inducing Oliver to take upon himself the office of respiration – a troublesome practice, but one which custom has rendered necessary to our easy existence; and for some time he lay gasping on a little flock mattress, rather unequally poised between this world and the next: the balance being decidedly in favour of the latter. Now, if, during this brief period, Oliver had been surrounded by careful grandmothers, anxious aunts, experienced nurses, and doctors of profound wisdom, he would most inevitably and indubitably have been killed in no time. There being nobody by, however, but a pauper old woman, who was rendered rather misty by an unwonted allowance of beer; and a parish surgeon who did such matters by contract; Oliver and Nature fought out the point between them. The result was, that, after a few struggles, Oliver breathed, sneezed, and proceeded to advertise to the inmates of the workhouse the fact of a new burden having been imposed upon the parish, by setting up as loud a cry as could reasonably have been expected from a male infant who had not been possessed of that very useful appendage, a voice, for a much longer space of time than three minutes and a quarter.

As Oliver gave this first proof of the free and proper action of his lungs, the patchwork coverlet which was carelessly flung over the iron bedstead, rustled; the pale face of a young woman was raised feebly from the pillow; and a faint voice imperfectly articulated the words, 'Let me see the child, and die.'

The surgeon had been sitting with his face turned towards the fire: giving the palms of his hands a warm and a rub alternately. As the young woman spoke, he rose, and advancing to the bed's head, said, with more kindness than might have been expected of him: 'Oh, you must not talk about dying yet.'

'Lor bless her dear heart, no!' interposed the nurse, hastily depositing in her pocket a green glass bottle, the contents of which she had been tasting in a corner with evident satisfaction. 'Lor bless her dear heart, when she has lived as long as I have, sir, and had thirteen children of her own, and all on 'em dead except two, and them in the wurkus with me, she'll know better than to take on in that way, bless her dear heart! Think what it is to be a mother, there's a dear young lamb, do.'

Apparently this consolatory perspective of a mother's prospects failed in producing its due effect. The patient shook her head, and stretched out her hand towards the child.

The surgeon deposited it in her arms. She imprinted her cold white lips passionately on its forehead; passed her hands over her face; gazed wildly round; shuddered; fell back – and died. They chafed her breast, hands, and temples, but the blood had stopped for ever. They talked of hope and comfort. They had been strangers too long.

'It's all over, Mrs Thingummy!' said the surgeon at last.

'Ah, poor dear, so it is!' said the nurse, picking up the cork of the green bottle, which had fallen out on the pillow, as she stooped to take up the child. 'Poor dear!'

'You needn't mind sending up to me, if the child cries, nurse,' said the surgeon, putting on his gloves with great deliberation. 'It's very likely it *will* be troublesome. Give it a little gruel if it is.' He put on his hat, and, pausing by the bedside on his way to the door, added, 'She was a good-looking girl, too; where did she come from?'

'She was brought here last night,' replied the old woman, 'by the overseer's order. She was found lying in the street. She had walked some distance, for her shoes were worn to pieces; but where she came from, or where she was going to, nobody knows.'

The surgeon leaned over the body, and raised the left hand. 'The old story,' he said, shaking his head: 'no wedding-ring, I see. Ah! Good-night!'

The medical gentleman walked away to dinner; and the nurse, having once more applied herself to the green bottle, sat down on a low chair before the fire, and proceeded to dress the infant.

What an excellent example of the power of dress, young Oliver Twist was! Wrapped in the blanket which had hitherto formed his only covering, he might have been the child of a nobleman or a beggar; it would have been hard for the haughtiest stranger to have assigned him his proper station in society. But now that he was enveloped in the old calico robes which had grown yellow in the same service, he was badged and ticketed, and fell into his place at once – a parish child – the orphan of a workhouse – the humble, half-starved drudge – to be cuffed and buffeted through the world – despised by all, and pitied by none.

Oliver cried lustily. If he could have known that he was an orphan, left to the tender mercies of church-wardens and overseers, perhaps he would have cried the louder.

CHAPTER 2

Treats of Oliver Twist's growth, education, and board

For the next eight or ten months, Oliver was the victim of a systematic course of treachery and deception. He was brought up by hand. The hungry and destitute situation of the infant orphan was duly reported by the workhouse authorities to the parish authorities. The parish authorities enquired with dignity of the workhouse authorities, whether there was no female then domiciled in 'the house' who was in a situation to impart to Oliver Twist, the consolation and nourishment of which he stood in need. The workhouse authorities replied with humility, that there was not. Upon this, the parish authorities magnanimously and humanely resolved, that Oliver should be 'farmed,' or, in other words, that he should be despatched to a branch-workhouse some three miles off, where twenty or thirty other juvenile offenders against the poor-laws, rolled about the floor all day, without the inconvenience of too much food or too much clothing, under the parental superintendence of an elderly female, who received the culprits at and for the consideration of sevenpence-halfpenny per small head per week. Sevenpence-halfpenny's worth per week is a good round diet for a child; a great deal may be got for sevenpence-halfpenny, quite enough to overload its stomach, and make it uncomfortable. The elderly female was a woman of wisdom and experience; she knew what was good for children; and she had a very accurate perception of what was good for herself. So, she appropriated the greater part of the weekly stipend to her own use, and consigned the rising parochial generation to even a shorter allowance than was originally provided for them. Thereby finding in the lowest depth a deeper still; and proving herself a very great experimental philosopher.

Everybody knows the story of another experimental philosopher who had a great theory about a horse being able to live without eating, and who demonstrated it so well, that he got his own horse down to a straw a day, and would unquestionably have rendered him a very spirited and rampacious animal on nothing at all, if he had not died, four and twenty hours before he was to have had his first comfortable bait of air. Unfortunately for the experimental philosophy of the female to whose protecting care Oliver Twist was delivered over, a similar result usually attended the operation of *her* system; for at the very moment when a child had contrived to exist upon the smallest possible portion of the weakest possible food, it did perversely happen in eight and a half cases out of ten, either that it sickened from want and cold, or fell into the fire from neglect, or got half smothered by accident; in any one of which cases, the miserable little being was usually summoned into another world, and there gathered to the fathers it had never known in this.

Occasionally, when there was some more than usually interesting inquest upon a parish child who had been overlooked in turning up a bedstead, or inadvertently scalded to death when there happened to be a washing – though the latter accident was very scarce, anything approaching to a washing being of rare occurrence in the farm – the jury would take it into their heads to ask troublesome questions, or the parishioners would rebelliously affix their signatures to a remonstrance. But these impertinences were speedily checked by the evidence of the surgeon, and the testimony of the beadle; the former of whom had always opened the body and found nothing inside (which was very probable indeed), and the latter of whom invariably swore whatever the parish wanted; which was very self-devotional. Besides, the board made periodical pilgrimages to the farm, and always sent the beadle the day before, to say they were going. The children were neat and clean to behold, when *they* went; and what more would the people have!

It cannot be expected that this system of farming would produce any very extraordinary or luxuriant crop. Oliver Twist's ninth birthday found him a pale thin child, somewhat diminutive in stature, and decidedly small in circumference. But nature or inheritance had implanted a good sturdy spirit in Oliver's breast. It had had plenty of room to expand, thanks to the spare diet of the establishment; and perhaps to this circumstance may be attributed his having any ninth birthday at all. Be this as it may, however, it *was* his ninth birthday; and he was keeping it in the coal-cellar with a select party of two other young gentlemen, who, after participating with him in a sound thrashing, had been locked up for atrociously presuming to be hungry, when Mrs Mann, the good lady of the house, was unexpectedly startled by the apparition of Mr Bumble, the beadle, striving to undo the wicket of the garden-gate.

'Goodness gracious! Is that you, Mr Bumble, sir?' said Mrs Mann, thrusting her head out of the window in well-affected ecstasies of joy. 'Susan, take Oliver and them two brats upstairs, and wash 'em directly.) My heart alive! Mr Bumble, how glad I am to see you, sure–ly!'

Now, Mr Bumble was a fat man, and a choleric; so, instead of responding to this open-hearted salutation in a kindred spirit, he gave the little wicket a tremendous shake, and then bestowed upon it a kick which could have emanated from no leg but a beadle's.

'Lor, only think,' said Mrs Mann, running out – for the three boys had been removed by this time – 'only think of that! That I should have forgotten that the gate was bolted on the inside, on account of them dear children! Walk in, sir; walk in, pray, Mr Bumble, do, sir.'

Although this invitation was accompanied with a curtsey that might have softened the heart of a church-warden, it by no means mollified the beadle.

'Do you think this respectful or proper conduct, Mrs Mann,' enquired Mr Bumble, grasping his cane, 'to keep the parish officers a-waiting at your garden-gate, when they come here upon porochial business connected with the porochial orphans? Are you aweer, Mrs Mann, that you are, as I may say, a porochial delegate, and a stipendiary?'

'I'm sure, Mr Bumble, that I was only a-telling one or two of the dear children as is so fond of you, that it was you a-coming,' replied Mrs Mann with great humility.

Mr Bumble had a great idea of his oratorical powers and his importance. He had displayed the one, and vindicated the other. He relaxed.

'Well, well, Mrs Mann,' he replied in a calmer tone; 'it may be as you say; it may be. Lead the way in, Mrs Mann, for I come on business, and have something to say.'

Mrs Mann ushered the beadle into a small parlour with a brick floor; placed a seat for him; and officiously deposited his cocked-hat and cane on the table before him. Mr Bumble wiped from his forehead the perspiration which his walk had engendered, glanced complacently at the cocked-hat, and smiled. Yes, he smiled. Beadles are but men: and Mr Bumble smiled.

'Now don't you be offended at what I'm a-going to say,' observed Mrs Mann, with captivating sweetness. 'You've had a long walk, you know, or I wouldn't mention it. Now, will you take a little drop of somethink, Mr Bumble?'

'Not a drop. Not a drop,' said Mr Bumble, waving his right hand in a dignified, but placid manner.

'I think you will,' said Mrs Mann, who had noticed the tone of the refusal, and the gesture that had accompanied it. 'Just a leetle drop, with a little cold water, and a lump of sugar.'

Mr Bumble coughed.

'Now, just a leetle drop,' said Mrs Mann persuasively.

'What is it?' enquired the beadle.

'Why, it's what I'm obliged to keep a little of in the house, to put into the blessed infants' Daffy, when they ain't well, Mr Bumble,' replied Mrs Mann as she opened a corner cupboard, and took down a bottle and glass. 'It's gin. I'll not deceive you, Mr B. It's gin.'

'Do you give the children Daffy, Mrs Mann?' enquired Bumble, following with his eyes the interesting process of mixing.

'Ah, bless 'em, that I do, dear as it is,' replied the nurse. 'I couldn't see 'em suffer before my very eyes, you know, sir.'

'No,' said Mr Bumble approvingly; 'no, you could

not. You are a humane woman, Mrs Mann.' (Here she set down the glass.) 'I shall take an early opportunity of mentioning it to the board, Mrs Mann.' (He drew it towards him.) 'You feel as a mother, Mrs Mann.' (He stirred the gin-and-water.) 'I – I drink your health with cheerfulness, Mrs Mann;' and he swallowed half of it.

'And now about business,' said the beadle, taking out a leathern pocketbook. 'The child that was half-baptised Oliver Twist, is nine year old today.'

'Bless him!' interposed Mrs Mann, inflaming her left eye with the corner of her apron.

'And notwithstanding a offered reward of ten pound, which was afterwards increased to twenty pound. Notwithstanding the most superlative, and, I may say, supernat'ral exertions on the part of this parish,' said Bumble, 'we have never been able to discover who is his father, or what was his mother's settlement, name, or con–dition.'

Mrs Mann raised her hands in astonishment; but added, after a moment's reflection, 'How comes he to have any name at all, then?'

The beadle drew himself up with great pride, and said, 'I inwented it.'

'You, Mr Bumble!'

'I, Mrs Mann. We name our fondlings in alphabetical order. The last was a S – Swubble, I named him. This was a T – Twist, I named *him*. The next one as comes will be Unwin, and the next Vilkins. I have got names ready made to the end of the alphabet, and all the way through it again, when we come to Z.'

'Why, you're quite a literary character, sir!' said Mrs Mann.

'Well, well,' said the beadle, evidently gratified with

the compliment; 'perhaps I may be. Perhaps I may be, Mrs Mann.' He finished the gin-and-water, and added, 'Oliver being now too old to remain here, the board have determined to have him back into the house. I have come out myself to take him there. So let me see him at once.'

'I'll fetch him directly,' said Mrs Mann, leaving the room for that purpose. Oliver, having had by this time as much of the outer coat of dirt which encrusted his face and hands, removed, as could be scrubbed off in one washing, was led into the room by his benevolent protectress.

'Make a bow to the gentleman, Oliver,' said Mrs Mann.

Oliver made a bow, which was divided between the beadle on the chair, and the cocked-hat on the table.

'Will you go along with me, Oliver?' said Mr Bumble, in a majestic voice.

Oliver was about to say that he would go along with anybody with great readiness, when, glancing upward, he caught sight of Mrs Mann, who had got behind the beadle's chair, and was shaking her fist at him with a furious countenance. He took the hint at once, for the fist had been too often impressed upon his body not to be deeply impressed upon his recollection.

'Will *she* go with me?' enquired poor Oliver.

'No, she can't,' replied Mr Bumble. 'But she'll come and see you sometimes.'

This was no very great consolation to the child. Young as he was, however, he had sense enough to make a feint of feeling great regret at going away. It was no very difficult matter for the boy to call tears into his eyes. Hunger and recent ill-usage are great assistants if you want to cry; and Oliver cried very naturally indeed. Mrs Mann gave him a thousand embraces, and, what Oliver wanted a great deal more, a piece of bread and butter, lest he should seem too hungry when he got to the workhouse. With the slice of bread in his hand, and the little brown-cloth parish cap on his head, Oliver was then led away by Mr Bumble from the wretched home where one kind word or look had never lighted the gloom of his infant years. And yet he burst into an agony of childish grief, as the cottage-gate closed after him. Wretched as were the little companions in misery he was leaving behind, they were the only friends he had ever known; and a sense of his loneliness in the great wide world sank into the child's heart for the first time.

Mr Bumble walked on with long strides; little Oliver, firmly grasping his gold-laced cuff, trotted beside him, enquiring at the end of every quarter of a mile whether they were 'nearly there'. To these interrogations Mr Bumble returned very brief and snappish replies; for the temporary blandness which gin-and-water awakens in some bosoms had by this time evaporated; and he was once again a beadle.

Oliver had not been within the walls of the workhouse a quarter of an hour, and had scarcely completed the demolition of a second slice of bread, when Mr Bumble, who had handed him over to the care of an old woman, returned; and, telling him it was a board night, informed him that the board had said he was to appear before it forthwith.

Not having a very clearly defined notion of what a live board was, Oliver was rather astounded by this intelligence, and was not quite certain whether he ought to laugh or cry. He had no time to think about the matter, however; for Mr Bumble gave him a tap on the head, with his cane, to wake him up; and another on the back to make him lively: and bidding him follow, conducted him into a large whitewashed room, where eight or ten fat gentlemen were sitting round a table. At the top of the table, seated in an armchair rather higher than the rest, was a particularly fat gentleman with a very round, red face.

'Bow to the board,' said Bumble. Oliver brushed away two or three tears that were lingering in his eyes; and seeing no board but the table, fortunately bowed to that.

'What's your name, boy?' said the gentleman in the high chair.

Oliver was frightened at the sight of so many gentlemen, which made him tremble: and the beadle gave him another tap behind, which made him cry. These two causes made him answer in a very low and hesitating voice; whereupon a gentleman in a white waistcoat said he was a fool. Which was a capital way of raising his spirits, and putting him quite at his ease.

'Boy,' said the gentleman in the high chair, 'listen to me. You know you're an orphan, I suppose?'

'What's that, sir?' enquired poor Oliver.

'The boy *is* a fool – I thought he was,' said the gentleman in the white waistcoat.

'Hush!' said the gentleman who had spoken first. 'You know you've got no father or mother, and that you were brought up by the parish, don't you?'

'Yes, sir,' replied Oliver, weeping bitterly.

'What are you crying for?' enquired the gentleman in the white waistcoat. And to be sure it was very extraordinary. What *could* the boy be crying for?

'I hope you say your prayers every night,' said another gentleman in a gruff voice: 'and pray for the people who feed you, and take care of you – like a Christian.'

'Yes, sir,' stammered the boy. The gentleman who spoke last was unconsciously right. It would have been *very* like a Christian, and a marvellously good Christian, too, if Oliver had prayed for the people who fed and took care of *him*. But he hadn't, because nobody had taught him.

'Well! You have come here to be educated, and taught a useful trade,' said the red-faced gentleman in the high chair.

'So you'll begin to pick oakum tomorrow morning at six o'clock,' added the surly one in the white waistcoat.

For the combination of both these blessings in the one simple process of picking oakum, Oliver bowed low by the direction of the beadle, and was then hurried away to a large ward: where, on a rough, hard bed, he sobbed himself to sleep. What a noble illustration of the tender laws of England! They let the paupers go to sleep!

Poor Oliver! He little thought, as he lay sleeping in happy unconsciousness of all around him, that the board had that very day arrived at a decision which would exercise the most material influence over all his future fortunes. But they had. And this was it:

The members of this board were very sage, deep, philosophical men; and when they came to turn their attention to the workhouse, they found out at once, what ordinary folks would never have discovered – the poor people liked it! It was a regular place of public entertainment for the poorer classes; a tavern where there was nothing to pay; a public breakfast, dinner, tea, and supper all the year round; a brick and mortar elysium, where it was all play and no work. 'Oho!' said the board, looking very knowing; 'we are the fellows to set this to rights; we'll stop it all, in no time.' So, they established the rule, that all poor people should have the alternative (for they would compel nobody, not they), of being starved by a gradual process in the house, or by a quick one out of it. With this view, they contracted with the waterworks to lay on an unlimited supply of water; and with a corn-factor to supply periodically small quantities of oatmeal; and issued three meals of thin gruel a day, with an onion twice a week, and half a roll on Sundays. They made a great many other wise and humane regulations, having reference to the ladies, which it is not necessary to repeat; kindly undertook to divorce poor married people, in consequence of the great expense of a suit in Doctors' Commons; and, instead of compelling a man to support his family, as they had theretofore done, took his family away from him, and made him a bachelor! There is no saying how many applicants for relief, under these last two heads, might have started up in all classes of society, if it had not been coupled with the workhouse; but the board were long-headed men, and had provided for this difficulty. The relief was inseparable from the workhouse and the gruel; and that frightened people.

For the first six months after Oliver Twist was removed, the system was in full operation. It was rather expensive at first, in consequence of the increase in the undertaker's bill, and the necessity of taking in the clothes of all the paupers, which fluttered loosely on their wasted, shrunken forms, after a week or two's gruel. But the number of workhouse inmates got thin as well as the paupers; and the board were in ecstasies.

The room in which the boys were fed, was a large stone hall, with a copper at one end: out of which the master, dressed in an apron for the purpose, and assisted by one or two women, ladled the gruel at mealtimes. Of this festive composition each boy had one porringer, and no more – except on occasions of great public rejoicing, when he had two ounces and a quarter of bread besides. The bowls never wanted washing. The boys polished them with their spoons till they shone again; and when they had performed this operation (which never took very long, the spoons being nearly as large as the bowls), they would sit staring at the copper, with such eager eyes, as if they could have devoured the very bricks of which it was composed; employing themselves, meanwhile, in sucking their fingers most assiduously, with the view of catching up any stray splashes of gruel that might have been cast thereon. Boys have generally excellent appetites. Oliver Twist and his companions suffered the tortures of slow starvation for three months: at last they got so voracious and wild with hunger, that one boy, who was tall for his age, and hadn't been used to that sort of thing (for his father had kept a small cook-shop), hinted darkly to his companions, that unless he had another basin of gruel *per diem*, he was afraid he might some night happen to eat the boy who slept next him, who happened to be a weakly youth of tender age. He had a wild, hungry eye; and they implicitly believed him. A council was held; lots were cast who should walk up to the master after supper that evening, and ask for more; and it fell to Oliver Twist.

The evening arrived; the boys took their places. The master, in his cook's uniform, stationed himself at the copper; his pauper assistants ranged themselves

Oliver asking for more

behind him; the gruel was served out; and a long grace was said over the short commons. The gruel disappeared; the boys whispered each other, and winked at Oliver; while his next neighbours nudged him. Child as he was, he was desperate with hunger, and reckless with misery. He rose from the table; and advancing to the master, basin and spoon in hand, said: somewhat alarmed at his own temerity: 'Please, sir, I want some more.'

The master was a fat, healthy man: but he turned very pale. He gazed in stupefied astonishment on the small rebel for some seconds, and then clung for support to the copper. The assistants were paralysed with wonder; the boys with fear.

'What!' said the master at length, in a faint voice.

'Please, sir,' replied Oliver, 'I want some more.'

The master aimed a blow at Oliver's head with the ladle; pinioned him in his arms; and shrieked aloud for the beadle.

The board were sitting in solemn conclave, when Mr Bumble rushed into the room in great excitement, and addressing the gentleman in the high chair, said, 'Mr Limbkins, I beg your pardon, sir! Oliver Twist has asked for more!'

There was a general start. Horror was depicted on every countenance.

'For *more!*' said Mr Limbkins. 'Compose yourself, Bumble, and answer me distinctly. Do I understand that he asked for more, after he had eaten the supper allotted by the dietary?'

'He did, sir,' replied Bumble.

'That boy will be hung,' said the gentleman in the white waistcoat. 'I know that boy will be hung.'

Nobody controverted the prophetic gentleman's

opinion. An animated discussion took place. Oliver was ordered into instant confinement; and a bill was next morning pasted on the outside of the gate, offering a reward of five pounds to anybody who would take Oliver Twist off the hands of the parish. In other words, five pounds and Oliver Twist were offered to any man or woman who wanted an apprentice to any trade, business, or calling.

'I never was more convinced of anything in my life,' said the gentleman in the white waistcoat, as he knocked at the gate and read the bill next morning: 'I never was more convinced of anything in my life, than I am that that boy will come to be hung.'

As I purpose to show in the sequel whether the white-waistcoated gentleman was right or not, I should perhaps mar the interest of this narrative (supposing it to possess any at all), if I ventured to hint just yet, whether the life of Oliver Twist had this violent termination or no.

CHAPTER 3

Relates how Oliver Twist was very near getting a place, which would not have been a sinecure

For a week after the commission of the impious and profane offence of asking for more, Oliver remained a close prisoner in the dark and solitary room to which he had been consigned by the wisdom and mercy of the board. It appears, at first sight, not unreasonable to suppose, that, if he had entertained a becoming feeling of respect for the prediction of the gentleman in the white waistcoat, he would have established that sage individual's prophetic character, once and for ever, by tying one end of his pocket-handkerchief to a hook in the wall, and attaching himself to the other. To the performance of this feat, however, there was one obstacle: namely, that pocket-handkerchiefs being decided articles of luxury, had been, for all future times and ages, removed from the noses of paupers by the express order of the board, in council assembled: solemnly given and pronounced under their hands and seals. There was a still greater obstacle in Oliver's youth and childishness. He only cried bitterly all day; and, when the long, dismal night came on, spread his little hands before his eyes to shut out the darkness, and crouching in the corner, tried to sleep: ever and anon waking with a start and tremble, and drawing himself closer and closer to the wall, as if to feel even its cold hard surface were a protection in the gloom and loneliness which surrounded him.

Let it not be supposed by the enemies of 'the system', that, during the period of his solitary incarceration, Oliver was denied the benefit of exercise, the pleasure of society, or the advantages of religious consolation. As for exercise, it was nice cold weather, and he was allowed to perform his ablutions every morning under the pump, in a stone yard, in the presence of Mr Bumble, who prevented his catching cold, and caused a tingling sensation to pervade his frame, by repeated applications of the cane. As for society, he was carried every other day into the hall where the boys dined, and there sociably flogged as a public warning and example. And so far from being denied the advantages of religious consolation, he was kicked into the same apartment every evening at prayer-time, and there permitted to listen to, and console his mind with, a general supplication of the boys, containing a special clause, therein inserted by authority of the board, in which they entreated to be made good, virtuous, contented, and obedient, and to be guarded from the sins and vices of Oliver Twist; whom the supplication distinctly set forth to be under the exclusive patronage and protection of the powers of wickedness, and an article direct from the manufactory of the very Devil himself.

It chanced one morning, while Oliver's affairs were in this auspicious and comfortable state, that Mr Gamfield, chimney-sweep, went his way down the High Street, deeply cogitating in his mind his ways and means of paying certain arrears of rent, for which his landlord had become rather pressing. Mr Gamfield's most sanguine estimate of his finances could not raise them within full five pounds of the desired amount; and, in a species of arithmetical desperation, he was alternately cudgelling his brains and his donkey, when, passing the workhouse, his eyes encountered the bill on the gate.

'Wo—o!' said Mr Gamfield to the donkey.

The donkey was in a state of profound abstraction: wondering, probably, whether he was destined to be regaled with a cabbage-stalk or two when he had disposed of the two sacks of soot with which the little cart was laden; so, without noticing the word of command, he jogged onward.

Mr Gamfield growled a fierce imprecation on the donkey generally, but more particularly on his eyes; and, running after him, bestowed a blow on his head, which would inevitably have beaten in any skull but a donkey's. Then, catching hold of the bridle, he gave his jaw a sharp wrench, by way of gentle reminder that he was not his own master; and by these means turned him round. He then gave him another blow on the head, just to stun him till he came back again. Having completed these arrangements, he walked up to the gate, to read the bill.

The gentleman with the white waistcoat was standing at the gate with his hands behind him, after having delivered himself of some profound sentiments in the boardroom. Having witnessed the little dispute between Mr Gamfield and the donkey, he smiled joyously when that person came up to read the bill, for he saw at once that Mr Gamfield was exactly the sort of master Oliver Twist wanted. Mr Gamfield smiled, too, as he perused the document; for five pounds was just the sum he had been wishing for; and, as to the boy with which it was encumbered, Mr Gamfield, knowing what the dietary of the workhouse was, well knew he would be a nice small pattern, just the very thing for register stoves. So, he spelt the bill through again, from beginning to end; and then, touching his fur cap in token of humility, accosted the gentleman in the white waistcoat.

'This here boy, sir, wot the parish wants to 'prentis,' said Mr Gamfield.

'Ay, my man,' said the gentleman in the white waistcoat, with a condescending smile. 'What of him?'

'If the parish vould like him to learn a right pleasant trade, in a good 'spectable chimbley-sweepin' bisness,' said Mr Gamfield, 'I wants a 'prentis, and I am ready to take him.'

'Walk in,' said the gentleman in the white waistcoat. Mr Gamfield having lingered behind, to give the donkey another blow on the head, and another wrench of the jaw, as a caution not to run away in his absence, followed the gentleman with the white waist-coat into the room where Oliver had first seen him.

'It's a nasty trade,' said Mr Limbkins, when Gamfield had again stated his wish.

'Young boys have been smothered in chimneys before now,' said another gentleman.

'That's a-cause they damped the straw afore they lit it in the chimbley to make 'em come down agin,' said Gamfield; 'that's all smoke, and no blaze; vereas smoke ain't o' no use at all in making a boy come down, for it only sinds him to sleep, and that's wot he likes. Boys is wery obstinit, and wery lazy, gen'lmen, and there's nothink like a good hot blaze to make 'em come down vith a run. It's humane too, gen'lmen, a-cause, even if they've stuck in the chimbley, roasting their feet makes 'em struggle to hextricate theirselves.'

The gentleman in the white waistcoat appeared very much amused by this explanation; but his mirth was speedily checked by a look from Mr Limbkins. The board then proceeded to converse among themselves for a few minutes, but in so low a tone, that the words 'saving of expenditure', 'looked well in the accounts,' 'have a printed report published', were alone audible. These only chanced to be heard, indeed, on account of their being very frequently repeated with great emphasis.

At length the whispering ceased; and the members of the board, having resumed their seats and their solemnity, Mr Limbkins said: 'We have considered your proposition, and we don't approve of it.'

'Not at all,' said the gentleman in the white waist-coat.

'Decidedly not,' added the other members.

As Mr Gamfield did happen to labour under the

slight imputation of having bruised three or four boys to death already, it occurred to him that the board had, perhaps, in some unaccountable freak, taken it into their heads that this extraneous circumstance ought to influence their proceedings. It was very unlike their general mode of doing business, if they had; but still, as he had no particular wish to revive the rumour, he twisted his cap in his hands, and walked slowly from the table.

'So you won't let me have him, gen'lmen?' said Mr Gamfield, pausing near the door.

'No,' replied Mr Limbkins; 'at least, as it's a nasty business, we think you ought to take something less than the premium we offered.'

Mr Gamfield's countenance brightened, as, with a quick step, he returned to the table, and said, 'What'll you give, gen'lmen? Come! Don't be too hard on a poor man. What'll you give?'

'I should say, three pound ten was plenty,' said Mr Limbkins.

'Ten shillings too much,' said the gentleman in the white waistcoat.

'Come!' said Gamfield; 'say four pound, gen'lmen. Say four pound, and you've got rid on him for good and all. There!'

'Three pound ten,' repeated Mr Limbkins, firmly.

'Come! I'll split the difference, gen'lmen,' urged Gamfield. 'Three pound fifteen.'

'Not a farthing more,' was the firm reply of Mr Limbkins.

'You're desperate hard upon me, gen'lmen,' said Gamfield, wavering.

'Pooh! pooh! nonsense!' said the gentleman in the white waistcoat. 'He'd be cheap with nothing at all, as

a premium. Take him, you silly fellow! He's just the boy
for you. He wants the stick, now and then: it'll do him
good: and his board needn't come very expensive, for
he hasn't been over-fed since he was born. Ha! ha! ha!'

Mr Gamfield gave an arch look at the faces round
the table, and, observing a smile on all of them,
gradually broke into a smile himself. The bargain was
made. Mr Bumble was at once instructed that Oliver
Twist and his indentures were to be conveyed before
the magistrate, for signature and approval, that very
afternoon.

In pursuance of this determination, little Oliver,
to his excessive astonishment, was released from
bondage, and ordered to put himself into a clean
shirt. He had hardly achieved this very unusual
gymnastic performance, when Mr Bumble brought
him, with his own hands, a basin of gruel, and the
holiday allowance of two ounces and a quarter of
bread. At this tremendous sight, Oliver began to cry
very piteously: thinking, not unnaturally, that the
board must have determined to kill him for some
useful purpose, or they never would have begun to
fatten him up in that way.

'Don't make your eyes red, Oliver, but eat your food
and be thankful.' said Mr Bumble, in a tone of
impressive pomposity. 'You're a-going to be made a
'prentice of, Oliver.'

'A 'prentice, sir!' said the child, trembling.

'Yes, Oliver,' said Mr Bumble. 'The kind and
blessed gentlemen which is so many parents to you,
Oliver: when you have none of your own: are a-going
to 'prentice you: and to set you up in life, and make a
man of you: although the expense to the parish is
three pound ten! – three pound ten, Oliver! – seventy

shillins – one hundred and forty sixpences! – and all for a naughty orphan which nobody can't love.'

As Mr Bumble paused to take breath, after delivering this address in an awful voice, the tears rolled down the poor child's face, and he sobbed bitterly.

'Come,' said Mr Bumble, somewhat less pompously, for it was gratifying to his feelings to observe the effect his eloquence had produced; 'Come, Oliver! Wipe your eyes with the cuffs of your jacket, and don't cry into your gruel; that's a very foolish action, Oliver.' It certainly was, for there was quite enough water in it already.

On their way to the magistrate, Mr Bumble instructed Oliver that all he would have to do, would be to look very happy, and say, when the gentleman asked him if he wanted to be apprenticed, that he should like it very much indeed; both of which injunctions Oliver promised to obey: the rather as Mr Bumble threw in a gentle hint, that if he failed in either particular, there was no telling what would be done to him. When they arrived at the office, he was shut up in a little room by himself, and admonished by Mr Bumble to stay there, until he came back to fetch him.

There the boy remained, with a palpitating heart, for half an hour. At the expiration of which time, Mr Bumble thrust in his head, unadorned with the cocked-hat, and said aloud: 'Now, Oliver, my dear, come to the gentleman.' As Mr Bumble said this, he put on a grim and threatening look, and added, in a low voice, 'Mind what I told you, you young rascal!'

Oliver stared innocently in Mr Bumble's face at this somewhat contradictory style of address; but that gentleman prevented his offering any remark thereupon, by leading him at once into an adjoining room:

the door of which was open. It was a large room, with a great window. Behind a desk, sat two old gentlemen with powdered heads: one of whom was reading the newspaper; while the other was perusing, with the aid of a pair of tortoiseshell spectacles, a small piece of parchment which lay before him. Mr Limbkins was standing in front of the desk on one side; and Mr Gamfield, with a partially washed face, on the other; while two or three bluff-looking men, in top-boots, were lounging about.

The old gentleman with the spectacles gradually dozed off, over the little bit of parchment; and there was a short pause, after Oliver had been stationed by Mr Bumble in front of the desk.

'This is the boy, your worship,' said Mr Bumble.

The old gentleman who was reading the newspaper raised his head for a moment, and pulled the other old gentleman by the sleeve; whereupon, the last-mentioned old gentleman woke up.

'Oh, is this the boy?' said the old gentleman.

'This is him, sir,' replied Mr Bumble. 'Bow to the magistrate, my dear.'

Oliver roused himself, and made his best obeisance. He had been wondering, with his eyes fixed on the magistrates' powder, whether all boards were born with that white stuff on their heads, and were boards from thenceforth on that account.

'Well,' said the old gentleman, 'I suppose he's fond of chimney-sweeping?'

'He dotes on it, your worship,' replied Bumble; giving Oliver a sly pinch, to intimate that he had better not say he didn't.

'And he *will* be a sweep, will he?' enquired the old gentleman.

'If we was to bind him to any other trade tomorrow, he'd run away simultaneous, your worship,' replied Bumble.

'And this man that's to be his master – you, sir – you'll treat him well, and feed him, and do all that sort of thing, will you?' said the old gentleman.

'When I says I will, I means I will,' replied Mr Gamfield doggedly.

'You're a rough speaker, my friend, but you look an honest, open-hearted man,' said the old gentleman: turning his spectacles in the direction of the candidate for Oliver's premium, whose villainous countenance was a regular stamped receipt for cruelty. But the magistrate was half blind and half childish, so he couldn't reasonably be expected to discern what other people did.

'I hope I am, sir,' said Mr Gamfield, with an ugly leer.

'I have no doubt you are, my friend,' replied the old gentleman: fixing his spectacles more firmly on his nose, and looking about him for the inkstand.

It was the critical moment of Oliver's fate. If the inkstand had been where the old gentleman thought it was, he would have dipped his pen into it, and signed the indentures, and Oliver would have been straightway hurried off. But, as it chanced to be immediately under his nose, it followed, as a matter of course, that he looked all over his desk for it, without finding it; and happening in the course of his search to look straight before him, his gaze encountered the pale and terrified face of Oliver Twist: who, despite all the admonitory looks and pinches of Bumble, was regarding the repulsive countenance of his future master, with a mingled expression of horror and fear, too palpable to be mistaken, even by a half-blind magistrate.

The old gentleman stopped, laid down his pen, and looked from Oliver to Mr Limbkins; who attempted to take snuff with a cheerful and unconcerned aspect.

'My boy!' said the old gentleman, leaning over the desk. Oliver started at the sound. He might be excused for doing so: for the words were kindly said; and strange sounds frighten one. He trembled violently, and burst into tears.

'My boy!' said the old gentleman, 'you look pale and alarmed. What is the matter?'

'Stand a little away from him, Beadle,' said the other magistrate: laying aside the paper, and leaning forward with an expression of interest. 'Now, boy, tell us what's the matter: don't be afraid.'

Oliver fell on his knees, and clasping his hands together, prayed that they would order him back to the dark room – that they would starve him – beat him – kill him if they pleased – rather than send him away with that dreadful man.

'Well!' said Mr Bumble, raising his hands and eyes with most impressive solemnity, 'Well! of all the artful and designing orphans that ever I see, Oliver, you are one of the most bare-facedest.'

'Hold your tongue, Beadle,' said the second old gentleman, when Mr Bumble had given vent to this compound adjective.

'I beg your worship's pardon,' said Mr Bumble, incredulous of his having heard aright. 'Did your worship speak to me?'

'Yes. Hold your tongue.'

Mr Bumble was stupefied with astonishment. A beadle ordered to hold his tongue! A moral revolution!

Oliver escapes being bound apprentice to the sweep

The old gentleman in the tortoiseshell spectacles looked at his companion; he nodded significantly.

'We refuse to sanction these indentures,' said the old gentleman: tossing aside the piece of parchment as he spoke.

'I hope,' stammered Mr Limbkins: 'I hope the magistrates will not form the opinion that the authorities have been guilty of any improper conduct, on the unsupported testimony of a mere child.'

'The magistrates are not called upon to pronounce any opinion on the matter,' said the second old gentleman sharply. 'Take the boy back to the workhouse, and treat him kindly. He seems to want it.'

That same evening, the gentleman in the white waistcoat most positively and decidedly affirmed, not only that Oliver would be hung, but that he would be drawn and quartered into the bargain. Mr Bumble shook his head with gloomy mystery, and said he wished he might come to good; whereunto Mr Gamfield replied, that he wished he might come to him; which, although he agreed with the beadle in most matters, would seem to be a wish of a totally opposite description.

The next morning, the public were once more informed that Oliver Twist was again To Let, and that five pounds would be paid to anybody who would take possession of him.

CHAPTER 4

*Oliver, being offered another place, makes
his first entry into public life*

In great families, when an advantageous place cannot
be obtained, either in possession, reversion, remainder,
or expectancy, for the young man who is growing up,
it is a very general custom to send him to sea. The
board, in imitation of so wise and salutary an example,
took counsel together on the expediency of shipping
off Oliver Twist, in some small trading vessel bound to
a good unhealthy port. This suggested itself as the very
best thing that could possibly be done with him: the
probability being, that the skipper would flog him to
death, in a playful mood, someday after dinner, or
would knock his brains out with an iron bar; both
pastimes being, as is pretty generally known, very
favourite and common recreations among gentlemen
of that class. The more the case presented itself to the
board, in this point of view, the more manifold the
advantages of the step appeared; so, they came to the
conclusion that the only way of providing for Oliver
effectually, was to send him to sea without delay.

Mr Bumble had been despatched to make various
preliminary enquiries, with the view of finding out
some captain or other who wanted a cabin-boy without any friends; and was returning to the workhouse
to communicate the result of his mission; when he
encountered at the gate, no less a person than Mr
Sowerberry, the parochial undertaker.

Mr Sowerberry was a tall, gaunt, large-jointed man,

attired in a suit of threadbare black, with darned cotton stockings of the same colour, and shoes to answer. His features were not naturally intended to wear a smiling aspect, but he was in general rather given to professional jocosity. His step was elastic, and his face betokened inward pleasantry, as he advanced to Mr Bumble, and shook him cordially by the hand.

'I have taken the measure of the two women that died last night, Mr Bumble,' said the undertaker.

'You'll make your fortune, Mr Sowerberry,' said the beadle, as he thrust his thumb and forefinger into the proffered snuffbox of the undertaker: which was an ingenious little model of a patent coffin. 'I say you'll make your fortune, Mr Sowerberry,' repeated Mr Bumble, tapping the undertaker on the shoulder, in a friendly manner, with his cane.

'Think so?' said the undertaker in a tone which half admitted and half disputed the probability of the event. 'The prices allowed by the board are very small, Mr Bumble.'

'So are the coffins,' replied the beadle; with precisely as near an approach to a laugh as a great official ought to indulge in.

Mr Sowerberry was much tickled at this: as of course he ought to be; and laughed a long time without cessation. 'Well, well, Mr Bumble,' he said at length, 'there's no denying that, since the new system of feeding has come in, the coffins are something narrower and more shallow than they used to be; but we must have some profit, Mr Bumble. Well-seasoned timber is an expensive article, sir; and all the iron handles come, by canal, from Birmingham.'

'Well, well,' said Mr Bumble, 'every trade has its drawbacks. A fair profit is, of course, allowable.'

45

'Of course, of course,' replied the undertaker; 'and if I don't get a profit upon this or that particular article, why, I make it up in the long-run, you see – he! he! he!'

'Just so,' said Mr Bumble.

'Though I must say,' continued the undertaker, resuming the current of observations which the beadle had interrupted: 'though I must say, Mr Bumble, that I have to contend against one very great disadvantage: which is, that all the stout people go off the quickest. The people who have been better off, and have paid rates for many years, are the first to sink when they come into the house; and let me tell you, Mr Bumble, that three or four inches over one's calculation makes a great hole in one's profits: especially when one has a family to provide for, sir.'

As Mr Sowerberry said this, with the becoming indignation of an ill-used man; and as Mr Bumble felt that it rather tended to convey a reflection on the honour of the parish; the latter gentleman thought it advisable to change the subject. Oliver Twist being uppermost in his mind, he made him his theme.

'By the by,' said Mr Bumble, 'you don't know anybody who wants a boy, do you? A porochial 'prentis, who is at present a deadweight; a millstone, as I may say; round the porochial throat? Liberal terms, Mr Sowerberry, liberal terms!' As Mr Bumble spoke, he raised his cane to the bill above him, and gave three distinct raps upon the words 'five pounds': which were printed thereon in Roman capitals of gigantic size.

'Gadso!' said the undertaker: taking Mr Bumble by the gilt-edged lapel of his official coat; 'that's just the very thing I wanted to speak to you about. You know –

dear me, what a very elegant button this is, Mr Bumble! I never noticed it before.'

'Yes, I think it is rather pretty,' said the beadle, glancing proudly downwards at the large brass buttons which embellished his coat. 'The die is the same as the porochial seal – the Good Samaritan healing the sick and bruised man. The board presented it to me on New-year's morning, Mr Sowerberry. I put it on, I remember, for the first time, to attend the inquest on that reduced tradesman, who died in a doorway at midnight.'

'I recollect,' said the undertaker. 'The jury brought in, "Died from exposure to the cold, and want of the common necessaries of life", didn't they?'

Mr Bumble nodded.

'And they made it a special verdict, I think,' said the undertaker, 'by adding some words to the effect, that if the relieving officer had – '

'Tush! Foolery!' interposed the beadle. 'If the board attended to all the nonsense that ignorant jurymen talk, they'd have enough to do.'

'Very true,' said the undertaker; 'they would indeed.'

'Juries,' said Mr Bumble, grasping his cane tightly, as was his wont when working into a passion: 'juries is ineddicated, vulgar, grovelling wretches.'

'So they are,' said the undertaker.

'They haven't no more philosophy nor political economy about 'em than that,' said the beadle, snapping his fingers contemptuously.

'No more they have,' acquiesced the undertaker.

'I despise 'em,' said the beadle, growing very red in the face.

'So do I,' rejoined the undertaker.

'And I only wish we'd a jury of the independent sort, in the house for a week or two,' said the beadle; 'the rules and regulations of the board would soon bring their spirit down for 'em.'

'Let 'em alone for that,' replied the undertaker. So saying, he smiled, approvingly: to calm the rising wrath of the indignant parish officer.

Mr Bumble lifted off his cocked hat; took a handkerchief from the inside of the crown; wiped from his forehead the perspiration which his rage had engendered; fixed the cocked hat on again; and, turning to the undertaker, said in a calmer voice: 'Well; what about the boy?'

'Oh!' replied the undertaker; 'why, you know, Mr Bumble, I pay a good deal towards the poor's rates.'

'Hem!' said Mr Bumble. 'Well?'

'Well,' replied the undertaker, 'I was thinking that if I pay so much towards 'em, I've a right to get as much out of 'em as I can, Mr Bumble; and so – and so – I think I'll take the boy myself.'

Mr Bumble grasped the undertaker by the arm, and led him into the building. Mr Sowerberry was closeted with the board for five minutes; and it was arranged that Oliver should go to him that evening 'upon liking' – a phrase which means, in the case of a parish apprentice, that if the master find, upon a short trial, that he can get enough work out of a boy without putting too much food into him, he shall have him for a term of years, to do what he likes with.

When little Oliver was taken before 'the gentlemen' that evening; and informed that he was to go, that night, as general house-lad to a cöffin-maker's; and that if he complained of his situation, or ever came back to the parish again, he would be sent to sea, there to be drowned, or knocked on the head, as the case might be, he evinced so little emotion, that they by common consent pronounced him a hardened young rascal, and ordered Mr Bumble to remove him forthwith.

Now, although it was very natural that the board, of all people in the world, should feel in a great state of virtuous astonishment and horror at the smallest tokens of want of feeling on the part of anybody, they were rather out, in this particular instance. The simple fact was, that Oliver, instead of possessing too little feeling, possessed rather too much; and was in a fair way of being reduced, for life, to a state of brutal stupidity and sullenness by the ill-usage he had received. He heard the news of his destination, in perfect silence; and, having had his luggage put into his hand – which was not very difficult to carry, inasmuch as it was all comprised within the limits of a brown paper parcel, about half a foot square by three inches deep – he pulled his cap over his eyes; and once more attaching himself to Mr Bumble's coat cuff, was led away by that dignitary to a new scene of suffering.

For some time, Mr Bumble drew Oliver along, without notice or remark; for the beadle carried his head very erect, as a beadle always should: and, it being a windy day, little Oliver was completely enshrouded by the skirts of Mr Bumble's coat as they blew open, and disclosed to great advantage his flapped waistcoat and drab plush knee-breeches. As they drew near to their destination, however, Mr Bumble thought it expedient to look down, and see that the boy was in good order for inspection by his new master: which he accordingly did, with a fit and becoming air of gracious patronage.

'Oliver!' said Mr Bumble.

'Yes, sir,' replied Oliver, in a low, tremulous voice.

'Pull that cap off your eyes, and hold up your head, sir.'

Although Oliver did as he was desired, at once; and passed the back of his unoccupied hand briskly across his eyes, he left a tear in them when he looked up at his conductor. As Mr Bumble gazed sternly upon him, it rolled down his cheek. It was followed by another, and another. The child made a strong effort, but it was an unsuccessful one. Withdrawing his other hand from Mr Bumble's, he covered his face with both; and wept until the tears sprung out from between his chin and bony fingers.

'Well!' exclaimed Mr Bumble, stopping short, and darting at his little charge a look of intense malignity. 'Well! Of *all* the ungratefullest, and worst-disposed boys as ever I see, Oliver, you are the – '

'No, no, sir,' sobbed Oliver, clinging to the hand which held the well-known cane; 'no, no, sir; I will be good indeed; indeed, indeed I will, sir! I am a very little boy, sir; and it is so – so – '

'So what?' enquired Mr Bumble in amazement.

'So lonely, sir! So very lonely!' cried the child. 'Everybody hates me. Oh! sir, don't, don't pray be cross to me!' The child beat his hand upon his heart; and looked in his companion's face, with tears of real agony.

Mr Bumble regarded Oliver's piteous and helpless look, with some astonishment, for a few seconds; hemmed three or four times in a husky manner; and, after muttering something about 'that troublesome cough', bade Oliver dry his eyes and be a good boy. Then once more taking his hand, he walked on with him in silence.

The undertaker, who had just put up the shutters of his shop, was making some entries in his daybook by the light of a most appropriately dismal candle, when Mr Bumble entered.

'Aha!' said the undertaker: looking up from the book, and pausing in the middle of a word; 'is that you, Bumble?'

'No one else, Mr Sowerberry,' replied the beadle. 'Here! I've brought the boy.' Oliver made a bow.

'Oh! that's the boy, is it?' said the undertaker: raising the candle above his head, to get a better view of Oliver. 'Mrs Sowerberry, will you have the goodness to come here a moment, my dear?'

Mrs Sowerberry emerged from a little room behind the shop, and presented the form of a short, thin, squeezed-up woman, with a vixenish countenance.

'My dear,' said Mr Sowerberry, deferentially, 'this is the boy from the workhouse that I told you of.' Oliver bowed again.

'Dear me!' said the undertaker's wife, 'he's very small.'

'Why, he *is* rather small,' replied Mr Bumble: looking at Oliver as if it were his fault that he was no bigger; 'he *is* small. There's no denying it. But he'll grow, Mrs Sowerberry – he'll grow.'

'Ah! I dare say he will,' replied the lady pettishly, 'on our victuals and our drink. I see no saving in parish children, not I; for they always cost more to keep than they're worth. However, men always think they know best. There! Get downstairs, little bag o' bones.' With this, the undertaker's wife opened a side door, and pushed Oliver down a steep flight of stairs into a stone cell, damp and dark: forming the anteroom to the coal-cellar, and denominated 'kitchen': wherein sat a slatternly girl, in shoes down at heel, and blue worsted stockings very much out of repair.

'Here, Charlotte,' said Mrs Sowerberry, who had followed Oliver down, 'give this boy some of the cold bits that were put by for Trip. He hasn't come home since the morning, so he may go without 'em. I dare say the boy isn't too dainty to eat 'em – are you, boy?'

Oliver, whose eyes had glistened at the mention of meat, and who was trembling with eagerness to devour it, replied in the negative; and a plateful of coarse broken victuals was set before him.

I wish some well-fed philosopher, whose meat and drink turn to gall within him; whose blood is ice, whose heart is iron; could have seen Oliver Twist clutching at the dainty viands that the dog had neglected. I wish he could have witnessed the horrible avidity with which Oliver tore the bits asunder with all the ferocity of famine. There is only one thing I should like better; and that would be to see the Philosopher making the same sort of meal himself, with the same relish.

'Well,' said the undertaker's wife, when Oliver had finished his supper: which she had regarded in silent horror, and with fearful auguries of his future appetite: 'have you done?'

There being nothing eatable within his reach, Oliver replied in the affirmative.

'Then come with me,' said Mrs Sowerberry: taking up a dim and dirty lamp, and leading the way upstairs; 'your bed's under the counter. You don't mind sleeping among the coffins, I suppose? But it doesn't much matter whether you do or don't, for you can't sleep anywhere else. Come; don't keep me here all night!'

Oliver lingered no longer, but meekly followed his new mistress.

CHAPTER 5

Oliver mingles with new associates. Going to a
funeral for the first time, he forms an unfavourable
notion of his master's business

Oliver, being left to himself in the undertaker's shop,
set the lamp down on a workman's bench, and gazed
timidly about him with a feeling of awe and dread,
which many people a good deal older than he will be
at no loss to understand. An unfinished coffin on
black trestles, which stood in the middle of the shop,
looked so gloomy and death-like that a cold tremble
came over him, every time his eyes wandered in the
direction of the dismal object: from which he almost
expected to see some frightful form slowly rear its
head, to drive him mad with terror. Against the wall
were ranged, in regular array, a long row of elm
boards cut into the same shape: looking in the dim
light, like high-shouldered ghosts with their hands in
their breeches-pockets. Coffin-plates, elm-chips,
bright-headed nails, and shreds of black cloth, lay
scattered on the floor; and the wall behind the counter was ornamented with a lively representation of
two mutes in very stiff neckcloths, on duty at a large
private door, with a hearse drawn by four black
steeds, approaching in the distance. The shop was
close and hot. The atmosphere seemed tainted with
the smell of coffins. The recess beneath the counter
in which his flock mattress was thrust, looked like
a grave.

Nor were these the only dismal feelings which

depressed Oliver. He was alone in a strange place; and we all know how chilled and desolate the best of us will sometimes feel in such a situation. The boy had no friends to care for, or to care for him. The regret of no recent separation was fresh in his mind; the absence of no loved and well-remembered face sank heavily into his heart. But his heart *was* heavy, notwithstanding; and he wished, as he crept into his narrow bed, that that were his coffin, and that he could be lain in a calm and lasting sleep in the churchyard ground, with the tall grass waving gently above his head, and the sound of the old deep bell to soothe him in his sleep.

Oliver was awakened in the morning, by a loud kicking at the outside of the shop-door; which, before he could huddle on his clothes, was repeated, in an angry and impetuous manner, about twenty-five times. When he began to undo the chain, the legs desisted, and a voice began.

'Open the door, will yer?' cried the voice which belonged to the legs which had kicked at the door.

'I will, directly, sir,' replied Oliver: undoing the chain, and turning the key.

'I suppose yer the new boy, ain't yer?' said the voice through the keyhole.

'Yes, sir,' replied Oliver.

'How old are yer?' enquired the voice.

'Ten, sir,' replied Oliver.

'Then I'll whop yer when I get in,' said the voice; 'you just see if I don't, that's all, my work'us brat!' and having made this obliging promise, the voice began to whistle.

Oliver had been too often subjected to the process to which the very expressive monosyllable just recorded bears reference, to entertain the smallest doubt that the owner of the voice, whoever he might be, would redeem his pledge, most honourably. He drew back the bolts with a trembling hand, and opened the door.

For a second or two, Oliver glanced up the street, and down the street, and over the way: impressed with the belief that the unknown, who had addressed him through the keyhole, had walked a few paces off, to warm himself; for nobody did he see but a big charity-boy, sitting on a post in front of the house, eating a slice of bread and butter: which he cut into wedges, the size of his mouth, with a clasp knife, and then consumed with great dexterity.

'I beg your pardon, sir,' said Oliver at length: seeing that no other visitor made his appearance; 'did you knock?'

'I kicked,' replied the charity-boy.

'Did you want a coffin, sir?' enquired Oliver, innocently.

At this the charity-boy looked monstrous fierce; and said that Oliver would want one before long, if he cut jokes with his superiors in that way.

'Yer don't know who I am, I suppose, Work'us?' said the charity-boy, in continuation: descending from the top of the post, meanwhile, with edifying gravity.

'No, sir,' rejoined Oliver.

'I'm Mister Noah Claypole,' said the charity-boy, 'and you're under me. Take down the shutters, yer idle young ruffian!' With this, Mr Claypole administered a kick to Oliver, and entered the shop with a dignified air, which did him great credit. It is difficult for a large-headed, small-eyed youth, of lumbering make and heavy countenance, to look dignified under any circumstances; but it is more especially so, when superadded to these personal attractions are a red nose and yellow smalls.

Oliver, having taken down the shutters, and broken a pane of glass in his efforts to stagger away beneath the weight of the first one to a small court at the side of the house in which they were kept during the day, was graciously assisted by Noah: who having consoled him with the assurance that 'he'd catch it', condescended to help him. Mr Sowerberry came down soon after. Shortly afterwards Mrs Sowerberry appeared. Oliver having 'caught it', in fulfilment of Noah's prediction, followed that young gentleman down the stairs to breakfast.

'Come near the fire, Noah,' said Charlotte. 'I saved a nice little bit of bacon for you from master's breakfast. Oliver, shut that door at Mister Noah's back, and take them bits that I've put out on the cover of the bread-pan. There's your tea; take it away to that box, and drink it there, and make haste, for they'll want you to mind the shop. D'ye hear?'

'D'ye hear, Work'us?' said Noah Claypole.

'Lor, Noah!' said Charlotte, 'what a rum creature you are! Why don't you let the boy alone?'

'Let him alone!' said Noah. 'Why everybody lets him alone enough, for the matter of that. Neither his father nor his mother will ever interfere with him. All his relations let him have his own way pretty well. Eh, Charlotte? He! he! he!'

'Oh, you queer soul!' said Charlotte, bursting into a hearty laugh, in which she was joined by Noah; after which they both looked scornfully at poor Oliver Twist, as he sat shivering on the box in the coldest corner of the room, and ate the stale pieces which had been specially reserved for him.

Noah was a charity-boy, but not a workhouse orphan. No chance-child was he, for he could trace his genealogy all the way back to his parents, who lived hard by; his mother being a washerwoman, and his father a drunken soldier, discharged with a wooden leg, and a diurnal pension of twopence-halfpenny and an unstatable fraction. The shop-boys in the neighbourhood had long been in the habit of branding Noah, in the public streets, with the ignominious epithets of 'leathers', 'charity', and the like; and Noah had borne them without reply. But, now that fortune has cast in his way a nameless orphan, at whom even the meanest could point the finger of scorn, he retorted on him with interest. This affords charming food for contemplation. It shows us what a beautiful thing human nature may be made to be; and how impartially the same amiable qualities are developed in the finest lord and the dirtiest charity-boy.

Oliver had been sojourning at the undertaker's some three weeks or a month. Mr and Mrs Sowerberry – the shop being shut up – were taking their supper in the little back-parlour, when Mr Sowerberry, after several deferential glances at his wife, said, 'My dear – ' He was going to say more; but, Mrs Sowerberry looking up, with a peculiarly unpropitious aspect, he stopped short.

'Well,' said Mrs Sowerberry, sharply.

'Nothing, my dear, nothing,' said Mr Sowerberry.

'Ugh, you brute!' said Mrs Sowerberry.

'Not at all, my dear,' said Mr Sowerberry humbly. 'I thought you didn't want to hear, my dear. I was only going to say – '

'Oh, don't tell me what you were going to say,' interposed Mrs Sowerberry. 'I am nobody; don't consult me, pray. *I* don't want to intrude upon your secrets.' As Mrs Sowerberry said this, she gave an hysterical laugh, which threatened violent consequences.

'But, my dear,' said Sowerberry, 'I want to ask your advice.'

'No, no, don't ask mine,' replied Mrs Sowerberry, in an affecting manner: 'ask somebody else's.' Here, there was another hysterical laugh, which frightened Mr Sowerberry very much. This is a very common and much-approved matrimonial course of treatment, which is often very effective. It at once reduced Mr Sowerberry to begging, as a special favour, to be allowed to say what Mrs Sowerberry was most curious to hear. After a short altercation of less than three quarters of an hour's duration, the permission was most graciously conceded.

'It's only about young Twist, my dear,' said Mr Sowerberry. 'A very good-looking boy, that, my dear.'

'He need be, for he eats enough,' observed the lady.

'There's an expression of melancholy in his face, my dear,' resumed Mr Sowerberry, 'which is very interesting. He would make a delightful mute, my love.'

Mrs Sowerberry looked up with an expression of considerable wonderment. Mr Sowerberry remarked it; and, without allowing time for any observation on the good lady's part, proceeded.

'I don't mean a regular mute to attend grown-up people, my dear, but only for children's practice. It would be very new to have a mute in proportion, my dear. You may depend upon it, it would have a superb effect.'

Mrs Sowerberry, who had a good deal of taste in the

undertaking way, was much struck by the novelty of this idea; but, as it would have been compromising her dignity to have said so, under existing circumstances, she merely enquired, with much sharpness, why such an obvious suggestion had not presented itself to her husband's mind before? Mr Sowerberry rightly construed this, as an acquiescence in his proposition; it was speedily determined, therefore, that Oliver should be at once initiated into the mysteries of the trade; and, with this view, that he should accompany his master on the very next occasion of his services being required.

The occasion was not long in coming. Half an hour after breakfast next morning, Mr Bumble entered the shop; and supporting his cane against the counter, drew forth his large leathern pocketbook, from which he selected a small scrap of paper, which he handed over to Sowerberry.

'Aha!' said the undertaker, glancing over it with a lively countenance; 'an order for a coffin, eh?'

'For a coffin first, and a porochial funeral afterwards,' replied Mr Bumble, fastening the strap of the leathern pocketbook, which, like himself, was very corpulent.

'Bayton,' said the undertaker, looking from the scrap of paper to Mr Bumble. 'I never heard the name before.'

Bumble shook his head, as he replied, 'Obstinate people, Mr Sowerberry; very obstinate. Proud, too, I'm afraid, sir.'

'Proud, eh?' exclaimed Mr Sowerberry with a sneer. 'Come, that's too much.'

'Oh, it's sickening,' replied the beadle. 'Antimonial, Mr Sowerberry!'

'So it is,' acquiesced the undertaker.

'We only heard of the family the night before last,' said the beadle; 'and we shouldn't have known anything about them, then, only a woman who lodges in the same house made an application to the porochial committee for them to send the porochial surgeon to see a woman as was very bad. He had gone out to dinner; but his 'prentice (which is a very clever lad) sent 'em some medicine in a blacking-bottle, offhand.'

'Ah, there's promptness,' said the undertaker.

'Promptness, indeed!' replied the beadle. 'But what's the consequence; what's the ungrateful behaviour of these rebels, sir? Why, the husband sends back word that the medicine won't suit his wife's complaint, and so she shan't take it – says she shan't take it, sir! Good, strong, wholesome medicine, as was given with great success to two Irish labourers and a coal heaver, only a week before – sent 'em for nothing, with a blackin'-bottle in – and he sends back word that she shan't take it, sir!'

As the atrocity presented itself to Mr Bumble's mind in full force, he struck the counter sharply with his cane, and became flushed with indignation.

'Well,' said the undertaker, 'I ne–ver–did – '

'Never did, sir!' ejaculated the beadle. 'No, nor nobody never did; but, now she's dead, we've got to bury her; and that's the direction, and the sooner it's done, the better.'

Thus saying, Mr Bumble put on his cocked hat wrong side first, in a fever of parochial excitement, and flounced out of the shop.

'Why, he was so angry, Oliver, that he forgot even to ask after you!' said Mr Sowerberry, looking after the beadle as he strode down the street.

'Yes, sir,' replied Oliver, who had carefully kept himself out of sight during the interview, and who was shaking from head to foot at the mere recollection of the sound of Mr Bumble's voice. He needn't have taken the trouble to shrink from Mr Bumble's glance, however; for that functionary, on whom the prediction of the gentleman in the white waistcoat had made a very strong impression, thought that now the under-taker had got Oliver upon trial the subject was better avoided, until such time as he should be firmly bound for seven years, and all danger of his being returned upon the hands of the parish should be thus effectually and legally overcome.

'Well,' said Mr Sowerberry, taking up his hat, 'the sooner this job is done, the better. Noah, look after the shop. Oliver, put on your cap, and come with me.' Oliver obeyed, and followed his master on his professional mission.

They walked on, for some time, through the most crowded and densely inhabited part of the town; and then, striking down a narrow street more dirty and miserable than any they had yet passed through, paused to look for the house which was the object of their search. The houses on either side were high and large, but very old, and tenanted by people of the poorest class: as their neglected appearance would have sufficiently denoted, without the concurrent testimony afforded by the squalid looks of the few men and women who, with folded arms and bodies half doubled, occasionally skulked along. A great many of the tenements had shop-fronts; but these were fast closed, and mouldering away, only the upper rooms being inhabited. Some houses which had become insecure from age and decay, were prevented from falling into the street, by huge beams of wood reared against the walls, and firmly planted in the road; but even these crazy dens seemed to have been selected as the nightly haunts of some houseless wretches, for many of the rough boards which supplied the place of door and window, were wrenched from their positions, to afford an aperture wide enough for the passage of a human body. The kennel was stagnant and filthy. The very rats, which here and there lay putrefying in its rottenness, were hideous with famine.

There was neither knocker nor bell-handle at the open door where Oliver and his master stopped; so, groping his way cautiously through the dark passage, and bidding Oliver keep close to him and not be afraid, the undertaker mounted to the top of the first flight of stairs. Stumbling against a door on the landing, he rapped at it with his knuckles.

It was opened by a young girl of thirteen or fourteen. The undertaker at once saw enough of what the room contained to know it was the apartment to which he had been directed. He stepped in; Oliver followed him.

There was no fire in the room, but a man was crouching mechanically over the empty stove. An old woman, too, had drawn a low stool to the cold hearth, and was sitting beside him. There were some ragged children in another corner; and in a small recess, opposite the door, there lay upon the ground something covered with an old blanket. Oliver shuddered as he cast his eyes towards the place, and crept involuntarily closer to his master; for though it was covered up, the boy felt that it was a corpse.

The man's face was thin and very pale; his hair and beard were grizzly; his eyes were bloodshot. The old woman's face was wrinkled; her two remaining teeth protruded over her under lip; and her eyes were bright and piercing. Oliver was afraid to look at either her or the man. They seemed so like the rats he had seen outside.

'Nobody shall go near her,' said the man, starting fiercely up, as the undertaker approached the recess. 'Keep back! Damn you, keep back, if you've a life to lose!'

'Nonsense, my good man,' said the undertaker, who was pretty well used to misery in all its shapes. 'Nonsense!'

'I tell you,' said the man: clenching his hands, and stamping furiously on the floor, 'I tell you I won't have her put into the ground. She couldn't rest there. The worms would worry her – not eat her – she is so worn away.'

The undertaker offered no reply to this raving; but producing a tape from his pocket, knelt down for a moment by the side of the body.

'Ah!' said the man: bursting into tears, and sinking on his knees at the feet of the dead woman; 'kneel down, kneel down – kneel round her, every one of you, and mark my words! I say she was starved to death. I never knew how bad she was, till the fever came upon her; and then her bones were starting through the skin. There was neither fire nor candle; she died in the dark – in the dark! She couldn't even see her children's faces, though we heard her gasping out their names. I begged for her in the streets: and they sent me to prison. When I came back, she was dying; and all the blood in my heart has dried up, for they starved her to death. I swear it before the God that saw it! They starved her!' He twined his hands in his hair; and, with a loud scream, rolled grovelling upon the floor: his eyes fixed, and the foam covering his lips.

The terrified children cried bitterly; but the old woman, who had hitherto remained as quiet as if she had been wholly deaf to all that passed, menaced them into silence. Having unloosed the cravat of the man who still remained extended on the ground, she tottered towards the undertaker.

'She was my daughter,' said the old woman, nodding her head in the direction of the corpse; and speaking with an idiotic leer, more ghastly than even the presence of death in such a place. 'Lord, Lord! Well, it is strange that I who gave birth to her, and was a woman then, should be alive and merry now, and she lying there: so cold and stiff! Lord, Lord! – to think of it; it's as good as a play – as good as a play!'

As the wretched creature mumbled and chuckled in her hideous merriment, the undertaker turned to go away.

'Stop, stop!' said the old woman in a loud whisper. 'Will she be buried tomorrow, or next day, or tonight? I laid her out; and I must walk, you know. Send me a large cloak: a good warm one: for it is bitter cold. We should have cake and wine, too, before we go! Never mind; send some bread – only a loaf of bread, and a cup of water. Shall we have some bread, dear?' she said eagerly: catching at the undertaker's coat, as he once more moved towards the door.

'Yes, yes,' said the undertaker, 'of course. Anything you like!' He disengaged himself from the old woman's grasp; and, drawing Oliver after him, hurried away.

The next day (the family having been meanwhile relieved with a half-quartern loaf and a piece of cheese, left with them by Mr Bumble himself) Oliver and his master returned to the miserable abode; where Mr Bumble had already arrived, accompanied by four men from the workhouse, who were to act as bearers. An old black cloak had been thrown over the rags of the old woman and the man; and the bare coffin having been screwed down, was hoisted on the shoulders of the bearers, and carried into the street.

'Now, you must put your best leg foremost, old lady!' whispered Sowerberry in the old woman's ear; 'we are rather late; and it won't do to keep the clergyman waiting. Move on, my men – as quick as you like!'

Thus directed, the bearers trotted on under their light burden; and the two mourners kept as near them, as they could. Mr Bumble and Sowerberry walked at a good smart pace in front; and Oliver, whose legs were not so long as his master's, ran by the side.

There was not so great a necessity for hurrying as Mr Sowerberry had anticipated, however; for when they reached the obscure corner of the churchyard in which the nettles grew, and where the parish graves were made, the clergyman had not arrived; and the clerk, who was sitting by the vestry-room fire, seemed to think it by no means improbable that it might be an hour or so, before he came. So, they put the bier on the brink of the grave; and the two mourners waited patiently in the damp clay, with a cold rain drizzling down, while the ragged boys whom the spectacle had attracted into the churchyard played a noisy game at hide-and-seek among the tombstones, or varied their amusements by jumping backwards and forwards over the coffin. Mr Sowerberry and Bumble, being personal friends of the clerk, sat by the fire with him, and read the paper.

At length, after a lapse of something more than an hour, Mr Bumble, and Sowerberry, and the clerk, were seen running towards the grave. Immediately afterwards, the clergyman appeared: putting on his surplice as he came along. Mr Bumble then thrashed a boy or two, to keep up appearances; and the reverend gentleman, having read as much of the burial service as could be compressed into four minutes, gave his surplice to the clerk, and walked away again.

'Now, Bill!' said Sowerberry to the grave-digger. 'Fill up!'

It was no very difficult task; for the grave was so full, that the uppermost coffin was within a few feet of the surface. The grave-digger shovelled in the earth; stamped it loosely down with his feet: shouldered his spade; and walked off, followed by the boys, who murmured very loud complaints at the fun being over so soon.

'Come, my good fellow!' said Bumble, tapping the man on the back. 'They want to shut up the yard.'

The man who had never once moved, since he had taken his station by the grave side, started, raised his head, stared at the person who had addressed him, walked forward for a few paces; and fell down in a swoon. The crazy old woman was too much occupied in bewailing the loss of her cloak (which the under-taker had taken off), to pay him any attention; so they threw a can of cold water over him; and when he came to, saw him safely out of the churchyard, locked the gate, and departed on their different ways.

'Well, Oliver,' said Sowerberry, as they walked home, 'how do you like it?'

'Pretty well, thank you, sir,' replied Oliver, with considerable hesitation. 'Not very much, sir.'

'Ah, you'll get used to it in time, Oliver,' said Sowerberry. 'Nothing when you *are* used to it, my boy.'

Oliver wondered, in his own mind, whether it had taken a very long time to get Mr Sowerberry used to it. But he thought it better not to ask the question; and walked back to the shop: thinking over all he had seen and heard.

CHAPTER 6

Oliver, being goaded by the taunts of Noah, rouses into action, and rather astonishes him

The month's trial over, Oliver was formally apprenticed. It was a nice sickly season just at this time. In commercial phrase, coffins were looking up; and, in the course of a few weeks, Oliver acquired a great deal of experience. The success of Mr Sowerberry's ingenious speculation, exceeded even his most sanguine hopes. The oldest inhabitants recollected no period at which measles had been so prevalent, or so fatal to infant existence; and many were the mournful processions which little Oliver headed, in a hatband reaching down to his knees, to the indescribable admiration and emotion of all the mothers in the town. As Oliver accompanied his master in most of his adult expeditions, too, in order that he might acquire that equanimity of demeanour and full command of nerve which are essential to a finished undertaker, he had many opportunities of observing the beautiful resignation and fortitude with which some strong-minded people bear their trials and losses.

For instance; when Sowerberry had an order for the burial of some rich old lady or gentleman, who was surrounded by a great number of nephews and nieces, who had been perfectly inconsolable during the previous illness, and whose grief had been wholly irrepressible even on the most public occasions, they would be as happy among themselves as need be – quite cheerful and contented – conversing together with as much freedom and gaiety, as if nothing whatever had happened to disturb them. Husbands, too, bore the loss of their wives with the most heroic calmness. Wives, again, put on weeds for their husbands, as if, so far from grieving in the garb of sorrow, they had made up their minds to render it as becoming and attractive as possible. It was observable, too, that ladies and gentlemen who were in passions of anguish during the ceremony of inter-ment, recovered almost as soon as they reached home, and became quite composed before the tea-drinking was over. All this was very pleasant and improving to see; and Oliver beheld it with great admiration.

That Oliver Twist was moved to resignation by the example of these good people, I cannot, although I am his biographer, undertake to affirm with any degree of confidence; but I can most distinctly say, that for many months he continued meekly to submit to the domination and ill-treatment of Noah Claypole: who used him far worse than before, now that his jealousy was roused by seeing the new boy promoted to the black stick and hatband, while he, the old one, remained stationary in the muffin-cap and leathers. Charlotte treated him ill, because Noah did; and Mrs

Sowerberry was his decided enemy, because Mr Sowerberry was disposed to be his friend; so, between these three on one side, and a glut of funerals on the other, Oliver was not altogether as comfortable as the hungry pig was, when he was shut up, by mistake, in the grain department of a brewery.

And now, I come to a very important passage in Oliver's history; for I have to record an act, slight and unimportant perhaps in appearance, but which indirectly produced a material change in all his future prospects and proceedings.

One day, Oliver and Noah had descended into the kitchen at the usual dinner-hour, to banquet upon a small joint of mutton – a pound and a half of the worst end of the neck – when Charlotte being called out of the way, there ensued a brief interval of time, which Noah Claypole, being hungry and vicious, considered he could not possibly devote to a worthier purpose than aggravating and tantalising young Oliver Twist.

Intent upon this innocent amusement, Noah put his feet on the tablecloth; and pulled Oliver's hair; and twitched his ears; and expressed his opinion that he was a 'sneak'; and furthermore announced his intention of coming to see him hanged, whenever that desirable event should take place; and entered upon various other topics of petty annoyance, like a malicious and ill-conditioned charity-boy as he was. But, none of these taunts producing the desired effect of making Oliver cry, Noah attempted to be more facetious still; and in this attempt, did what many small wits, with far greater reputations than Noah, sometimes do to this day, when they want to be funny. He got rather personal.

'Work'us,' said Noah, 'how's your mother?'

'She's dead,' replied Oliver; 'don't you say anything about her to me!'

Oliver's colour rose as he said this; he breathed quickly; and there was a curious working of the mouth and nostrils, which Mr Claypole thought must be the immediate precursor of a violent fit of crying. Under this impression he returned to the charge.

'What did she die of, Work'us?' said Noah.

'Of a broken heart, some of our old nurses told me,' replied Oliver: more as if he were talking to himself, than answering Noah. 'I think I know what it must be to die of that!'

'Tol de rol lol lol, right fol lairy, Work'us,' said Noah, as a tear rolled down Oliver's cheek. 'What's set you a-snivelling now?'

'Not *you*,' replied Oliver, hastily brushing the tear away. 'Don't think it.'

'Oh, not me, eh!' sneered Noah.

'No, not you,' replied Oliver, sharply. 'There; that's enough. Don't say anything more to me about her; you'd better not!'

'Better not!' exclaimed Noah. 'Well! Better not! Work'us, don't be impudent. *Your* mother, too! She was a nice 'un, she was. Oh, Lor!' And here, Noah nodded his head expressively; and curled up as much of his small red nose as muscular action could collect together, for the occasion.

'Yer know, Work'us,' continued Noah, emboldened by Oliver's silence, and speaking in a jeering tone of affected pity: of all tones the most annoying: 'Yer know, Work'us, it can't be helped now; and of course yer couldn't help it then; and I'm very sorry for it; and I'm sure we all are, and pity yer very much.

But yer must know, Work'us, yer mother was a regular right-down bad 'un.'

'What did you say?' enquired Oliver, looking up very quickly.

'A regular right-down bad 'un, Work'us,' replied Noah, coolly. 'And it's a great deal better, Work'us, that she died when she did, or else she'd have been hard labouring in Bridewell, or transported, or hung; which is more likely than either, isn't it?'

Crimson with fury, Oliver started up; overthrew the chair and table; seized Noah by the throat; shook him, in the violence of his rage, till his teeth chattered in his head; and, collecting his whole force into one heavy blow, felled him to the ground.

A minute ago, the boy had looked the quiet, mild, dejected creature that harsh treatment had made him. But his spirit was roused at last; the cruel insult to his dead mother had set his blood on fire. His breast heaved; his attitude was erect; his eye bright and vivid; his whole person changed, as he stood glaring over the cowardly tormentor who now lay crouching at his feet; and defied him with an energy he had never known before.

'He'll murder me!' blubbered Noah. 'Charlotte! missis! Here's the new boy a-murdering of me! Help! help! Oliver's gone mad! Char—lotte!'

Noah's shouts were responded to, by a loud scream from Charlotte, and a louder from Mrs Sowerberry; the former of whom rushed into the kitchen by a side-door, while the latter paused on the staircase till she was quite certain that it was consistent with the preservation of human life, to come further down.

'Oh, you little wretch!' screamed Charlotte: seizing Oliver with her utmost force, which was about equal to that of a moderately strong man in particularly good training, 'Oh, you little un–grate–ful, mur–de–rous, horrid villain!' And between every syllable, Charlotte gave Oliver a blow with all her might: accompanying it with a scream, for the benefit of society.

Charlotte's fist was by no means a light one; but, lest it should not be effectual in calming Oliver's wrath, Mrs Sowerberry plunged into the kitchen, and assisted to hold him with one hand, while she scratched his face with the other. In this favourable position of affairs, Noah rose from the ground, and pommelled him behind.

This was rather too violent exercise to last long. When they were all wearied out, and could tear and beat no longer, they dragged Oliver, struggling and shouting, but nothing daunted, into the dust-cellar, and there locked him up. This being done, Mrs Sowerberry sunk into a chair, and burst into tears.

'Bless her, she's going off!' said Charlotte. 'A glass of water, Noah, dear. Make haste!'

'Oh! Charlotte,' said Mrs Sowerberry: speaking as well as she could, through a deficiency of breath, and a sufficiency of cold water, which Noah had poured over her head and shoulders. 'Oh! Charlotte, what a mercy we have not all been murdered in our beds!'

'Ah! mercy indeed, ma'am,' was the reply. 'I only hope this'll teach master not to have any more of these dreadful creatures, that are born to be murderers and robbers from their very cradle. Poor Noah! He was all but killed, ma'am, when I come in.'

'Poor fellow!' said Mrs Sowerberry: looking piteously on the charity-boy.

Noah, whose top waistcoat-button might have been

Oliver plucks up a spirit

somewhere on a level with the crown of Oliver's head, rubbed his eyes with the inside of his wrists while this commiseration was bestowed upon him, and performed some affecting tears and sniffs.

'What's to be done!' exclaimed Mrs Sowerberry. 'Your master's not at home; there's not a man in the house, and he'll kick that door down in ten minutes.' Oliver's vigorous plunges against the bit of timber in question, rendered this occurrence highly probable.

'Dear, dear! I don't know, ma'am,' said Charlotte, 'unless we send for the police-officers.'

'Or the millingtary,' suggested Mr Claypole.

'No, no,' said Mrs Sowerberry: bethinking herself of Oliver's old friend. 'Run to Mr Bumble, Noah, and tell him to come here directly, and not to lose a minute; never mind your cap! Make haste! You can hold a knife to that black eye, as you run along. It'll keep the swelling down.'

Noah stopped to make no reply, but started off at his fullest speed; and very much it astonished the people who were out walking, to see a charity-boy tearing through the streets pell-mell, with no cap on his head, and a clasp-knife at his eye.

CHAPTER 7

Oliver continues refractory

Noah Claypole ran along the streets at his swiftest pace, and paused not once for breath, until he reached the workhouse-gate. Having rested here, for a minute or so, to collect a good burst of sobs and an imposing show of tears and terror, he knocked loudly at the

wicket; and presented such a rueful face to the aged
pauper who opened it, that even he, who saw nothing
but rueful faces about him at the best of times, started
back in astonishment.

'Why, what's the matter with the boy!' said the old
pauper.

'Mr Bumble! Mr Bumble!' cried Noah, with well-
affected dismay: and in tones so loud and agitated,
that they not only caught the ear of Mr Bumble
himself, who happened to be hard by, but alarmed
him so much that he rushed into the yard without his
cocked hat – which is a very curious and remarkable
circumstance: as showing that even a beadle, acted
upon by a sudden and powerful impulse, may be
afflicted with a momentary visitation of loss of self-
possession, and forgetfulness of personal dignity.

'Oh, Mr Bumble, sir!' said Noah: 'Oliver, sir –
Oliver has – '

'What? What?' interposed Mr Bumble: with a gleam
of pleasure in his metallic eyes. 'Not run away; he
hasn't run away, has he Noah?'

'No, sir, no. Not run away, sir, but he's turned
wicious,' replied Noah. 'He tried to murder me, sir;
and then he tried to murder Charlotte; and then
missis. Oh! what dreadful pain it is! Such agony,
please, sir!' And here, Noah writhed and twisted his
body into an extensive variety of eel-like positions;
thereby giving Mr Bumble to understand that, from
the violent and sanguinary onset of Oliver Twist, he
had sustained severe internal injury and damage, from
which he was at that moment suffering the acutest
torture.

When Noah saw that the intelligence he communi-
cated perfectly paralysed Mr Bumble, he imparted

additional effect thereunto, by bewailing his dreadful wounds ten times louder than before; and when he observed a gentleman in a white waistcoat crossing the yard, he was more tragic in his lamentations than ever: rightly conceiving it highly expedient to attract the notice, and rouse the indignation, of the gentleman aforesaid.

The gentleman's notice was very soon attracted; for he had not walked three paces, when he turned angrily round, and enquired what that young cur was howling for, and why Mr Bumble did not favour him with something which would render the series of vocular exclamations so designated, an involuntary process?

'It's a poor boy from the free-school, sir,' replied Mr Bumble, 'who has been nearly murdered – all but murdered, sir – by young Twist.'

'By Jove!' exclaimed the gentleman in the white waistcoat, stopping short. 'I knew it! I felt a strange presentiment from the very first, that that audacious young savage would come to be hung!'

'He has likewise attempted, sir, to murder the female servant,' said Mr Bumble, with a face of ashy paleness.

'And his missis,' interposed Mr Claypole.

'And his master, too, I think you said, Noah?' added Mr Bumble.

'No! he's out, or he would have murdered him,' replied Noah. 'He said he wanted to.'

'Ah! said he wanted to, did he, my boy?' enquired the gentleman in the white waistcoat.

'Yes, sir,' replied Noah. 'And please, sir, missis wants to know whether Mr Bumble can spare time to step up there, directly, and flog him – 'cause master's out.'

'Certainly, my boy; certainly,' said the gentleman in

the white waistcoat: smiling benignly, and patting Noah's head, which was about three inches higher than his own. 'You're a good boy – a very good boy. Here's a penny for you. Bumble, just step up to Sowerberry's with your cane, and see what's best to be done. Don't spare him, Bumble.'

'No, I will not, sir,' replied the beadle: adjusting the wax-end which was twisted round the bottom of his cane, for purposes of parochial flagellation.

'Tell Sowerberry not to spare him either. They'll never do anything with him, without stripes and bruises,' said the gentleman in the white waistcoat.

'I'll take care, sir,' replied the beadle. And the cocked hat and cane having been, by this time, adjusted to their owner's satisfaction, Mr Bumble and Noah Claypole betook themselves with all speed to the undertaker's shop.

Here the position of affairs had not at all improved. Sowerberry had not yet returned, and Oliver continued to kick, with undiminished vigour, at the cellar-door. The accounts of his ferocity, as related by Mrs Sowerberry and Charlotte, were of so startling a nature, that Mr Bumble judged it prudent to parley, before opening the door. With this view he gave a kick at the outside, by way of prelude; and, then, applying his mouth to the keyhole, said, in a deep and impressive tone: 'Oliver!'

'Come; you let me out!' replied Oliver, from the inside.

'Do you know this here voice, Oliver?' said Mr Bumble.

'Yes,' replied Oliver.

'Ain't you afraid of it, sir? Ain't you a-trembling while I speak, sir?' said Mr Bumble.

'No!' replied Oliver, boldly.

An answer so different from the one he had expected to elicit, and was in the habit of receiving, staggered Mr Bumble not a little. He stepped back from the keyhole; drew himself up to his full height; and looked from one to another of the three bystanders, in mute astonishment.

'Oh, you know, Mr Bumble, he must be mad,' said Mrs Sowerberry. 'No boy in half his senses could venture to speak so to you.'

'It's not Madness, ma'am,' replied Mr Bumble, after a few moments of deep meditation. 'It's Meat.'

'What?' exclaimed Mrs Sowerberry.

'Meat, ma'am, meat,' replied Bumble, with stern emphasis. 'You've over-fed him, ma'am. You've raised a artificial soul and spirit in him, ma'am, unbecoming a person of his condition: as the board, Mrs Sowerberry, who are practical philosophers, will tell you. What have paupers to do with soul or spirit? It's quite enough that we let 'em have live bodies. If you had kept the boy on gruel, ma'am, this would never have happened.'

'Dear, dear!' ejaculated Mrs Sowerberry, piously raising her eyes to the kitchen ceiling: 'this comes of being liberal!'

The liberality of Mrs Sowerberry to Oliver, had consisted in a profuse bestowal upon him of all the dirty odds and ends which nobody else would eat; so there was a great deal of meekness and self-devotion in her voluntarily remaining under Mr Bumble's heavy accusation. Of which, to do her justice, she was wholly innocent, in thought, word, or deed.

'Ah!' said Mr Bumble, when the lady brought her eyes down to earth again; 'the only thing that can be

78

done now, that I know of, is to leave him in the cellar for a day or so, till he's a little starved down; and then to take him out, and keep him on gruel all through his apprenticeship. He comes of a bad family. Excitable natures, Mrs Sowerberry! Both the nurse and doctor said, that that mother of his made her way here, against difficulties and pain that would have killed any well-disposed woman, weeks before.'

At this point of Mr Bumble's discourse, Oliver, just hearing enough to know that some new allusion was being made to his mother, recommenced kicking, with a violence that rendered every other sound inaudible. Sowerberry returned at this juncture. Oliver's offence having been explained to him, with such exaggerations as the ladies thought best calculated to rouse his ire, he unlocked the cellar door in a twinkling, and dragged his rebellious apprentice out, by the collar.

Oliver's clothes had been torn in the beating he had received; his face was bruised and scratched; and his hair scattered over his forehead. The angry flush had not disappeared, however, and when he was pulled out of his prison, he scowled boldly on Noah, and looked quite undismayed.

'Now, you are a nice young fellow, ain't you?' said Sowerberry; giving Oliver a shake, and a box on the ear.

'He called my mother names,' replied Oliver.

'Well, and what if he did, you little ungrateful wretch?' said Mrs Sowerberry. 'She deserved what he said, and worse.'

'She didn't,' said Oliver.

'She did,' said Mrs Sowerberry.

'It's a lie,' said Oliver.

Mrs Sowerberry burst into a flood of tears.

This flood of tears left Mr Sowerberry no alternative. If he had hesitated for one instant to punish Oliver most severely, it must be quite clear to every experienced reader that he would have been, according to all precedents in disputes of matrimony established, a brute, an unnatural husband, an insulting creature, a base imitation of a man, and various other agreeable characters too numerous for recital within the limits of this chapter. To do him justice, he was, as far as his power went – it was not very extensive – kindly disposed towards the boy; perhaps, because it was his interest to be so; perhaps, because his wife disliked him. The flood of tears, however, left him no resource; so he at once gave him a drubbing, which satisfied even Mrs Sowerberry herself, and rendered Mr Bumble's subsequent application of the parochial cane, rather unnecessary. For the rest of the day, he was shut up in the back kitchen, in company with a pump and a slice of bread, and, at night, Mrs Sowerberry, after making various remarks outside the door, by no means complimentary to the memory of his mother, looked into the room, and, amidst the jeers and pointings of Noah and Charlotte, ordered him upstairs to his dismal bed.

It was not until he was left alone in the silence and stillness of the gloomy workshop of the undertaker, that Oliver gave way to the feelings which the day's treatment may be supposed likely to have awakened in a mere child. He had listened to their taunts with a look of contempt; he had borne the lash without a cry: for he felt that pride swelling in his heart which would have kept down a shriek to the last, though they had roasted him alive. But now, when there were none to see or hear him, he fell upon his knees on the floor, and, hiding his face in his hands, wept such tears as, God send for the credit of our nature, few so young may ever have cause to pour out before him!

For a long time Oliver remained motionless in this attitude. The candle was burning low in the socket when he rose to his feet. Having gazed cautiously round him, and listened intently, he gently undid the fastenings of the door, and looked abroad.

It was a cold, dark night. The stars seemed, to the boy's eyes, farther from the earth than he had ever seen them before; there was no wind; and the sombre shadows thrown by the trees upon the ground, looked sepulchral and death-like, from being so still. He softly reclosed the door. Having availed himself of the expiring light of the candle to tie up in a handkerchief the few articles of wearing apparel he had, sat himself down upon a bench, to wait for morning.

With the first ray of light that struggled through the crevices in the shutters, Oliver arose, and again unbarred the door. One timid look around – one moment's pause of hesitation – he had closed it behind him, and was in the open street.

He looked to the right and to the left, uncertain whither to fly. He remembered to have seen the waggons, as they went out, toiling up the hill. He took the same route; and arriving at a footpath across the fields: which he knew, after some distance, led out again into the road: struck into it, and walked quickly on.

Along this same footpath, Oliver well remembered he had trotted beside Mr Bumble, when he first carried him to the workhouse from the farm. His way lay directly in front of the cottage. His heart beat quickly when he bethought himself of this; and he half resolved to turn back. He had come a long way though, and should lose a great deal of time by doing so. Besides, it was so early that there was very little fear of his being seen; so he walked on.

He reached the house. There was no appearance of its inmates stirring at that early hour. Oliver stopped, and peeped into the garden. A child was weeding one of the little beds; as he stopped, he raised his pale face and disclosed the features of one of his former companions. Oliver felt glad to see him, before he went; for, though younger than himself, he had been his little friend and playmate. They had been beaten and starved, and shut up together, many and many a time.

'Hush, Dick!' said Oliver, as the boy ran to the gate, and thrust his thin arm between the rails to greet him. 'Is anyone up?'

'Nobody but me,' replied the child.

'You mustn't say you saw me, Dick,' said Oliver. 'I am running away. They beat and ill-use me, Dick; and I am going to seek my fortune, some long way off. I don't know where. How pale you are!'

'I heard the doctor tell them I was dying,' replied the child with a faint smile. 'I am very glad to see you, dear; but don't stop, don't stop!'

'Yes, yes, I will, to say goodbye to you,' replied Oliver. 'I shall see you again, Dick. I know I shall! You will be well and happy!'

'I hope so,' replied the child. 'After I am dead, but not before. I know the doctor must be right, Oliver, because I dream so much of Heaven, and Angels, and kind faces that I never see when I am awake. Kiss me,' said the child, climbing up the low gate, and flinging his little arms round Oliver's neck. 'Goodbye, dear! God bless you!'

The blessing was from a young child's lips, but it was the first that Oliver had ever heard invoked upon his head: and through the struggles and sufferings, and troubles and changes, of his after life, he never once forgot it.

CHAPTER 8

Oliver walks to London. He encounters on the road a strange sort of young gentleman

Oliver reached the stile at which the by-path terminated; and once more gained the highroad. It was eight o'clock now. Though he was nearly five miles away from the town, he ran, and hid behind the hedges, by turns, till noon: fearing that he might be pursued and overtaken. Then he sat down to rest by the side of the milestone, and began to think, for the first time, where he had better go and try to live.

The stone by which he was seated, bore, in large characters, an intimation that it was just seventy miles from that spot to London. The name awakened a new train of ideas in the boy's mind. London! – that great large place! – nobody – not even Mr Bumble – could ever find him there! He had often heard the old men in the workhouse, too, say that no lad of spirit need want in London; and that there were ways of living in that vast city, which those who had been bred up in country parts had no idea of. It was the very place for a homeless boy, who must die in the streets unless someone helped him. As these things passed through his thoughts, he jumped upon his feet, and again walked forward.

He had diminished the distance between himself and London by full four miles more, before he recollected how much he must undergo ere he could hope to reach his place of destination. As this consideration forced itself upon him, he slackened his pace a little, and meditated upon his means of getting there. He had a crust of bread, a coarse shirt, and two pairs of stockings, in his bundle. He had a penny too – a gift of Sowerberry's after some funeral in which he had acquitted himself more than ordinarily well – in his pocket. 'A clean shirt,' thought Oliver, 'is a very comfortable thing; and so are two pairs of darned stockings; and so is a penny; but they are small helps to a sixty-five miles' walk in winter time.' But Oliver's thoughts, like those of most other people, although they were extremely ready and active to point out his difficulties, were wholly at a loss to suggest any feasible mode of surmounting them; so, after a good deal of thinking to no particular purpose, he changed his little bundle over to the other shoulder, and trudged on.

Oliver walked twenty miles that day; and all that time tasted nothing but the crust of dry bread, and a few draughts of water, which he begged at the cottage-doors by the roadside. When the night came, he turned into a meadow; and, creeping close under a hayrick, determined to lie there, till morning. He felt frightened at first, for the wind moaned dismally over the empty fields: and he was cold and hungry, and more alone than he had ever felt before. Being very tired with his walk, however, he soon fell asleep and forgot his troubles.

He felt cold and stiff, when he got up next morning, and so hungry that he was obliged to exchange the penny for a small loaf, in the very first village through which he passed. He had walked no more than twelve miles, when night closed in again. His feet were sore, and his legs so weak that they trembled beneath him. Another night passed in the bleak damp air, made him worse; when he set forward on his journey next morning, he could hardly crawl along.

He waited at the bottom of a steep hill till a stagecoach came up, and then begged of the outside passengers; but there were very few who took any notice of him: and even those told him to wait till they got to the top of the hill, and then let them see how far he could run for a halfpenny. Poor Oliver tried to keep up with the coach a little way, but was unable to do it, by reason of his fatigue and sore feet. When the outsides saw this, they put their halfpence back into their pockets again, declaring that he was an idle young dog, and didn't deserve anything; and the coach rattled away and left only a cloud of dust behind.

In some villages, large painted boards were fixed up: warning all persons who begged within the district, that they would be sent to jail. This frightened Oliver very much, and made him glad to get out of those villages with all possible expedition. In others, he would stand about the inn-yards, and look mournfully at every one who passed: a proceeding which generally terminated in the landlady's ordering one of the post-boys who were lounging about, to drive that strange boy out of the place, for she was sure he had come to steal something. If he begged at a farmer's house, ten to one but they threatened to set the dog on him; and when he showed his nose in a shop, they talked about the beadle – which brought Oliver's heart into his mouth – very often the only thing he had there, for many hours together.

In fact, if it had not been for a good-hearted turnpike-man, and a benevolent old lady, Oliver's troubles would have been shortened by the very same process which had put an end to his mother's; in other words, he would most assuredly have fallen dead upon the king's highway. But the turnpike-man gave him a meal of bread and cheese; and the old lady, who had a shipwrecked grandson wandering barefoot in some distant part of the earth, took pity upon the poor orphan, and gave him what little she could afford – and more – with such kind and gentle words, and such tears of sympathy and compassion, that they sank deeper into Oliver's soul, than all the sufferings he had ever undergone.

Early on the seventh morning after he had left his native place, Oliver limped slowly into the little town of Barnet. The window-shutters were closed; the street was empty; not a soul had awakened to the business of the day. The sun was rising in all its splendid beauty; but the light only served to show the boy his own lonesomeness and desolation, as he sat, with bleeding feet and covered with dust, upon a doorstep.

By degrees, the shutters were opened; the window-blinds were drawn up; and people began passing to and fro. Some few stopped to gaze at Oliver for a moment or two, or turned round to stare at him as they hurried by; but none relieved him, or troubled themselves to enquire how he came there. He had no heart to beg. And there he sat.

He had been crouching on the step for some time: wondering at the great number of public houses (every other house in Barnet was a tavern, large or small), gazing listlessly at the coaches as they passed through, and thinking how strange it seemed that they could do, with ease, in a few hours, what it had taken him a whole week of courage and determination beyond his years to accomplish: when he was roused by observing that a boy, who had passed him carelessly some minutes before, had returned, and was now surveying him most earnestly from the opposite side of the way. He took little heed of this at first; but the boy remained in the same attitude of close observation so long, that Oliver raised his head, and returned his steady look. Upon this, the boy crossed over; and, walking close up to Oliver, said, 'Hullo, my covey! What's the row?'

The boy who addressed this enquiry to the young wayfarer, was about his own age: but one of the queerest-looking boys that Oliver had ever seen. He was a snub-nosed, flat-browed, common-faced boy enough, and as dirty a juvenile as one would wish to see; but he had about him all the airs and manners of a man. He was short of his age: with rather bow-legs, and little, sharp, ugly eyes. His hat was stuck on the top of his head so lightly, that it threatened to fall off every moment – and would have done so, very often, if the wearer had not had a knack of every now and then giving his head a sudden twitch, which brought it back to its old place again. He wore a man's coat, which reached nearly to his heels. He had turned the cuffs back, halfway up his arm, to get his hands out of the sleeves; apparently with the ultimate view of thrusting them into the pockets of his corduroy trousers; for there he kept them. He was, altogether, as roistering and swaggering a young gentleman as ever stood four feet six, or something less, in his bluchers.

'Hullo, my covey! What's the row?' said this strange young gentleman to Oliver.

'I am very hungry and tired,' replied Oliver: the tears standing in his eyes as he spoke. 'I have walked a long way. I have been walking these seven days.'

'Walking for sivin days!' said the young gentleman. 'Oh, I see. Beak's order, eh? But,' he added, noticing Oliver's look of surprise, 'I suppose you don't know what a beak is, my flash com–pan–i–on.'

Oliver mildly replied, that he had always heard a bird's mouth described by the term in question.

'My eyes, how green!' exclaimed the young gentleman. 'Why, a beak's a madgst'rate; and when you walk by a beak's order, it's not straight forerd, but always a-going up, and nivir a-coming down agin. Was you never on the mill?'

'What mill?' enquired Oliver.

'What mill! Why, *the* mill – the mill as takes up so little room that it'll work inside a Stone Jug; and always goes better when the wind's low with people, than when it's high; a-cos then they can't get workmen. But come,' said the young gentleman; 'you want grub, and you shall have it. I'm at low-water-mark myself – only one bob and a magpie; but, *as far as* it goes, I'll fork out and stump. Up with you on your pins. There! Now then! Morrice!'

Assisting Oliver to rise, the young gentleman took him to an adjacent chandler's shop, where he purchased a sufficiency of ready-dressed ham and a half-quartern loaf, or, as he himself expressed it, 'a fourpenny bran!' the ham being kept clean and preserved from dust, by the ingenious expedient of making a hole in the loaf by pulling out a portion of the crumb, and stuffing it therein. Taking the bread under his arm, the young gentleman turned into a small public house, and led the way to a taproom in the rear of the premises. Here, a pot of beer was brought in, by direction of the mysterious youth; and Oliver, falling to, at his new friend's bidding, made a long and hearty meal, during the progress of which, the strange boy eyed him from time to time with great attention.

'Going to London?' said the strange boy, when Oliver had at length concluded.

'Yes.'

'Got any lodgings?'

'No.'

'Money?'

'No.'

The strange boy whistled; and put his arms into his pockets, as far as the big coat sleeves would let them go.

'Do you live in London?' enquired Oliver.

'Yes. I do, when I'm at home,' replied the boy. 'I suppose you want some place to sleep in tonight, don't you?'

'I do, indeed,' answered Oliver. 'I have not slept under a roof since I left the country.'

'Don't fret your eyelids on that score,' said the young gentleman. 'I've got to be in London tonight; and I know a 'spectable old genelman as lives there, wot'll give you lodgings for nothink, and never ask for the change – that is, if any genelman he knows interduces you. And don't he know me? Oh, no! Not in the least! By no means. Certainly not!'

The young gentleman smiled, as if to intimate that the latter fragments of discourse were playfully ironical; and finished the beer as he did so.

This unexpected offer of shelter was too tempting

to be resisted; especially as it was immediately followed up, by the assurance that the old gentleman referred to, would doubtless provide Oliver with a comfortable place, without loss of time. This led to a more friendly and confidential dialogue; from which Oliver discovered that his friend's name was Jack Dawkins, and that he was a peculiar pet and *protégé* of the elderly gentleman before mentioned.

Mr Dawkins's appearance did not say a vast deal in favour of the comforts which his patron's interest obtained for those whom he took under his protection; but, as he had a rather flighty and dissolute mode of conversing, and furthermore avowed that among his intimate friends he was better known by the *sobriquet* of 'The artful Dodger,' Oliver concluded that, being of a dissipated and careless turn, the moral precepts of his benefactor had hitherto been thrown away upon him. Under this impression, he secretly resolved to cultivate the good opinion of the old gentleman as quickly as possible; and, if he found the Dodger incorrigible, as he more than half suspected he should, to decline the honour of his farther acquaintance.

As John Dawkins objected to their entering London before nightfall, it was nearly eleven o'clock when they reached the turnpike at Islington. They crossed from the Angel into St John's Road; struck down the small street which terminates at Sadler's Wells Theatre; through Exmouth Street and Coppice Row; down the little court by the side of the workhouse; across the classic ground which once bore the name of Hockley-in-the-Hole; thence into Little Saffron Hill; and so into Saffron Hill the Great: along which the Dodger scudded at a rapid pace, directing Oliver to follow close at his heels.

Although Oliver had enough to occupy his attention in keeping sight of his leader, he could not help bestowing a few hasty glances on either side of the way, as he passed along. A dirtier or more wretched place he had never seen. The street was very narrow and muddy, and the air was impregnated with filthy odours. There were a good many small shops; but the only stock in trade appeared to be heaps of children, who, even at that time of night, were crawling in and out at the doors, or screaming from the inside. The sole places that seemed to prosper amid the general blight of the place, were the public houses; and in them, the lowest orders of Irish were wrangling with might and main. Covered ways and yards, which here and there diverged from the main street, disclosed little knots of houses, where drunken men and women were positively wallowing in filth; and from several of the doorways, great ill-looking fellows were cautiously emerging, bound, to all appearance, on no very well-disposed or harmless errands.

Oliver was just considering whether he hadn't better run away, when they reached the bottom of the hill. His conductor, catching him by the arm, pushed open the door of a house near Field Lane; and, drawing him into the passage, closed it behind them.

'Now, then!' cried a voice from below, in reply to a whistle from the Dodger.

'Plummy and slam!' was the reply.

This seemed to be some watchword or signal that all was right; for the light of a feeble candle gleamed on the wall at the remote end of the passage; and a man's face peeped out, from where a balustrade of the old kitchen staircase had been broken away.

'There's two on you,' said the man, thrusting the

candle farther out, and shading his eyes with his hand. 'Who's the t'other one?'

'A new pal,' replied Jack Dawkins, pulling Oliver forward.

'Where did he come from?'

'Greenland. Is Fagin upstairs?'

'Yes, he's a-sortin' the wipes. Up with you!' The candle was drawn back, and the face disappeared.

Oliver, groping his way with one hand, and having the other firmly grasped by his companion, ascended with much difficulty the dark and broken stairs: which his conductor mounted with an ease and expedition that showed he was well acquainted with them. He threw open the door of a back-room, and drew Oliver in after him.

The walls and ceiling of the room were perfectly black with age and dirt. There was a deal table before the fire: upon which were a candle, stuck in a ginger-beer bottle, two or three pewter pots, a loaf and butter, and a plate. In a frying-pan, which was on the fire, and which was secured to the mantelshelf by a string, some sausages were cooking; and standing over them, with a toasting-fork in his hand, was a very old shrivelled Jew, whose villainous-looking and repulsive face was obscured by a quantity of matted red hair. He was dressed in a greasy flannel gown, with his throat bare; and seemed to be dividing his attention between the frying-pan and a clotheshorse, over which a great number of silk handkerchiefs were hanging. Several rough beds made of old sacks, were huddled side by side on the floor. Seated round the table were four or five boys, none older than the Dodger, smoking long clay pipes, and drinking spirits with the air of middle-aged men. These all crowded about their associate as

Oliver introduced to the respectable old gentleman

he whispered a few words to the Jew; and then turned round and grinned at Oliver. So did the Jew himself, toasting-fork in hand.

'This is him, Fagin,' said Jack Dawkins; 'my friend Oliver Twist.'

The Jew grinned; and, making a low obeisance to Oliver, took him by the hand, and hoped he should have the honour of his intimate acquaintance. Upon this, the young gentlemen with the pipes came round him, and shook both his hands very hard – especially the one in which he held his little bundle. One young gentleman was very anxious to hang up his cap for him; and another was so obliging as to put his hands in his pockets, in order that, as he was very tired, he might not have the trouble of emptying them, himself, when he went to bed. These civilities would probably have been extended much farther, but for a liberal exercise of the Jew's toasting-fork on the heads and shoulders of the affectionate youths who offered them.

'We are very glad to see you, Oliver, very,' said the Jew. 'Dodger, take off the sausages; and draw a tub near the fire for Oliver. Ah! you're a-staring at the pocket-handkerchiefs! eh, my dear! There are a good many of 'em, ain't there? We've just looked 'em out, ready for the wash; that's all, Oliver; that's all. Ha! ha! ha!'

The latter part of this speech, was hailed by a boisterous shout from all the hopeful pupils of the merry old gentleman. In the midst of which, they went to supper.

Oliver ate his share, and the Jew then mixed him a glass of hot gin and water: telling him he must drink it off directly, because another gentleman wanted the tumbler. Oliver did as he was desired. Immediately afterwards he felt himself gently lifted on to one of the sacks; and then he sunk into a deep sleep.

CHAPTER 9

*Containing further particulars concerning the
pleasant old gentleman, and his hopeful pupils*

It was late next morning when Oliver awoke, from a sound, long sleep. There was no other person in the room but the old Jew, who was boiling some coffee in a saucepan for breakfast, and whistling softly to himself as he stirred it round and round, with an iron spoon. He would stop every now and then to listen when there was the least noise below: and when he had satisfied himself, he would go on, whistling and stirring again, as before.

Although Oliver had roused himself from sleep, he was not thoroughly awake. There is a drowsy state, between sleeping and waking, when you dream more in five minutes with your eyes half open, and yourself half conscious of everything that is passing around you, than you would in five nights with your eyes fast closed, and your senses wrapped in perfect unconsciousness. At such times, a mortal knows just enough of what his mind is doing, to form some glimmering conception of its mighty powers, its bouncing from earth and spurning time and space, when freed from the restraint of its corporeal associate.

Oliver was precisely in this condition. He saw the Jew with his half-closed eyes; heard his low whistling; and recognised the sound of the spoon grating against the saucepan's sides; and yet the selfsame senses were mentally engaged, at the same time, in busy action with almost everybody he had ever known.

When the coffee was done, the Jew drew the saucepan to the hob. Standing, then, in an irresolute attitude for a few minutes, as if he did not well know how to employ himself, he turned round and looked at Oliver, and called him by his name. He did not answer, and was to all appearances asleep.

After satisfying himself upon this head, the Jew stepped gently to the door: which he fastened. He then drew forth: as it seemed to Oliver, from some trap in the floor: a small box, which he placed carefully on the table. His eyes glistened as he raised the lid, and looked in. Dragging an old chair to the table, he sat down; and took from it a magnificent gold watch, sparkling with jewels.

'Aha!' said the Jew, shrugging up his shoulders, and distorting every feature with a hideous grin. 'Clever dogs! Clever dogs! Staunch to the last! Never told the old parson where they were. Never peached upon old Fagin! And why should they? It wouldn't have loosened the knot, or kept the drop up, a minute longer. No, no, no! Fine fellows! Fine fellows!'

With these, and other muttered reflections of the like nature, the Jew once more deposited the watch in its place of safety. At least half a dozen more were severally drawn forth from the same box, and surveyed with equal pleasure; besides rings, brooches, bracelets, and other articles of jewellery, of such magnificent materials, and costly workmanship, that Oliver had no idea, even of their names.

Having replaced these trinkets, the Jew took out another: so small that it lay in the palm of his hand.

There seemed to be some very minute inscription on it; for the Jew laid it flat upon the table, and, shading it with his hand, pored over it, long and earnestly. At length he put it down, as if despairing of success; and, leaning back in his chair, muttered: 'What a fine thing capital punishment is! Dead men never repent; dead men never bring awkward stories to light. Ah! it's a fine thing for the trade! Five of 'em strung up in a row, and none left to play booty, or turn white-livered!'

As the Jew uttered these words, his bright dark eyes, which had been staring vacantly before him, fell on Oliver's face; the boy's eyes were fixed on his in mute curiosity; and although the recognition was only for an instant – for the briefest space of time that can possibly be conceived – it was enough to show the old man that he had been observed. He closed the lid of the box with a loud crash; and, laying his hand on a bread knife which was on the table, started furiously up. He trembled very much though; for, even in his terror, Oliver could see that the knife quivered in the air.

'What's that?' said the Jew. 'What do you watch me for? Why are you awake? What have you seen? Speak out, boy! Quick – quick! for your life!'

'I wasn't able to sleep any longer, sir,' replied Oliver, meekly. 'I am very sorry if I have disturbed you, sir.'

'You were not awake an hour ago?' said the Jew, scowling fiercely on the boy.

'No! No, indeed!' replied Oliver.

'Are you sure?' cried the Jew: with a still fiercer look than before: and a threatening attitude.

'Upon my word I was not, sir,' replied Oliver, earnestly. 'I was not, indeed, sir.'

'Tush, tush, my dear!' said the Jew, abruptly resuming his old manner, and playing with the knife a

little, before he laid it down; as if to induce the belief
that he had caught it up, in mere sport. 'Of course I
know that, my dear. I only tried to frighten you.
You're a brave boy. Ha! ha! you're a brave boy,
Oliver!' The Jew rubbed his hands with a chuckle, but
glanced uneasily at the box, notwithstanding.

'Did you see any of these pretty things, my dear?'
said the Jew, laying his hand upon it after a short
pause.

'Yes, sir,' replied Oliver.

'Ah!' said the Jew, turning rather pale. 'They –
they're mine, Oliver; my little property. All I have to
live upon, in my old age. The folks call me a miser, my
dear. Only a miser; that's all.'

Oliver thought the old gentleman must be a decided
miser to live in such a dirty place, with so many
watches; but, thinking that perhaps his fondness for
the Dodger and the other boys, cost him a good deal of
money, he only cast a deferential look at the Jew, and
asked if he might get up.

'Certainly, my dear, certainly,' replied the old
gentleman. 'Stay. There's a pitcher of water in the
corner by the door. Bring it here; and I'll give you
a basin to wash in, my dear.'

Oliver got up; walked across the room; and stooped
for an instant to raise the pitcher. When he turned his
head, the box was gone.

He had scarcely washed himself, and made everything tidy, by emptying the basin out of the window,
agreeably to the Jew's directions, when the Dodger
returned: accompanied by a very sprightly young
friend, whom Oliver had seen smoking on the previous night, and who was now formally introduced to
him as Charley Bates. The four sat down, to breakfast,

on the coffee, and some hot rolls and ham which the Dodger had brought home in the crown of his hat.

'Well,' said the Jew, glancing slyly at Oliver, and addressing himself to the Dodger, 'I hope you've been at work this morning, my dears?'

'Hard,' replied the Dodger.

'As Nails,' added Charley Bates.

'Good boys, good boys!' said the Jew. 'What have *you* got Dodger?'

'A couple of pocketbooks,' replied that young gentleman.

'Lined?' enquired the Jew, with eagerness.

'Pretty well,' replied the Dodger, producing two pocketbooks; one green, and the other red.

'Not so heavy as they might be,' said the Jew, after looking at the insides carefully; 'but very neat and nicely made. Ingenious workman, ain't he, Oliver?'

'Very, indeed, sir,' said Oliver. At which Mr Charles Bates laughed uproariously: very much to the amazement of Oliver, who saw nothing to laugh at, in anything that had passed.

'And what have you got, my dear?' said Fagin to Charley Bates.

'Wipes,' replied Master Bates; at the same time producing four pocket-handkerchiefs.

'Well,' said the Jew, inspecting them closely; 'they're very good ones, very. You haven't marked them well, though, Charley; so the marks shall be picked out with a needle, and we'll teach Oliver how to do it. Shall us, Oliver, eh? Ha! ha! ha!'

'If you please, sir,' said Oliver.

'You'd like to be able to make pocket-handkerchiefs as easy as Charley Bates. wouldn't you, my dear?' said the Jew.

'Very much, indeed, if you'll teach me, sir,' replied Oliver.

Master Bates saw something so exquisitely ludicrous in this reply, that he burst into another laugh; which laugh, meeting the coffee he was drinking, and carrying it down some wrong channel, very nearly terminated in his premature suffocation.

'He is so jolly green!' said Charley when he recovered, as an apology to the company for his unpolite behaviour.

The Dodger said nothing, but he smoothed Oliver's hair over his eyes, and said he'd know better, by and by; upon which the old gentleman, observing Oliver's colour mounting, changed the subject by asking whether there had been much of a crowd at the execution that morning? This made him wonder more and more; for it was plain from the replies of the two boys that they had both been there; and Oliver naturally wondered how they could possibly have found time to be so very industrious.

When the breakfast was cleared away, the merry old gentleman and the two boys played at a very curious and uncommon game, which was performed in this way. The merry old gentleman, placing a snuffbox in one pocket of his trousers, a notecase in the other, and a watch in his waistcoat pocket, with a guard-chain round his neck, and sticking a mock diamond pin in his shirt: buttoned his coat tight round him, and putting his spectacle-case and handkerchief in his pockets, trotted up and down the room with a stick, in imitation of the manner in which old gentlemen walk about the streets any hour in the day. Sometimes he stopped at the fireplace, and sometimes at the door, making believe that he was staring with all his might into shop-windows. At such times, he would look constantly round him, for fear of thieves, and would keep slapping all his pockets in turn, to see that he hadn't lost anything, in such a very funny and natural manner, that Oliver laughed till the tears ran down his face. All this time, the two boys followed him closely about: getting out of his sight, so nimbly, every time he turned round, that it was impossible to follow their motions. At last, the Dodger trod upon his toes, or ran upon his boot accidentally, while Charley Bates stumbled up against him behind; and in that one moment they took from him, with the most extraordinary rapidity, snuffbox, notecase, watch-guard, chain, shirt-pin, pocket-handkerchief, even the spectacle-case. If the old gentleman felt a hand in any one of his pockets, he cried out where it was; and then the game began all over again.

When this game had been played a great many times, a couple of young ladies called to see the young gentlemen; one of whom was named Bet, and the other Nancy. They wore a good deal of hair, not very neatly turned up behind, and were rather untidy about the shoes and stockings. They were not exactly pretty, perhaps; but they had a great deal of colour in their faces, and looked quite stout and hearty. Being remarkably free and agreeable in their manners, Oliver thought them very nice girls indeed. As there is no doubt they were.

These visitors stopped a long time. Spirits were produced, in consequence of one of the young ladies complaining of a coldness in her inside; and the conversation took a very convivial and improving turn. At length, Charley Bates expressed his opinion that it was time to pad the hoof. This, it occurred to

Oliver, must be French for going out; for, directly afterwards, the Dodger, and Charley, and the two young ladies, went away together, having been kindly furnished by the amiable old Jew with money to spend.

'There, my dear,' said Fagin. 'That's a pleasant life, isn't it? They have gone out for the day.'

'Have they done work, sir?' enquired Oliver.

'Yes,' said the Jew; 'that is, unless they should unexpectedly come across any, when they are out; and they won't neglect it, if they do, my dear, depend upon it. Make 'em your models, my dear. Make 'em your models,' tapping the fire-shovel on the hearth to add force to his words; 'do everything they bid you, and take their advice in all matters – especially the Dodger's, my dear. He'll be a great man himself, and will make you one too, if you take pattern by him – Is my handkerchief hanging out of my pocket, my dear?' said the Jew, stopping short.

'Yes, sir,' said Oliver.

'See if you can take it out, without my feeling it: as you saw them do, when we were at play this morning.'

Oliver held up the bottom of the pocket with one hand, as he had seen the Dodger hold it, and drew the handkerchief lightly out of it with the other.

'Is it gone?' cried the Jew.

'Here it is, sir,' said Oliver, showing it in his hand.

'You're a clever boy, my dear,' said the playful old gentleman, patting Oliver on the head approvingly. 'I never saw a sharper lad. Here's a shilling for you. If you go on, in this way, you'll be the greatest man of the time. And now come here, and I'll show you how to take the marks out of the handkerchiefs.'

Oliver wondered what picking the old gentleman's

pocket in play, had to do with his chances of being a great man. But, thinking that the Jew, being so much his senior, must know best, he followed him quietly to the table, and was soon deeply involved in his new study.

CHAPTER 10

Oliver becomes better acquainted with the characters of his new associates; and purchases experience at a high price. Being a short, but very important chapter, in this history

For many days, Oliver remained in the Jew's room, picking the marks out of the pocket-handkerchiefs, (of which a great number were brought home), and sometimes taking part in the game already described: which the two boys and the Jew played, regularly, every morning. At length, he began to languish for fresh air, and took many occasions of earnestly entreating the old gentleman to allow him to go out to work, with his two companions.

Oliver was rendered the more anxious to be actively employed, by what he had seen of the stern morality of the old gentleman's character. Whenever the Dodger or Charley Bates came home at night, empty-handed, he would expatiate with great vehemence on the misery of idle and lazy habits; and would enforce upon them the necessity of an active life, by sending them supperless to bed. On one occasion, indeed, he even went so far as to knock them both down a flight of stairs; but this was carrying out his virtuous precepts to an unusual extent.

At length, one morning, Oliver obtained the permission he had so eagerly sought. There had been no handkerchiefs to work upon, for two or three days, and the dinners had been rather meagre. Perhaps these were reasons for the old gentleman's giving his assent; but, whether they were or no, he told Oliver he might go, and placed him under the joint guardianship of Charley Bates, and his friend the Dodger.

The three boys sallied out; the Dodger with his coat-sleeves tucked up, and his hat cocked, as usual; Master Bates sauntering along with his hands in his pockets; and Oliver between them, wondering where they were going, and what branch of manufacture he would be instructed in, first.

The pace at which they went, was such a very lazy, ill-looking saunter, that Oliver soon began to think his companions were going to deceive the old gentleman, by not going to work at all. The Dodger had a vicious propensity, too, of pulling the caps from the heads of small boys and tossing them down areas; while Charley Bates exhibited some very loose notions concerning the rights of property, by pilfering divers apples and onions from the stalls at the kennel sides, and thrusting them into pockets which were so surprisingly capacious, that they seemed to undermine his whole suit of clothes in every direction. These things looked so bad, that Oliver was on the point of declaring his intention of seeking his way back, in the best way he could; when his thoughts were suddenly directed into another channel, by a very mysterious change of behaviour on the part of the Dodger.

They were just emerging from a narrow court not far from the open square in Clerkenwell, which is yet called, by some strange perversion of terms, 'The Green': when the Dodger made a sudden stop; and, laying his finger on his lip, drew his companions back again, with the greatest caution and circumspection.

'What's the matter?' demanded Oliver.

'Hush!' replied the Dodger. 'Do you see that old cove at the bookstall?'

'The old gentleman over the way?' said Oliver. 'Yes, I see him.'

'He'll do,' said the Dodger.

'A prime plant,' observed Master Charley Bates.

Oliver looked from one to the other, with the greatest surprise; but he was not permitted to make any enquiries; for the two boys walked stealthily across the road, and slunk close behind the old gentleman towards whom his attention had been directed. Oliver walked a few paces after them; and, not knowing whether to advance or retire, stood looking on in silent amazement.

The old gentleman was a very respectable-looking personage, with a powdered head and gold spectacles. He was dressed in a bottle-green coat with a black velvet collar; wore white trousers; and carried a smart bamboo cane under his arm. He had taken up a book from the stall, and there he stood, reading away, as hard as if he were in his elbow-chair, in his own study. It is very possible that he fancied himself there, indeed; for it was plain, from his abstraction, that he saw not the bookstall, nor the street, nor the boys; nor, in short, anything but the book itself: which he was reading straight through: turning over the leaf when he got to the bottom of a page, beginning at the top line of the next one, and going regularly on, with the greatest interest and eagerness.

What was Oliver's horror and alarm as he stood a few paces off, looking on with his eyelids as wide open as they would possibly go, to see the Dodger plunge his hand into the old gentleman's pocket, and draw from thence a handkerchief! To see him hand the same to Charley Bates; and finally to behold them, both, running away round the corner at full speed!

In an instant the whole mystery of the handkerchiefs, and the watches, and the jewels, and the Jew, rushed upon the boy's mind. He stood, for a moment, with the blood so tingling through all his veins from terror, that he felt as if he were in a burning fire; then, confused and frightened, he took to his heels; and, not knowing what he did, made off as fast as he could lay his feet to the ground.

This was all done in a minute's space. In the very instant when Oliver began to run, the old gentleman, putting his hand to his pocket, and missing his handkerchief, turned sharp round. Seeing the boy scudding away at such a rapid pace, he very naturally concluded him to be the depredator; and, shouting 'Stop thief!' with all his might, made off after him, book in hand.

But the old gentleman was not the only person who raised the hue-and-cry. The Dodger and Master Bates, unwilling to attract public attention by running down the open street, had merely retired into the very first doorway round the corner. They no sooner heard the cry, and saw Oliver running, than, guessing exactly how the matter stood, they issued forth with great promptitude; and, shouting 'Stop thief!' too, joined in the pursuit like good citizens.

Although Oliver had been brought up by philosophers, he was not theoretically acquainted with the

Oliver amazed at the Dodger's mode of 'going to work'

beautiful axiom that self-preservation is the first law of nature. If he had been, perhaps he would have been prepared for this. Not being prepared, however, it alarmed him the more; so away he went like the wind, with the old gentleman and the two boys roaring and shouting behind him.

'Stop thief! Stop thief!' There is a magic in the sound. The tradesman leaves his counter, and the carman his waggon; the butcher throws down his tray; the baker his basket; the milkman his pail; the errand-boy his parcels; the schoolboy his marbles; the paviour his pickaxe; the child his battledore. Away they run, pell-mell, helter-skelter, slap-dash: tearing, yelling, screaming, knocking down the passengers as they turn the corners, rousing up the dogs, and astonishing the fowls: and streets, squares, and courts, re-echo with the sound.

'Stop thief! Stop thief!' The cry is taken up by a hundred voices, and the crowd accumulate at every turning. Away they fly, splashing through the mud, and rattling along the pavements: up go the windows, out run the people, onward bear the mob, a whole audience desert Punch in the very thickest of the plot, and, joining the rushing throng, swell the shout, and lend fresh vigour to the cry, 'Stop thief! Stop thief!'

'Stop thief! Stop thief!' There is a passion *for hunting something* deeply implanted in the human breast. One wretched breathless child, panting with exhaustion; terror in his looks; agony in his eyes; large drops of perspiration streaming down his face; strains every nerve to make head upon his pursuers; and as they follow on his track, and gain upon him every instant, they hail his decreasing strength with still louder shouts, and whoop and scream with joy.

'Stop thief!' Ay, stop him for God's sake, were it only in mercy!

Stopped at last! A clever blow. He is down upon the pavement, and the crowd eagerly gather round him: each new-comer, jostling and struggling with the others to catch a glimpse. 'Stand aside!' 'Give him a little air!' 'Nonsense! he don't deserve it.' 'Where's the gentleman?' 'Here he is, coming down the street.' 'Make room there for the gentleman!' 'Is this the boy, sir?' 'Yes.'

Oliver lay, covered with mud and dust, and bleeding from the mouth, looking wildly round upon the heap of faces that surrounded him, when the old gentleman was officiously dragged and pushed into the circle by the foremost of the pursuers.

'Yes,' said the gentleman, 'I am afraid it is the boy.'

'Afraid!' murmured the crowd. 'That's a good 'un!'

'Poor fellow!' said the gentleman, 'he has hurt himself.'

'*I* did that, sir,' said a great lubberly fellow, stepping forward; 'and preciously I cut my knuckle agin' his mouth. *I* stopped him, sir.'

The fellow touched his hat with a grin, expecting something for his pains; but, the old gentleman, eyeing him with an expression of dislike, looked anxiously round, as if he contemplated running away himself: which it is very possible he might have attempted to do, and thus have afforded another chase, had not a police officer (who is generally the last person to arrive in such cases) at that moment made his way through the crowd, and seized Oliver by the collar.

'Come, get up,' said the man, roughly.

'It wasn't me indeed, sir. Indeed, indeed, it was

two other boys,' said Oliver, clasping his hands passionately, and looking round. 'They are here somewhere.'

'Oh no, they ain't,' said the officer. He meant this to be ironical, but it was true besides; for the Dodger and Charley Bates had filed off down the first convenient court they came to. 'Come, get up!'

'Don't hurt him,' said the old gentleman, compassionately.

'Oh no, I won't hurt him,' replied the officer, tearing his jacket half off his back, in proof thereof. 'Come, I know you; it won't do. Will you stand upon your legs, you young devil?'

Oliver, who could hardly stand, made a shift to raise himself on his feet, and was at once lugged along the streets by the jacket-collar, at a rapid pace. The gentleman walked on with them by the officer's side; and as many of the crowd as could achieve the feat, got a little ahead, and stared back at Oliver from time to time. The boys shouted in triumph; and on they went.

CHAPTER II

Treats of Mr Fang the police magistrate; and furnishes a slight specimen of his mode of administering justice

The offence had been committed within the district, and indeed in the immediate neighbourhood of, a very notorious metropolitan police office. The crowd had only the satisfaction of accompanying Oliver through two or three streets, and down a place called Mutton Hill, when he was led beneath a low archway, and up a dirty court, into this dispensary of summary justice, by the back way. It was a small paved yard into which they turned, and here they encountered a stout man with a bunch of whiskers on his face, and a bunch of keys in his hand.

'What's the matter now?' said the man carelessly.

'A young fogle-hunter,' replied the man who had Oliver in charge.

'Are you the party that's been robbed, sir?' enquired the man with the keys.

'Yes, I am,' replied the old gentleman; 'but I am not sure that this boy actually took the handkerchief. I – I would rather not press the case.'

'Must go before the magistrate now, sir,' replied the man. 'His worship will be disengaged in half a minute. Now, young gallows!'

This was an invitation for Oliver to enter through a door which he unlocked as he spoke, and which led into a stone cell. Here he was searched; and nothing being found upon him, locked up.

This cell was in shape and size something like an area cellar, only not so light. It was most intolerably dirty; for it was Monday morning; and it had been tenanted by six drunken people, who had been locked up, elsewhere, since Saturday night. But this is little. In our station-houses, men and women are every night confined on the most trivial *charges* – the word is worth noting – in dungeons, compared with which, those in Newgate, occupied by the most atrocious felons, tried, found guilty, and under sentence of death, are palaces. Let anyone who doubts this, compare the two.

The old gentleman looked almost as rueful as Oliver when the key grated in the lock. He turned with a sigh to the book, which had been the innocent cause of all this disturbance.

'There is something in that boy's face,' said the old gentleman to himself as he walked slowly away, tapping his chin with the cover of the book, in a thoughtful manner; 'something that touches and interests me. *Can* he be innocent? He looked like – By the by,' exclaimed the old gentleman, halting very abruptly, and staring up into the sky, 'Bless my soul! Where have I seen something like that look before?'

After musing for some minutes, the old gentleman walked, with the same meditative face, into a back ante room opening from the yard; and there, retiring into a corner, called up before his mind's eye a vast amphitheatre of faces over which a dusky curtain had hung for many years. 'No,' said the old gentleman, shaking his head; 'it must be imagination.'

He wandered over them again. He had called them into view, and it was not easy to replace the shroud that had so long concealed them. There were the faces of friends, and foes, and of many that had been almost strangers peering intrusively from the crowd; there were the faces of young and blooming girls that were now old women; there were faces that the grave had changed and closed upon, but which the mind, superior to its power, still dressed in their old freshness and beauty, calling back the lustre of the eyes, the brightness of the smile, the beaming of the soul through its mask of clay, and whispering of beauty beyond the tomb, changed but to be heightened, and taken from earth only to be set up as a light, to shed a soft and gentle glow upon the path to Heaven.

But the old gentleman could recall no one countenance of which Oliver's features bore a trace. So, he heaved a sigh over the recollections he had awakened; and being, happily for himself, an absent old gentleman, buried them again in the pages of the musty book.

He was roused by a touch on the shoulder, and a request from the man with the keys to follow him into the office. He closed his book hastily; and was at once ushered into the imposing presence of the renowned Mr Fang.

The office was a front parlour, with a panelled wall. Mr Fang sat behind a bar, at the upper end; and on one side the door was a sort of wooden pen in which poor little Oliver was already deposited: trembling very much at the awfulness of the scene.

Mr Fang was a lean, long-backed, stiff-necked, middle-sized man, with no great quantity of hair, and what he had, growing on the back and sides of his head. His face was stern, and much flushed. If he were really not in the habit of drinking rather more than was exactly good for him, he might have brought an action against his countenance for libel, and have recovered heavy damages.

The old gentleman bowed respectfully; and advancing to the magistrate's desk, said, suiting the action to the word, 'That is my name and address, sir.' He then withdrew a pace or two; and, with another polite and gentlemanly inclination of the head, waited to be questioned.

Now, it so happened that Mr Fang was at that moment perusing a leading article in a newspaper of the morning, adverting to some recent decision of his, and commending him, for the three hundred and fiftieth time, to the special and particular notice of the Secretary of State for the Home Department. He was out of temper; and he looked up with an angry scowl.

'Who are you?' said Mr Fang.

The old gentleman pointed, with some surprise, to his card.

'Officer!' said Mr Fang, tossing the card contemptuously away with the newspaper. 'Who is this fellow?'

'My name, sir,' said the old gentleman, speaking *like* a gentleman, 'my name, sir, is Brownlow. Permit me to enquire the name of the magistrate who offers a gratuitous and unprovoked insult to a respectable person, under the protection of the bench.' Saying this, Mr Brownlow looked round the office as if in search of some person who would afford him the required information.

'Officer!' said Mr Fang, throwing the paper on one side, 'what's this fellow charged with?'

'He's not charged at all, your worship,' replied the officer. 'He appears against the boy, your worship.'

His worship knew this perfectly well; but it was a good annoyance, and a safe one.

'Appears against the boy, does he?' said Fang, surveying Mr Brownlow contemptuously from head to foot. 'Swear him!'

'Before I am sworn, I must beg to say one word,' said Mr Brownlow: 'and that is, that I really never, without actual experience, could have believed – '

'Hold your tongue, sir!' said Mr Fang, peremptorily.

'I will not, sir!' replied the old gentleman.

'Hold your tongue this instant, or I'll have you turned out of the office!' said Mr Fang. 'You're an insolent, impertinent fellow. How dare you bully a magistrate!'

At this point of the enquiry, Oliver raised his head; and, looking round with imploring eyes, murmured a feeble prayer for a draught of water.

'Stuff and nonsense!' said Mr Fang: 'don't try to make a fool of me.'

'I think he really is ill, your worship,' remonstrated the officer.

'I know better,' said Mr Fang.

'Take care of him, officer,' said the old gentleman, raising his hands instinctively; 'he'll fall down.'

'Stand away, officer,' cried Fang; 'let him, if he likes.'

Oliver availed himself of the kind permission, and fell to the floor in a fainting fit. The men in the office looked at each other, but no one dared to stir.

'I knew he was shamming,' said Fang, as if this were incontestable proof of the fact. 'Let him lie there; he'll soon be tired of that.'

'How do you propose to deal with the case, sir?' enquired the clerk in a low voice.

'Summarily,' replied Mr Fang. 'He stands committed for three months – hard labour of course. Clear the office.'

The door was opened for this purpose, and a couple of men were preparing to carry the insensible boy to his cell; when an elderly man of decent but poor appearance, clad in an old suit of black, rushed hastily into the office, and advanced towards the bench.

'Stop, stop! Don't take him away! For Heaven's sake stop a moment!' cried the new-comer, breathless with haste.

Although the presiding Genii in such an office as this, exercise a summary and arbitrary power over the liberties, the good name, the character, almost the lives, of Her Majesty's subjects, especially of the poorer class; and although, within such walls, enough fantastic tricks are daily played to make the angels blind with weeping; they are closed to the public, save through the medium of the daily press. Mr Fang was consequently not a little indignant to see an unbidden guest enter in such irreverent disorder.

'What is this? Who is this? Turn this man out. Clear the office!' cried Mr Fang.

'I *will* speak,' cried the man; 'I will not be turned out. I saw it all. I keep the bookstall. I demand to be sworn. I will not be put down. Mr Fang, you must hear me. You must not refuse, sir.'

The man was right. His manner was determined; and the matter was growing rather too serious to be hushed up.

'Swear the man,' growled Mr Fang, with a very ill grace. 'Now, man, what have you got to say?'

'This,' said the man: 'I saw three boys: two others and the prisoner here: loitering on the opposite side of the way, when this gentleman was reading. The robbery was committed by another boy. I saw it done; and I saw that this boy was perfectly amazed and stupefied by it.' Having by this time recovered a little breath, the worthy bookstall-keeper proceeded to relate, in a more coherent manner, the exact circumstances of the robbery.

'Why didn't you come here before?' said Fang, after a pause.

'I hadn't a soul to mind the shop,' replied the man. 'Everybody who could have helped me, had joined in the pursuit. I could get nobody till five minutes ago; and I've run here all the way.'

'The prosecutor was reading, was he?' enquired Fang, after another pause.

Weak, and thin, and pallid, he awoke at last from what seemed to have been a long and troubled dream. Feebly raising himself in the bed, with his head resting on his trembling arm, he looked anxiously around.

'What room is this? Where have I been brought to?' said Oliver. 'This is not the place I went to sleep in.'

He uttered these words in a feeble voice, being very faint and weak; but they were overheard at once. The curtain at the bed's head was hastily drawn back, and a motherly old lady, very neatly and precisely dressed, rose as she undrew it, from an armchair close by, in which she had been sitting at needlework.

'Hush, my dear,' said the old lady softly. 'You must be very quiet, or you will be ill again; and you have been very bad – as bad as bad could be, pretty nigh. Lie down again; there's a dear!' With those words, the old lady very gently placed Oliver's head upon the pillow; and, smoothing back his hair from his forehead, looked so kindly and lovingly in his face, that he could not help placing his little withered hand in hers, and drawing it round his neck.

'Save us!' said the old lady, with tears in her eyes, 'what a grateful little dear it is. Pretty creetur! What would his mother feel if she had sat by him as I have, and could see him now!'

'Perhaps she does see me,' whispered Oliver, folding his hands together; 'perhaps she has sat by me. I almost feel as if she had.'

'That was the fever, my dear,' said the old lady mildly.

'I suppose it was,' replied Oliver, 'because Heaven is a long way off; and they are too happy there, to come down to the bedside of a poor boy. But if she knew I was ill, she must have pitied me, even there; for she was very ill herself before she died. She can't know anything about me though,' added Oliver after a moment's silence. 'If she had seen me hurt, it would have made her sorrowful; and her face has always looked sweet and happy, when I have dreamed of her.'

The old lady made no reply to this; but wiping her eyes first, and her spectacles, which lay on the counter-pane, afterwards, as if they were part and parcel of those features, brought some cool stuff for Oliver to drink; and then, patting him on the cheek, told him he must lie very quiet, or he would be ill again.

So, Oliver kept very still; partly because he was anxious to obey the kind old lady in all things; and partly, to tell the truth, because he was completely exhausted with what he had already said. He soon fell into a gentle doze, from which he was awakened by the light of a candle: which, being brought near the bed, showed him a gentleman with a very large and loud-ticking gold watch in his hand, who felt his pulse, and said he was a great deal better.

'You *are* a great deal better, are you not, my dear?' said the gentleman.

'Yes, thank you, sir,' replied Oliver.

'Yes, I know you are,' said the gentleman: 'You're hungry too, a'n't you?'

'No, sir,' answered Oliver.

'Hem!' said the gentleman. 'No, I know you're not. He is not hungry, Mrs Bedwin,' said the gentleman: looking very wise.

The old lady made a respectful inclination of the head, which seemed to say that she thought the doctor was a very clever man. The doctor appeared much of the same opinion himself.

'Oh no, no,' returned Oliver quickly; 'but the eyes look so sorrowful; and where I sit, they seem fixed upon me. It makes my heart beat,' added Oliver in a low voice, 'as if it was alive, and wanted to speak to me, but couldn't.'

'Lord save us!' exclaimed the old lady, starting; 'don't talk in that way, child. You're weak and nervous after your illness. Let me wheel your chair round to the other side; and then you won't see it. There!' said the old lady, suiting the action to the word; 'you don't see it now, at all events.'

Oliver *did* see it in his mind's eye as distinctly as if he had not altered his position; but he thought it better not to worry the kind old lady; so he smiled gently when she looked at him; and Mrs Bedwin, satisfied that he felt more comfortable, salted and broke bits of toasted bread into the broth, with all the bustle befitting so solemn a preparation. Oliver got through it with extraordinary expedition. He had scarcely swallowed the last spoonful, when there came a soft rap at the door. 'Come in,' said the old lady; and in walked Mr Brownlow.

Now, the old gentleman came in as brisk as need be; but, he had no sooner raised his spectacles on his forehead, and thrust his hands behind the skirts of his dressing-gown to take a good long look at Oliver, than his countenance underwent a very great variety of odd contortions. Oliver looked very worn and shadowy from sickness, and made an ineffectual attempt to stand up, out of respect to his benefactor, which terminated in his sinking back into the chair again; and the fact is, if the truth must be told, that Mr Brownlow's heart, being large enough for any six ordinary old gentlemen of humane disposition, forced a supply of tears into his eyes, by some hydraulic process which we are not sufficiently philosophical to be in a condition to explain.

'Poor boy, poor boy!' said Mr Brownlow, clearing his throat. 'I'm rather hoarse this morning, Mrs Bedwin. I'm afraid I have caught cold.'

'I hope not, sir,' said Mrs Bedwin. 'Everything you have had, has been well aired, sir.'

'I don't know, Bedwin. I don't know,' said Mr Brownlow; 'I rather think I had a damp napkin at dinner-time yesterday; but never mind that. How do you feel, my dear?'

'Very happy, sir,' replied Oliver. 'And very grateful indeed, sir, for your goodness to me.'

'Good boy,' said Mr Brownlow, stoutly. 'Have you given him any nourishment, Bedwin? Any slops, eh?'

'He has just had a basin of beautiful strong broth, sir,' replied Mrs Bedwin: drawing herself up slightly, and laying a strong emphasis on the last word: to intimate that between slops, and broth well compounded, there existed no affinity or connection whatsoever.

'Ugh!' said Mr Brownlow, with a slight shudder; 'a couple of glasses of port wine would have done him a great deal more good. Wouldn't they, Tom White, eh?'

'My name is Oliver, sir,' replied the little invalid: with a look of great astonishment.

'Oliver,' said Mr Brownlow; 'Oliver what? Oliver White, eh?'

'No sir, Twist, Oliver Twist.'

'Queer name!' said the old gentleman. 'What made you tell the magistrate your name was White?'

'I never told him so, sir,' returned Oliver in amazement.

This sounded so like a falsehood, that the old gentleman looked somewhat sternly in Oliver's face. It was impossible to doubt him; there was truth in every one of its thin and sharpened lineaments.

'Some mistake,' said Mr Brownlow. But, although his motive for looking steadily at Oliver no longer existed, the old idea of the resemblance between his features and some familiar face came upon him so strongly, that he could not withdraw his gaze.

'I hope you are not angry with me, sir?' said Oliver, raising his eyes beseechingly.

'No, no,' replied the old gentleman. 'Why! what's this? Bedwin, look there!'

As he spoke, he pointed hastily to the picture above Oliver's head, and then to the boy's face. There was its living copy. The eyes, the head, the mouth; every feature was the same. The expression was for the instant, so precisely alike, that the minutest line seemed copied with startling accuracy!

Oliver knew not the cause of this sudden exclamation; for, not being strong enough to bear the start it gave him, he fainted away. A weakness on his part, which affords the narrative an opportunity of relieving the reader from suspense, in behalf of the two young pupils of the Merry Old Gentleman; and of recording –

That when the Dodger, and his accomplished friend Master Bates, joined in the hue-and-cry which was raised at Oliver's heels, in consequence of their executing an illegal conveyance of Mr Brownlow's personal property, as has been already described, they were actuated by a very laudable and becoming regard for themselves; and forasmuch as the freedom of the subject and the liberty of the individual are among the first and proudest boasts of a true-hearted Englishman, so, I need hardly beg the reader to observe, that this action should tend to exalt them in the opinion of all public and patriotic men, in almost as great a degree as this strong proof of their anxiety for their own preservation and safety goes to corroborate and confirm the little code of laws which certain profound and sound-judging philosophers have laid down as the mainsprings of all Nature's deeds and actions: the said philosophers very wisely reducing the good lady's proceedings to matters of maxim and theory: and, by a very neat and pretty compliment to her exalted wisdom and understanding, putting entirely out of sight any considerations of heart, or generous impulse and feeling. For, these are matters totally beneath a female who is acknowledged by universal admission to be far above the numerous little foibles and weaknesses of her sex.

If I wanted any further proof of the strictly philosophical nature of the conduct of these young gentlemen in their very delicate predicament, I should at once find it in the fact (also recorded in a foregoing part of this narrative), of their quitting the pursuit, when the general attention was fixed upon Oliver; and making immediately for their home by the shortest possible cut. Although I do not mean to assert that it is usually the practice of renowned and learned sages, to shorten the road to any great conclusion (their course indeed being rather to lengthen the distance, by various circumlocutions and discursive staggerings, like unto those in which drunken men under the pressure of a too mighty flow of ideas, are prone to indulge); still, I do mean to say, and do say distinctly, that it is the invariable practice of many mighty philosophers, in carrying out their theories, to evince great wisdom and foresight in providing against every possible contingency which can be supposed at all likely to affect themselves. Thus, to do a great right, you may do a little wrong; and you may take any means which the end to be attained, will justify; the amount of the right, or the amount of the wrong, or indeed the distinction between the two, being left entirely to the philosopher concerned, to be settled and determined by his clear, comprehensive, and impartial view of his own particular case.

It was not until the two boys had scoured, with great rapidity, through a most intricate maze of narrow streets and courts, that they ventured to halt beneath a low and dark archway. Having remained silent here, just long enough to recover breath to speak, Master Bates uttered an exclamation of amusement and delight; and, bursting into an uncontrollable fit of laughter, flung himself upon a doorstep, and rolled thereon in a transport of mirth.

'What's the matter?' enquired the Dodger.

'Ha! ha! ha!' roared Charley Bates.

'Hold your noise,' remonstrated the Dodger, looking cautiously round. 'Do you want to be grabbed, stupid?'

'I can't help it,' said Charley, 'I can't help it! To see him splitting away at that pace, and cutting round the corners, and knocking up against the posts, and starting on again as if he was made of iron as well as them, and me with the wipe in my pocket, singing out arter him – oh, my eye!' The vivid imagination of Master Bates, presented the scene before him in too strong colours. As he arrived at this apostrophe, he again rolled upon the doorstep, and laughed louder than before.

'What'll Fagin say?' enquired the Dodger; taking advantage of the next interval of breathlessness on the part of his friend to propound the question.

'What?' repeated Charley Bates.

'Ah, what?' said the Dodger.

'Why, what should he say?' enquired Charley: stopping rather suddenly in his merriment; for the Dodger's manner was impressive. 'What should he say?'

Mr Dawkins whistled for a couple of minutes; then, taking off his hat, scratched his head, and nodded thrice.

'What do you mean?' said Charley.

'Toor rul lol loo, gammon and spinnage, the frog he wouldn't, and high cockolorum,' said the Dodger: with a slight sneer on his intellectual countenance.

This was explanatory, but not satisfactory. Master Bates felt it so; and again said, 'What do you mean?'

The Dodger made no reply; but putting his hat on again, and gathering the skirts of his long-tailed coat under his arm, thrust his tongue into his cheek, slapped the bridge of his nose some half-dozen times in a familiar but expressive manner, and turning on his heel, slunk down the court. Master Bates followed, with a thoughtful countenance.

The noise of footsteps on the creaking stairs, a few minutes after the occurrence of this conversation, roused the merry old gentleman as he sat over the fire with a saveloy and a small loaf in his left hand; a pocketknife in his right; and a pewter pot on the trivet. There was a rascally smile on his white face as he turned round, and, looking sharply out from under his thick red eyebrows, bent his ear towards the door, and listened.

'Why, how's this?' muttered the Jew: changing countenance; 'only two of 'em? Where's the third? They can't have got into trouble. Hark!'

The footsteps approached nearer; they reached the landing. The door was slowly opened; and the Dodger and Charley Bates entered, closing it behind them.

CHAPTER 13

Some new acquaintances are introduced to the intelligent reader, connected with whom various pleasant matters are related, appertaining to this history

'Where's Oliver?' said the Jew, rising with a menacing look. 'Where's the boy?'

The young thieves eyed their preceptor as if they were alarmed at his violence; and looked uneasily at each other. But they made no reply.

'What's become of the boy?' said the Jew, seizing the Dodger tightly by the collar, and threatening him with horrid imprecations. 'Speak out, or I'll throttle you!'

Mr Fagin looked so very much in earnest, that Charley Bates, who deemed it prudent in all cases to be on the safe side, and who conceived it by no means improbable that it might be his turn to be throttled second, dropped upon his knees, and raised a loud, well-sustained, and continuous roar – something between a mad bull and a speaking trumpet.

'Will you speak?' thundered the Jew: shaking the Dodger so much that his keeping in the big coat at all, seemed perfectly miraculous.

'Why, the traps have got him, and that's all about it,'

133

said the Dodger, sullenly. 'Come, let go o' me, will you!' And, swinging himself, at one jerk, clean out of the big coat, which he left in the Jew's hands, the Dodger snatched up the toasting-fork and made a pass at the merry old gentleman's waistcoat; which, if it had taken effect, would have let a little more merriment out, than could have been easily replaced.

The Jew stepped back in this emergency, with more agility than could have been anticipated in a man of his apparent decrepitude; and, seizing up the pot, prepared to hurl it at his assailant's head. But Charley Bates, at this moment, calling his attention by a perfectly terrific howl, he suddenly altered its destination, and flung it full at that young gentleman.

'Why, what the blazes is in the wind now?' growled a deep voice. 'Who pitched that 'ere at me? It's well it's the beer, and not the pot, as hit me, or I'd have settled somebody. I might have know'd, as nobody but an infernal, rich, plundering, thundering old Jew could afford to throw away any drink but water – and not that, unless he done the River Company every quarter. Wot's it all about, Fagin? D— me, if my neck-handkercher an't lined with beer! Come in you sneaking warmint; wot are you stopping outside for, as if you was ashamed of your master! Come in!'

The man who growled out these words, was a stoutly-built fellow of about five-and-thirty, in a black velveteen coat, very soiled drab breeches, lace-up half boots, and grey cotton stockings, which enclosed a bulky pair of legs, with large swelling calves – the kind of legs, which in such costume, always look in an unfinished and incomplete state without a set of fetters to garnish them. He had a brown hat on his head, and a dirty belcher handkerchief round his neck: with the long frayed ends of which he smeared the beer from his face as he spoke. He disclosed, when he had done so, a broad heavy countenance with a beard of three days' growth, and two scowling eyes: one of which displayed various parti-coloured symptoms of having been recently damaged by a blow.

'Come in, d'ye hear?' growled this engaging ruffian.

A white shaggy dog, with his face scratched and torn in twenty different places, skulked into the room.

'Why didn't you come in afore?' said the man. 'You're getting too proud to own me afore company, are you? Lie down!'

This command was accompanied with a kick, which sent the animal to the other end of the room. He appeared well used to it, however; for he coiled himself up in a corner very quietly, without uttering a sound, and winking his very ill-looking eyes twenty times in a minute, appeared to occupy himself in taking a survey of the apartment.

'What are you up to? Ill-treating the boys, you covetous, avaricious, in–sa–ti–a–ble old fence?' said the man, seating himself deliberately. 'I wonder they don't murder you! *I* would if I was them. If I'd been your 'prentice, I'd have done it long ago, and – no I couldn't have sold you afterwards, for you're fit for nothing but keeping as a curiosity of ugliness in a glass bottle, and I suppose they don't blow glass bottles large enough.'

'Hush! hush! Mr Sikes,' said the Jew, trembling; 'don't speak so loud.'

'None of your mistering,' replied the ruffian; 'you always mean mischief when you come that. You know my name: out with it! I shan't disgrace it when the time comes.'

'Well, well, then – Bill Sikes,' said the Jew, with abject humility. 'You seem out of humour, Bill.'

'Perhaps I am,' replied Sikes; 'I should think *you* was rather out of sorts too, unless you mean as little harm when you throw pewter pots about, as you do when you blab and –'

'Are you mad?' said the Jew, catching the man by the sleeve, and pointing towards the boys.

Mr Sikes contented himself with tying an imaginary knot under his left ear, and jerking his head over on the right shoulder; a piece of dumb show which the Jew appeared to understand perfectly. He then, in cant terms, with which his whole conversation was plentifully besprinkled, but which would be quite unintelligible if they were recorded here, demanded a glass of liquor.

'And mind you don't poison it,' said Mr Sikes, laying his hat upon the table.

This was said in jest; but if the speaker could have seen the evil leer with which the Jew bit his pale lip as he turned round to the cupboard, he might have thought the caution not wholly unnecessary, or the wish (at all events) to improve upon the distiller's ingenuity not very far from the old gentleman's merry heart.

After swallowing two or three glasses of spirits, Mr Sikes condescended to take some notice of the young gentlemen; which gracious act led to a conversation, in which the cause and manner of Oliver's capture were circumstantially detailed, with such alterations and improvements on the truth, as to the Dodger appeared most advisable under the circumstances.

'I'm afraid,' said the Jew, 'that he may say something which will get us into trouble.'

'That's very likely,' returned Sikes with a malicious grin. 'You're blowed upon, Fagin.'

'And I'm afraid, you see – ' added the Jew, speaking as if he had not noticed the interruption; and regarding the other closely as he did so, 'I'm afraid that, if the game was up with us, it might be up with a good many more, and that it would come out rather worse for you than it would for me, my dear.'

The man started, and turned round upon the Jew. But the old gentleman's shoulders were shrugged up to his ears; and his eyes were vacantly staring on the opposite wall.

There was a long pause. Every member of the respectable coterie appeared plunged in his own reflections; not excepting the dog, who by a certain malicious licking of his lips seemed to be meditating an attack upon the legs of the first gentleman or lady he might encounter in the streets when he went out.

'Somebody must find out wot's been done at the office,' said Mr Sikes in a much lower tone than he had taken since he came in.

The Jew nodded assent.

'If he hasn't peached, and is committed, there's no fear till he comes out again,' said Mr Sikes, 'and then he must be taken care on. You must get hold of him somehow.'

Again the Jew nodded.

The prudence of this line of action, indeed, was obvious; but, unfortunately, there was one very strong objection to its being adopted. This was, that the Dodger, and Charley Bates, and Fagin, and Mr William Sikes, happened, one and all, to entertain a violent and deeply-rooted antipathy to going near a police-officer on any ground or pretext whatever.

How long they might have sat and looked at each other, in a state of uncertainty not the most pleasant of its kind, it is difficult to guess. It is not necessary to make any guesses on the subject, however; for the sudden entrance of the two young ladies whom Oliver had seen on a former occasion, caused the conversation to flow afresh.

'The very thing!' said the Jew. 'Bet will go; won't you, my dear?'

'Wheres?' enquired the young lady.

'Only just up to the office, my dear,' said the Jew coaxingly.

It is due to the young lady to say that she did not positively affirm that she would not, but that she merely expressed an emphatic and earnest desire to be 'blessed' if she would; a polite and delicate evasion of the request, which shows the young lady to have been possessed of that natural good breeding which cannot bear to inflict upon a fellow-creature, the pain of a direct and pointed refusal.

The Jew's countenance fell. He turned from this young lady, who was gaily, not to say gorgeously attired, in a red gown, green boots, and yellow curl-papers, to the other female.

'Nancy, my dear,' said the Jew in a soothing manner, 'what do *you* say?'

'That it won't do; so it's no use a-trying it on, Fagin,' replied Nancy.

'What do you mean by that?' said Mr Sikes, looking up in a surly manner.

'What I say, Bill,' replied the lady collectedly.

'Why, you're just the very person for it,' reasoned Mr Sikes: 'nobody about here knows anything of you.'

'And as I don't want 'em to, neither,' replied Nancy

in the same composed manner, 'it's rather more no than yes with me, Bill.'

'She'll go, Fagin,' said Sikes.

'No, she won't, Fagin,' said Nancy.

'Yes she will, Fagin,' said Sikes.

And Mr Sikes was right. By dint of alternate threats, promises, and bribes, the lady in question was ultimately prevailed upon to undertake the commission. She was not, indeed, withheld by the same considerations as her agreeable friend; for, having recently removed into the neighbourhood of Field Lane from the remote but genteel suburb of Ratcliffe, she was not under the same apprehension of being recognised by any of her numerous acquaintances.

Accordingly, with a clean white apron tied over her gown, and her curl-papers tucked up under a straw bonnet – both articles of dress being provided from the Jew's inexhaustible stock – Miss Nancy prepared to issue forth on her errand.

'Stop a minute, my dear,' said the Jew, producing a little covered basket. 'Carry that in one hand. It looks more respectable, my dear.'

'Give her a door-key to carry in her t'other one, Fagin,' said Sikes; 'it looks real and genivine like.'

'Yes, yes, my dear, so it does,' said the Jew, hanging a large street-door key on the forefinger of the young lady's right hand. 'There; very good! Very good indeed, my dear!' said the Jew, rubbing his hands.

'Oh, my brother! My poor, dear, sweet, innocent little brother!' exclaimed Nancy, bursting into tears, and wringing the little basket and the street-door key in an agony of distress. 'What has become of him! Where have they taken him to! Oh, do have pity, and tell me what's been done with the dear boy, gentlemen; do, gentlemen, if you please, gentlemen!'

Having uttered these words in a most lamentable and heart-broken tone: to the immeasurable delight of her hearers: Miss Nancy paused, winked to the company, nodded smilingly round, and disappeared.

'Ah! she's a clever girl, my dears,' said the Jew, turning round to his young friends, and shaking his head gravely, as if in mute admonition to them to follow the bright example they had just beheld.

'She's a honour to her sex,' said Mr Sikes, filling his glass, and smiting the table with his enormous fist. 'Here's her health, and wishing they was all like her!'

While these, and many other encomiums, were being passed on the accomplished Nancy, that young lady made the best of her way to the police-office; whither, notwithstanding a little natural timidity consequent upon walking through the streets alone and unprotected, she arrived in perfect safety shortly afterwards.

Entering by the back way, she tapped softly with the key at one of the cell-doors, and listened. There was no sound within: so she coughed and listened again. Still there was no reply: so she spoke.

'Nolly, dear?' murmured Nancy in a gentle voice; 'Nolly?'

There was nobody inside but a miserable shoeless criminal, who had been taken up for playing the flute, and who, the offence against society having been clearly proved, had been very properly committed by Mr Fang to the House of Correction for one month; with the appropriate and amusing remark that since he had so much breath to spare, it would be more wholesomely expended on the treadmill than in a musical instrument. He made no answer: being occupied in mentally bewailing the loss of the flute, which had been confiscated for the use of the county; so Nancy passed on to the next cell, and knocked there.

'Well!' cried a faint and feeble voice.

'Is there a little boy here?' enquired Nancy, with a preliminary sob.

'No,' replied the voice; 'God forbid!'

This was a vagrant of sixty-five, who was going to prison for *not* playing the flute; or, in other words, for begging in the streets, and doing nothing for his livelihood. In the next cell, was another man, who was going to the same prison for hawking tin saucepans without a license; thereby doing something for his living, in defiance of the Stamp-office.

But, as neither of these criminals answered to the name of Oliver, or knew anything about him, Nancy made straight up to the bluff officer in the striped waistcoat; and with the most piteous wailings and lamentations, rendered more piteous by a prompt and efficient use of the street-door key and the little basket, demanded her own dear brother.

'*I* haven't got him, my dear,' said the old man.

'Where is he?' screamed Nancy, in a distracted manner.

'Why, the gentleman's got him,' replied the officer.

'What gentleman? Oh, gracious heavens! What gentleman?' exclaimed Nancy.

In reply to this incoherent questioning, the old man informed the deeply affected sister that Oliver had been taken ill in the office, and discharged in consequence of a witness having proved the robbery to have been committed by another boy, not in custody; and that the prosecutor had carried him away, in an insensible condition, to his own residence: of and concerning which, all the informant knew was, that it was somewhere at Pentonville, he having heard that word mentioned in the directions to the coachman.

In a dreadful state of doubt and uncertainty, the agonised young woman staggered to the gate, and then, exchanging her faltering walk for a swift run, returned by the most devious and complicated route she could think of, to the domicile of the Jew.

Mr Bill Sikes no sooner heard the account of the expedition delivered, than he very hastily called up the white dog, and, putting on his hat, expeditiously departed: without devoting any time to the formality of wishing the company good-morning.

'We must know where he is, my dears; he must be found,' said the Jew, greatly excited. 'Charley, do nothing but skulk about, till you bring home some news of him! Nancy, my dear, I must have him found. I trust to you, my dear – to you and the Artful for everything! Stay, stay,' added the Jew, unlocking a drawer with a shaking hand; 'there's money, my dears. I shall shut up this shop tonight. You'll know where to find me! Don't stop here a minute. Not an instant, my dears!'

With these words, he pushed them from the room: and carefully double-locking and barring the door behind them, drew from its place of concealment the box which he had unintentionally disclosed to Oliver. Then, he hastily proceeded to dispose the watches and jewellery beneath his clothing.

A rap at the door startled him in this occupation.

'Who's there?' he cried in a shrill tone.

'Me!' replied the voice of the Dodger, through the keyhole.

'What now?' cried the Jew impatiently.

'Is he to be kidnapped to the other ken, Nancy says?' enquired the Dodger.

'Yes,' replied the Jew, 'wherever she lays hands on him. Find him, find him out, that's all! I shall know what to do next; never fear.'

The boy murmured a reply of intelligence; and hurried downstairs after his companions.

'He has not peached so far,' said the Jew, as he pursued his occupation. 'If he means to blab us among his new friends, we may stop his mouth yet.'

CHAPTER 14

Comprising further particulars of Oliver's stay at Mr Brownlow's, with the remarkable prediction which one Mr Grimwig uttered concerning him, when he went out on an errand

Oliver soon recovering from the fainting-fit into which Mr Brownlow's abrupt exclamation had thrown him, the subject of the picture was carefully avoided, both by the old gentleman and Mrs Bedwin, in the conversation that ensued: which indeed bore no reference to Oliver's history or prospects, but was confined to such topics as might amuse without exciting him. He was still too weak to get up to breakfast; but, when he came down into the house-keeper's room next day, his first act was to cast an eager glance at the wall, in the hope of again looking on the face of the beautiful lady. His expectations were disappointed, however, for the picture had been removed.

'Ah!' said the housekeeper, watching the direction of Oliver's eyes. 'It is gone, you see.'

'I see it is, ma'am,' replied Oliver. 'Why have they taken it away?'

'It has been taken down, child, because Mr Brownlow said, that as it seemed to worry you, perhaps it might prevent your getting well, you know,' rejoined the old lady.

'Oh, no, indeed. It didn't worry me, ma'am,' said Oliver. 'I liked to see it. I quite loved it.'

'Well, well!' said the old lady, good-humouredly; 'you get well as fast as ever you can, dear, and it shall be hung up again. There! I promise you that! Now, let us talk about something else.'

This was all the information Oliver could obtain about the picture at that time. As the old lady had been so kind to him in his illness, he endeavoured to think no more of the subject just then; so he listened attentively to a great many stories she told him, about an amiable and handsome daughter of hers, who was married to an amiable and handsome man, and lived in the country; and about a son, who was clerk to a merchant in the West Indies; and who was, also, such a good young man, and wrote such dutiful letters home four times a-year, that it brought the tears into her eyes to talk about them. When the old lady had expatiated, a long time, on the excellences of her children, and the merits of her kind good husband besides, who had been dead and gone, poor dear soul! just six-and-twenty years, it was time to have tea. After tea she began to teach Oliver cribbage: which he learnt as quickly as she could teach: and at which game they played, with great interest and gravity, until it was time for the invalid to have some warm wine and water, with a slice of dry toast, and then to go cosily to bed.

They were happy days, those of Oliver's recovery. Everything was so quiet, and neat, and orderly; everybody was kind and gentle; that after the noise and turbulence in the midst of which he had always lived, it seemed like Heaven itself. He was no sooner strong enough to put his clothes on, properly, than Mr Brownlow caused a complete new suit, and a new cap, and a new pair of shoes, to be provided for him. As Oliver was told that he might do what he liked with the old clothes, he gave them to a servant who had been very kind to him, and asked her to sell them to a Jew, and keep the money for herself. This she very readily did; and, as Oliver looked out of the parlour window, and saw the Jew roll them up in his bag and walk away, he felt quite delighted to think that they were safely gone, and that there was now no possible danger of his ever being able to wear them again. They were sad rags, to tell the truth; and Oliver had never had a new suit before.

One evening, about a week after the affair of the picture, as he was sitting talking to Mrs Bedwin, there came a message down from Mr Brownlow, that if Oliver Twist felt pretty well, he should like to see him in his study, and talk to him a little while.

'Bless us, and save us! Wash your hands, and let me part your hair nicely for you, child,' said Mrs Bedwin. 'Dear heart alive! If we had known he would have asked for you, we would have put you a clean collar on, and made you as smart as sixpence!'

Oliver did as the old lady bade him; and, although she lamented grievously, meanwhile, that there was not even time to crimp the little frill that bordered his shirt-collar; he looked so delicate and handsome, despite that important personal advantage, that she went so far as to say: looking at him with great complacency from head to foot, that she really didn't think it would have been possible, on the longest notice, to have made much difference in him for the better.

Thus encouraged, Oliver tapped at the study door. On Mr Brownlow calling to him to come in, he found himself in a little back room, quite full of books, with a window, looking into some pleasant little gardens. There was a table drawn up before the window, at which Mr Brownlow was seated reading. When he saw Oliver, he pushed the book away from him, and told him to come near the table, and sit down. Oliver complied; marvelling where the people could be found to read such a great number of books as seemed to be written to make the world wiser. Which is still a marvel to more experienced people than Oliver Twist, every day of their lives.

'There are a good many books, are there not, my boy?' said Mr Brownlow, observing the curiosity with which Oliver surveyed the shelves that reached from the floor to the ceiling.

'A great number, sir,' replied Oliver. 'I never saw so many.'

'You shall read them, if you behave well,' said the old gentleman kindly; 'and you will like that, better than looking at the outsides – that is, in some cases; because there *are* books of which the backs and covers are by far the best parts.'

'I suppose they are those heavy ones, sir,' said Oliver, pointing to some large quartos, with a good deal of gilding about the binding.

'Not always those,' said the old gentleman, patting Oliver on the head, and smiling as he did so; 'there are other equally heavy ones, though of a much smaller size. How should you like to grow up a clever man, and write books, eh?'

'I think I would rather read them, sir,' replied Oliver.

'What! wouldn't you like to be a book-writer?' said the old gentleman.

Oliver considered a little while; and at last said, he should think it would be a much better thing to be a bookseller; upon which the old gentleman laughed heartily, and declared he had said a very good thing. Which Oliver felt glad to have done, though he by no means knew what it was.

'Well, well,' said the old gentleman, composing his features. 'Don't be afraid! We won't make an author of you, while there's an honest trade to be learnt, or brick-making to turn to.'

'Thank you, sir,' said Oliver. At the earnest manner of his reply, the old gentleman laughed again; and said something about a curious instinct, which Oliver, not understanding, paid no very great attention to.

'Now,' said Mr Brownlow, speaking if possible in a kinder, but at the same time in a much more serious manner, than Oliver had ever known him assume yet, 'I want you to pay great attention, my boy, to what I am going to say. I shall talk to you without any reserve; because I am sure you are as well able to understand me, as many older persons would be.'

'Oh, don't tell me you are going to send me away, sir, pray!' exclaimed Oliver, alarmed at the serious tone of the old gentleman's commencement! 'Don't turn me out of doors to wander in the streets again.

Let me stay here, and be a servant. Don't send me back to the wretched place I came from. Have mercy upon a poor boy, sir!'

'My dear child,' said the old gentleman, moved by the warmth of Oliver's sudden appeal; 'you need not be afraid of my deserting you, unless you give me cause.'

'I never, never will, sir,' interposed Oliver.

'I hope not,' rejoined the old gentleman. 'I do not think you ever will. I have been deceived, before, in the objects whom I have endeavoured to benefit; but I feel strongly disposed to trust you, nevertheless; and I am more interested in your behalf than I can well account for, even to myself. The persons on whom I have bestowed my dearest love, lie deep in their graves; but, although the happiness and delight of my life lie buried there too, I have not made a coffin of my heart, and sealed it up, for ever, on my best affections. Deep affliction has but strengthened and refined them.'

As the old gentleman said this in a low voice: more to himself than to his companion: and as he remained silent for a short time afterwards: Oliver sat quite still.

'Well, well!' said the old gentleman at length, in a more cheerful tone, 'I only say this, because you have a young heart; and knowing that I have suffered great pain and sorrow, you will be more careful, perhaps, not to wound me again. You say you are an orphan, without a friend in the world; all the enquiries I have been able to make, confirm the statement. Let me hear your story; where you come from; who brought you up; and how you got into the company in which I found you. Speak the truth, and you shall not be friendless while I live.'

Oliver's sobs checked his utterance for some minutes; when he was on the point of beginning to relate how he had been brought up at the farm, and carried to the workhouse by Mr Bumble, a peculiarly impatient little double-knock was heard at the street-door: and the servant, running upstairs, announced Mr Grimwig.

'Is he coming up?' enquired Mr Brownlow.

'Yes, sir,' replied the servant. 'He asked if there were any muffins in the house; and, when I told him yes, he said he had come to tea.'

Mr Brownlow smiled; and, turning to Oliver, said that Mr Grimwig was an old friend of his, and he must not mind his being a little rough in his manners; for he was a worthy creature at bottom, as he had reason to know.

'Shall I go downstairs, sir?' enquired Oliver.

'No,' replied Mr Brownlow, 'I would rather you remained here.'

At this moment, there walked into the room: supporting himself by a thick stick: a stout old gentleman, rather lame in one leg, who was dressed in a blue coat, striped waistcoat, nankeen breeches and gaiters, and a broad-brimmed white hat, with the sides turned up with green. A very small-plaited shirt frill stuck put from his waistcoat; and a very long steel watch-chain, with nothing but a key at the end, dangled loosely below it. The ends of his white neckerchief were twisted into a ball about the size of an orange; the variety of shapes into which his countenance was twisted, defy description. He had a manner of screwing his head on one side when he spoke; and of looking out of the corners of his eyes at the same time: which irresistibly reminded the beholder of a parrot.

In this attitude, he fixed himself, the moment he made his appearance; and, holding out a small piece of orange-peel at arm's length, exclaimed, in a growling, discontented voice, 'Look here! do you see this! Isn't it a most wonderful and extraordinary thing that I can't call at a man's house but I find a piece of this poor surgeon's-friend on the staircase? I've been lamed with orange-peel once, and I know orange-peel will be my death at last. It will, sir: orange-peel will be my death, or I'll be content to eat my own head, sir!'

This was the handsome offer with which Mr Grimwig backed and confirmed nearly every assertion he made; and it was the more singular in his case, because, even admitting for the sake of argument, the possibility of scientific improvements being ever brought to that pass which will enable a gentleman to eat his own head in the event of his being so disposed, Mr Grimwig's head was such a particularly large one, that the most sanguine man alive could hardly entertain a hope of being able to get through it at a sitting – to put entirely out of the question, a very thick coating of powder.

'I'll eat my head, sir,' repeated Mr Grimwig, striking his stick upon the ground. 'Hallo! what's that!' looking at Oliver, and retreating a pace or two.

'This is young Oliver Twist, whom we were speaking about,' said Mr Brownlow.

Oliver bowed.

'You don't mean to say that's the boy who had the fever, I hope?' said Mr Grimwig, recoiling a little more. 'Wait a minute! Don't speak! Stop – ' continued Mr Grimwig, abruptly, losing all dread of the fever in his triumph at the discovery; 'that's the boy who had the orange! If that's not the boy, sir, who had the orange, and threw this bit of peel upon the staircase, I'll eat my head, and his too.'

'No, no, he has not had one,' said Mr Brownlow, laughing. 'Come! Put down your hat; and speak to my young friend.'

'I feel strongly on this subject, sir,' said the irritable old gentleman, drawing off his gloves. 'There's always more or less orange-peel on the pavement in our street; and I *know* it's put there by the surgeon's boy at the corner. A young woman stumbled over a bit last night, and fell against my garden-railings; directly she got up I saw her look towards his infernal red lamp with the pantomime-light. "Don't go to him," I called out of the window, "he's an assassin! A mantrap!" So he is. If he is not – ' Here the irascible old gentleman gave a great knock on the ground with his stick; which was always understood, by his friends, to imply the customary offer, whenever it was not expressed in words. Then, still keeping his stick in his hand, he sat down; and, opening a double eyeglass, which he wore attached to a broad black riband, took a view of Oliver: who, seeing that he was the object of inspection, coloured, and bowed again.

'That's the boy, is it?' said Mr Grimwig, at length.

'That is the boy,' replied Mr Brownlow.

'How are you, boy?' said Mr Grimwig.

'A great deal better, thank you, sir,' replied Oliver.

Mr Brownlow, seeming to apprehend that his singular friend was about to say something disagreeable, asked Oliver to step downstairs and tell Mrs Bedwin they were ready for tea; which, as he did not half like the visitor's manner, he was very happy to do.

'He is a nice-looking boy, is he not?' enquired Mr Brownlow.

'I don't know,' replied Mr Grimwig, pettishly.

'Don't know?'

'No. I don't know. I never see any difference in boys. I only know two sorts of boys. Mealy boys, and beef-faced boys.'

'And which is Oliver?'

'Mealy. I know a friend who has a beef-faced boy; a fine boy, they call him; with a round head, and red cheeks, and glaring eyes; a horrid boy; with a body and limbs that appear to be swelling out of the seams of his blue clothes; with the voice of a pilot, and the appetite of a wolf. I know him! The wretch!'

'Come,' said Mr Brownlow, 'these are not the characteristics of young Oliver Twist; so he needn't excite your wrath.'

'They are not,' replied Mr Grimwig. 'He may have worse.'

Here, Mr Brownlow coughed impatiently; which appeared to afford Mr Grimwig the most exquisite delight.

'He may have worse, I say,' repeated Mr Grimwig. 'Where does he come from? Who is he? What is he? He has had a fever. What of that? Fevers are not peculiar to good people; are they? Bad people have fevers sometimes; haven't they, eh? I knew a man who was hung in Jamaica for murdering his master. He had had a fever six times; he wasn't recommended to mercy on that account. Pooh! nonsense!'

Now, the fact was, that in the inmost recesses of his own heart, Mr Grimwig was strongly disposed to admit that Oliver's appearance and manner were unusually prepossessing; but he had a strong appetite for contradiction, sharpened on this occasion by the finding of the orange-peel; and, inwardly determining that no man should dictate to him whether a boy was well-looking or not, he had resolved, from the first, to oppose his friend. When Mr Brownlow admitted that on no one point of enquiry could he yet return a satisfactory answer; and that he had postponed any investigation into Oliver's previous history until he thought the boy was strong enough to bear it; Mr Grimwig chuckled maliciously. And he demanded, with a sneer, whether the housekeeper was in the habit of counting the plate at night; because, if she didn't find a tablespoon or two missing some sun-shiny morning, why, he would be content to – and so forth.

All this, Mr Brownlow, although himself somewhat of an impetuous gentleman: knowing his friend's peculiarities, bore with great good humour; as Mr Grimwig, at tea, was graciously pleased to express his entire approval of the muffins, matters went on very smoothly; and Oliver, who made one of the party, began to feel more at his ease than he had yet done in the fierce old gentleman's presence.

'And when are you going to hear a full, true, and particular account of the life and adventures of Oliver Twist?' asked Grimwig of Mr Brownlow, at the conclusion of the meal: looking sideways at Oliver, as he resumed the subject.

'Tomorrow morning,' replied Mr Brownlow. 'I would rather he was alone with me at the time. Come up to me tomorrow morning at ten o'clock, my dear.'

'Yes, sir,' replied Oliver. He answered with some hesitation, because he was confused by Mr Grimwig's looking so hard at him.

'I'll tell you what,' whispered that gentleman to Mr Brownlow; 'he won't come up to you tomorrow morning. I saw him hesitate. He is deceiving you, my good friend.'

'I'll swear he is not,' replied Mr Brownlow, warmly.

'If he is not,' said Mr Grimwig. 'I'll – ' and down went the stick.

'I'll answer for that boy's truth with my life!' said Mr Brownlow, knocking the table.

'And I for his falsehood with my head!' rejoined Mr Grimwig, knocking the table also.

'We shall see,' said Mr Brownlow, checking his rising anger.

'We will,' replied Mr Grimwig, with a provoking smile; 'we will.'

As fate would have it, Mrs Bedwin chanced to bring in, at this moment, a small parcel of books, which Mr Brownlow had that morning purchased of the identical bookstall-keeper, who has already figured in this history; having laid them on the table, she prepared to leave the room.

'Stop the boy, Mrs Bedwin!' said Mr Brownlow; 'there is something to go back.'

'He has gone, sir,' replied Mrs Bedwin.

'Call after him,' said Mr Brownlow; 'it's particular. He is a poor man, and they are not paid for. There are some books to be taken back, too.'

The street door was opened. Oliver ran one way; and the girl ran another; and Mrs Bedwin stood on the step and screamed for the boy; but there was no boy in sight. Oliver and the girl returned, in a breathless state, to report that there were no tidings of him.

'Dear me, I am very sorry for that,' exclaimed Mr Brownlow; 'I particularly wished those books to be returned tonight.'

'Send Oliver with them,' said Mr Grimwig, with, an

ironical smile; 'he will be sure to deliver them safely, you know.'

'Yes: do let me take them, if you please, sir,' said Oliver. 'I'll run all the way, sir.'

The old gentleman was just going to say that Oliver should not go out on any account; when a most malicious cough from Mr Grimwig determined him that he should; and that, by the prompt discharge of the commission, he should prove to him the injustice of his suspicions: on this head at least: at once.

'You *shall* go, my dear,' said the old gentleman. 'The books are on a chair by my table. Fetch them down.'

Oliver, delighted to be of use, brought down the books under his arm in a great bustle; and waited, cap in hand, to hear what message he was to take.

'You are to say,' said Mr Brownlow, glancing steadily at Grimwig; 'you are to say that you have brought those books back; and that you have come to pay the four pound ten I owe him. This is a five-pound note, so you will have to bring me back, ten shillings change.'

'I won't be ten minutes, sir,' replied Oliver, eagerly. Having buttoned up the banknote in his jacket pocket, and placed the books carefully under his arm, he made a respectful bow, and left the room. Mrs Bedwin followed him to the street door, giving him many directions about the nearest way, and the name of the bookseller, and the name of the street: all of which Oliver said he clearly understood. Having superadded many injunctions to be sure and not take cold, the old lady at length permitted him to depart.

'Bless his sweet face!' said the old lady, looking after him. 'I can't bear, somehow, to let him go out of my sight.'

At this moment, Oliver looked gaily round, and nodded before he turned the corner. The old lady smilingly returned his salutation, and, closing the door, went back to her own room.

'Let me see; he'll be back in twenty minutes, at the longest,' said Mr Brownlow, pulling out his watch, and placing it on the table. 'It will be dark by that time.'

'Oh! you really expect him to come back, do you?' enquired Mr Grimwig.

'Don't you?' asked Mr Brownlow, smiling.

The spirit of contradiction was strong in Mr Grimwig's breast, at the moment; and it was rendered stronger by his friend's confident smile.

'No,' he said, smiting the table with his fist, 'I do not. The boy has a new suit of clothes on his back, a set of valuable books under his arm, and a five-pound note in his pocket. He'll join his old friends the thieves, and laugh at you. If ever that boy returns to this house, sir, I'll eat my head.'

With these words he drew his chair closer to the table; and there the two friends sat, in silent expectation, with the watch between them.

It is worthy of remark, as illustrating the importance we attach to our own judgements, and the pride with which we put forth our most rash and hasty conclusions, that, although Mr Grimwig was not by any means a bad-hearted man, and though he would have been unfeignedly sorry to see his respected friend duped and deceived, he really did most earnestly and strongly hope at that moment, that Oliver Twist might not come back.

It grew so dark, that the figures on the dial-plate were scarcely discernible; but there the two old gentlemen continued to sit, in silence, with the watch between them.

CHAPTER 15

*Showing how very fond of Oliver Twist, the
merry old Jew and Miss Nancy were*

In the obscure parlour of a low public house, in the
filthiest part of Little Saffron Hill; a dark and gloomy
den, where a flaring gaslight burnt all day in the
wintertime; and where no ray of sun ever shone in the
summer: there sat, brooding over a little pewter
measure and a small glass, strongly impregnated with
the smell of liquor, a man in a velveteen coat, drab
shorts, half boots and stockings, whom even by that
dim light no experienced agent of police would have
hesitated to recognise as Mr William Sikes. At his feet,
sat a white-coated, red-eyed dog; who occupied himself, alternately, in winking at his master with both
eyes at the same time; and in licking a large, fresh cut
on one side of his mouth, which appeared to be the
result of some recent conflict.

'Keep quiet, you warmint! Keep quiet!' said Mr
Sikes, suddenly breaking silence. Whether his medit-
ations were so intense as to be disturbed by the dog's
winking, or whether his feelings were so wrought upon
by his reflections that they required all the relief
derivable from kicking an unoffending animal to allay
them, is matter for argument and consideration.
Whatever was the cause, the effect was a kick and a
curse, bestowed upon the dog simultaneously.

Dogs are not generally apt to revenge injuries
inflicted upon them by their masters; but Mr Sikes's
dog, having faults of temper in common with his

owner, and labouring, perhaps, at this moment, under a powerful sense of injury, made no more ado but at once fixed his teeth in one of the half boots. Having given it a hearty shake, he retired, growling, under a form; just escaping the pewter measure which Mr Sikes levelled at his head.

'You would, would you?' said Sikes, seizing the poker in one hand, and deliberately opening with the other a large clasp-knife, which he drew from his pocket. 'Come here, you born devil! Come here! D'ye hear?'

The dog no doubt heard; because Mr Sikes spoke in the very harshest key of a very harsh voice; but, appearing to entertain some unaccountable objection to having his throat cut, he remained where he was, and growled more fiercely than before: at the same time grasping the end of the poker between his teeth, and biting at it like a wild beast.

This resistance only infuriated Mr Sikes the more; who, dropping on his knees, began to assail the animal most furiously. The dog jumped from right to left, and from left to right: snapping, growling, barking; the man thrust and swore, and struck and blasphemed; and the struggle was reaching a most critical point for one or other; when, the door suddenly opening, the dog darted out: leaving Bill Sikes with the poker and the clasp-knife in his hands.

There must always be two parties to a quarrel, says the old adage. Mr Sikes, being disappointed of the dog's participation, at once transferred his share in the quarrel to the new-comer.

'What the devil do you come in between me and my dog for?' said Sikes, with a fierce gesture.

'I didn't know, my dear, I didn't know,' replied Fagin, humbly; for the Jew was the newcomer.

OLIVER TWIST

'Didn't know, you white-livered thief!' growled Sikes. 'Couldn't you hear the noise?'

'Not a sound of it, as I'm a living man, Bill,' replied the Jew.

'Oh no! You hear nothing, you don't,' retorted Sikes with a fierce sneer. 'Sneaking in and out, so as nobody hears how you come or go! I wish you had been the dog, Fagin, half a minute ago.'

'Why?' enquired the Jew with a forced smile.

' 'Cause the government, as cares for the lives of such men as you, as haven't half the pluck of curs, lets a man kill a dog how he likes,' replied Sikes, shutting up the knife with a very expressive look; 'that's why.'

The Jew rubbed his hands; and, sitting down at the table, affected to laugh at the pleasantry of his friend. He was obviously very ill at ease, however.

'Grin away,' said Sikes, replacing the poker, and surveying him with savage contempt; 'grin away. You'll never have the laugh at me, though, unless it's behind a nightcap. I've got the upper hand over you, Fagin; and, d – me, I'll keep it. There! If I go, you go; so take care of me.'

'Well, well, my dear,' said the Jew, 'I know all that; we – we – have a mutual interest, Bill – a mutual interest.'

'Humph,' said Sikes, as if he thought the interest lay rather more on the Jew's side than on his. 'Well, what have you got to say to me?'

'It's all passed safe through the melting-pot,' replied Fagin, 'and this is your share. It's rather more than it ought to be, my dear; but as I know you'll do me a good turn another time, and – '

'Stow that gammon,' interposed the robber, impatiently. 'Where is it? Hand over!'

'Yes, yes, Bill; give me time, give me time,' replied the Jew, soothingly. 'Here it is! All safe!' As he spoke, he drew forth an old cotton handkerchief from his breast; and untying a large knot in one corner, produced a small brown-paper packet. Sikes, snatching it from him, hastily opened it; and proceeded to count the sovereigns it contained.

'This is all, is it?' enquired Sikes.

'All,' replied the Jew.

'You haven't opened the parcel and swallowed one or two as you come along, have you?' enquired Sikes, suspiciously. 'Don't put on an injured look at the question; you've done it many a time. Jerk the tinkler.'

These words, in plain English, conveyed an injunction to ring the bell. It was answered by another Jew: younger than Fagin, but nearly as vile and repulsive in appearance.

Bill Sikes merely pointed to the empty measure. The Jew, perfectly understanding the hint, retired to fill it: previously exchanging a remarkable look with Fagin, who raised his eyes for an instant, as if in expectation of it, and shook his head in reply; so slightly that the action would have been almost imperceptible to an observant third person. It was lost upon Sikes, who was stooping at the moment to tie the bootlace which the dog had torn. Possibly, if he had observed the brief interchange of signals, he might have thought that it boded no good to him.

'Is anybody here, Barney?' enquired Fagin; speaking, now that Sikes was looking on, without raising his eyes from the ground.

'Dot a shoul,' replied Barney; whose words: whether they came from the heart or not: made their way through the nose.

'Nobody?' enquired Fagin, in a tone of surprise: which perhaps might mean that Barney was at liberty to tell the truth.

'Dobody but Biss Dadsy,' replied Barney.

'Nancy!' exclaimed Sikes. 'Where? Strike me blind, if I don't honour that 'ere girl, for her native talents.'

'She's bid havid a plate of boiled beef id the bar,' replied Barney.

'Send her here,' said Sikes, pouring out a glass of liquor. 'Send her here.'

Barney looked timidly at Fagin, as if for permission; the Jew remaining silent, and not lifting his eyes from the ground, he retired; and presently returned, ushering in Nancy; who was decorated with the bonnet, apron, basket, and street-door key, complete.

'You are on the scent, are you, Nancy?' enquired Sikes, proffering the glass.

'Yes, I am, Bill,' replied the young lady, disposing of its contents; 'and tired enough of it I am, too. The young brat's been ill and confined to the crib; and – '

'Ah, Nancy, dear!' said Fagin, looking up.

Now, whether a peculiar contraction of the Jew's red eyebrows, and a half-closing of his deeply-set eyes, warned Miss Nancy that she was disposed to be too communicative, is not a matter of much importance. The fact is all we need care for here; and the fact is, that she suddenly checked herself, and with several gracious smiles upon Mr Sikes, turned the conversation to other matters. In about ten minutes' time, Mr Fagin was seized with a fit of coughing; upon which Nancy pulled her shawl over her shoulders, and declared it was time to go. Mr Sikes, finding that he was walking a short part of her way himself, expressed his intention of accompanying her; they went away together, followed, at a little distance, by the dog, who slunk out of a backyard as soon as his master was out of sight.

The Jew thrust his head out of the room door when Sikes had left it; looked after him as he walked up the dark passage; shook his clenched fist; muttered a deep curse; and then, with a horrible grin, reseated himself at the table; where he was soon deeply absorbed in the interesting pages of the Hue-and-Cry.

Meanwhile, Oliver Twist, little dreaming that he was within so very short a distance of the merry old gentleman, was on his way to the bookstall. When he got into Clerkenwell, he accidentally turned down a by-street which was not exactly in his way; but not discovering his mistake until he had got halfway down it, and knowing it must lead in the right direction, he did not think it worth while to turn back; and so marched on, as quickly as he could, with the books under his arm.

He was walking along, thinking how happy and contented he ought to feel; and how much he would give for only one look at poor little Dick, who, starved and beaten, might be weeping bitterly at that very moment; when he was startled by a young woman screaming out very loud, 'Oh, my dear brother!' And he had hardly looked up, to see what the matter was, when he was stopped by having a pair of arms thrown tight round his neck.

'Don't,' cried Oliver, struggling. 'Let go of me. Who is it? What are you stopping me for?'

The only reply to this, was a great number of loud lamentations from the young woman who had embraced him; and who had a little basket and a street-door key in her hand.

'Oh my gracious!' said the young woman. 'I've found him! Oh! Oliver! Oliver! Oh you naughty boy, to make me suffer sich distress on your account! Come home, dear, come. Oh, I've found him. Thank gracious goodness heavins, I've found him!' With these incoherent exclamations, the young woman burst into another fit of crying, and got so dreadfully hysterical, that a couple of women who came up at the moment asked a butcher's boy with a shiny head of hair anointed with suet, who was also looking on, whether he didn't think he had better run for the doctor. To which, the butcher's boy: who appeared of a lounging, not to say indolent disposition: replied, that he thought not.

'Oh, no, no, never mind,' said the young woman, grasping Oliver's hand; 'I'm better now. Come home directly, you cruel boy! Come!'

'What's the matter, ma'am?' enquired one of the women.

'Oh, ma'am,' replied the young woman, 'he ran away, near a month ago, from his parents, who are hard-working and respectable people; and went and joined a set of thieves and bad characters; and almost broke his mother's heart.'

'Young wretch!' said one woman.

'Go home, do, you little brute,' said the other.

'I am not,' replied Oliver, greatly alarmed. 'I don't know her. I haven't any sister, or father and mother either. I'm an orphan; I live at Pentonville.'

'Only hear him, how he braves it out!' cried the young woman.

'Why, it's Nancy!' exclaimed Oliver; who now saw her face for the first time; and started back, in irrepressible astonishment.

'You see he knows me!' cried Nancy, appealing to the bystanders. 'He can't help himself. Make him come home, there's good people, or he'll kill his dear mother and father, and break my heart!'

'What the devil's this?' said a man, bursting out of a beer-shop, with a white dog at his heels; 'young Oliver! Come home to your poor mother, you young dog! Come home directly.'

'I don't belong to them. I don't know them. Help! help!' cried Oliver, struggling in the man's powerful grasp.

'Help!' repeated the man. 'Yes; I'll help you, you young rascal! What books are these? You've been a-stealing 'em, have you? Give 'em here.' With these words, the man tore the volumes from his grasp, and struck him on the head.

'That's right!' cried a looker-on, from a garret-window. 'That's the only way of bringing him to his senses!'

'To be sure!' cried a sleepy-faced carpenter; casting an approving look at the garret-window.

'It'll do him good!' said the two women.

'And he shall have it, too!' rejoined the man, administering another blow, and seizing Oliver by the collar. 'Come on, you young villain! Here, Bull's-eye, mind him, boy! Mind him!'

Weak with recent illness; stupefied by the blows and the suddenness of the attack; terrified by the fierce growling of the dog, and the brutality of the man; overpowered by the conviction of the bystanders that he really was the hardened little wretch he was described to be; what could one poor child do! Dark-ness had set in; it was a low neighbourhood; no help was near; resistance was useless. In another moment,

Oliver claimed by his affectionate friends

he was dragged into a labyrinth of dark narrow courts, and was forced along them at a pace which rendered the few cries he dared to give utterance to, unintelligible. It was of little moment. indeed, whether they were intelligible or no; for there was nobody to care for them, had they been ever so plain.

The gas-lamps were lighted; Mrs Bedwin was waiting anxiously at the open door; the servant had run up the street twenty times to see if there were any traces of Oliver; and still the two old gentlemen sat, per-severingly, in the dark parlour, with the watch between them.

CHAPTER 16

Relates what became of Oliver Twist, after
he had been claimed by Nancy

The narrow streets and courts, at length, terminated in a large open space; scattered about which, were pens for beasts, and other indications of a cattle-market. Sikes slackened his pace when they reached this spot: the girl being quite unable to support any longer, the rapid rate at which they had hitherto walked. Turning to Oliver, he roughly commanded him to take hold of Nancy's hand.

'Do you hear?' growled Sikes, as Oliver hesitated, and looked round.

They were in a dark corner, quite out of the track of passengers. Oliver saw, but too plainly, that resistance would be of no avail. He held out his hand, which Nancy clasped tight in hers.

'Give me the other,' said Sikes, seizing Oliver's unoccupied hand. 'Here, Bull's-eye!'

The dog looked up, and growled.

'See here, boy!' said Sikes, putting his other hand to Oliver's throat; 'if he speaks ever so soft a word, hold him! D'ye mind!'.

The dog growled again; and licking his lips, eyed Oliver as if he were anxious to attach himself to his windpipe without delay.

'He's as willing as a Christian, strike me blind if he isn't!' said Sikes, regarding the animal with a kind of grim and ferocious approval. 'Now, you know what you've got to expect, master, so call away as quick as you like; the dog will soon stop that game. Get on, young 'un!'

Bull's-eye wagged his tail in acknowledgment of this unusually endearing form of speech; and, giving vent to another admonitory growl for the benefit of Oliver, led the way onward.

It was Smithfield that they were crossing, although it might have been Grosvenor Square, for anything Oliver knew to the contrary. The night was dark and foggy. The lights in the shops could scarcely struggle through the heavy mist, which thickened every moment and shrouded the streets and houses in gloom; rendering the strange place still stranger in Oliver's eyes; and making his uncertainty the more dismal and depressing.

They had hurried on a few paces, when a deep church-bell struck the hour. With its first stroke, his two conductors stopped, and turned their heads in the direction whence the sound proceeded.

'Eight o'clock, Bill,' said Nancy, when the bell ceased.

'What's the good of telling me that; I can hear it, can't I!' replied Sikes.

'I wonder whether *they* can hear it,' said Nancy.

'Of course they can,' replied Sikes. 'It was Bartlemy time when I was shopped; and there warn't a penny trumpet in the fair, as I couldn't hear the squeaking on. Arter I was locked up for the night, the row and din outside made the thundering old jail so silent, that I could almost have beat my brains out against the iron plates of the door.'

'Poor fellows!' said Nancy, who still had her face turned towards the quarter in which the bell had sounded. 'Oh, Bill, such fine young chaps as them!'

'Yes; that's all you women think of,' answered Sikes. 'Fine young chaps! Well, they're as good as dead, so it don't much matter.'

With this consolation, Mr Sikes appeared to repress a rising tendency to jealousy, and, clasping Oliver's wrist more firmly, told him to step out again.

'Wait a minute!' said the girl: 'I wouldn't hurry by, if it was you that was coming out to be hung, the next time eight o'clock struck, Bill. I'd walk round and round the place till I dropped, if the snow was on the ground, and I hadn't a shawl to cover me.'

'And what good would that do?' enquired the unsentimental Mr Sikes. 'Unless you could pitch over a file and twenty yards of good stout rope, you might as well be walking fifty mile off, or not walking at all, for all the good it would do me. Come on, and don't stand preaching there.'

The girl burst into a laugh; drew her shawl more closely round her; and they walked away. But Oliver felt her hand tremble, and, looking up in her face as they passed a gas-lamp, saw that it had turned a deadly white.

They walked on, by little-frequented and dirty ways, for a full half-hour: meeting very few people, and those appearing from their looks to hold much the same position in society as Mr Sikes himself. At length they turned into a very filthy narrow street, nearly full of old-clothes shops: the dog running forward, as if conscious that there was no further occasion for his keeping on guard, stopped before the door of a shop that was closed and apparently untenanted; the house was in a ruinous condition, and on the door was nailed a board, intimating that it was to let: which looked as if it had hung there for many years.

'All right,' cried Sikes, glancing cautiously about.

Nancy stooped below the shutters, and Oliver heard the sound of a bell. They crossed to the opposite side of the street, and stood for a few moments under a lamp. A noise, as if a sash-window were gently raised, was heard; and soon afterwards the door softly opened. Mr Sikes then seized the terrified boy by the collar with very little ceremony; and all three were quickly inside the house.

The passage was perfectly dark. They waited, while the person who had let them in, chained and barred the door.

'Anybody here?' enquired Sikes.

'No,' replied a voice, which Oliver thought he had heard before.

'Is the old 'un here?' asked the robber.

'Yes,' replied the voice; 'and precious down in the mouth he has been. Won't he be glad to see you? Oh, no!'

The style of this reply, as well as the voice which delivered it, seemed familiar to Oliver's ears; but it was impossible to distinguish even the form of the speaker in the darkness.

'Let's have a glim,' said Sikes, 'or we shall go breaking our necks, or treading on the dog. Look after your legs if you do!'

'Stand still a moment, and I'll get you one,' replied the voice. The receding footsteps of the speaker were heard; and, in another minute, the form of Mr John Dawkins, otherwise the artful Dodger, appeared. He bore in his right hand a tallow candle stuck in the end of a cleft stick.

The young gentleman did not stop to bestow any other mark of recognition upon Oliver than a humorous grin; but, turning away, beckoned the visitors to follow him down a flight of stairs. They crossed an empty kitchen; and, opening the door of a low earthy-smelling room, which seemed to have been built in a small back-yard, were received with a shout of laughter.

'Oh, my wig, my wig!' cried Master Charles Bates, from whose lungs the laughter had proceeded; 'here he is! oh, cry, here he is! Oh, Fagin, look at him! Fagin, do look at him! I can't bear it; it is such a jolly game, I can't bear it. Hold me, somebody, while I laugh it out.'

With this irrepressible ebullition of mirth, Master Bates laid himself flat on the floor: and kicked convulsively for five minutes, in an ecstasy of facetious joy. Then jumping to his feet, he snatched the cleft stick from the Dodger; and, advancing to Oliver, viewed him round and round; while the Jew, taking off his nightcap, made a great number of low bows to the bewildered boy. The Artful, meantime, who was of a rather saturnine disposition, and seldom gave way to merriment when it interfered with business, rifled Oliver's pockets with steady assiduity.

'Look at his togs, Fagin!' said Charley, putting the

Oliver's reception by Fagin and the boys

light so close to his new jacket as nearly to set him on fire. 'Look at his togs! Superfine cloth, and the heavy swell cut! Oh, my eye, what a game! And his books, too! Nothing but a gentleman, Fagin!'

'Delighted to see you looking so well, my dear,' said the Jew, bowing with mock humility. 'The Artful shall give you another suit, my dear, for fear you should spoil that Sunday one. Why didn't you write, my dear, and say you were coming? We'd have got something warm for supper.'

At this, Master Bates roared again: so loud, that Fagin himself relaxed, and even the Dodger smiled; but as the Artful drew forth the five-pound note at that instant, it is doubtful whether the sally or the discovery awakened his merriment.

'Hallo! what's that?' enquired Sikes, stepping forward as the Jew seized the note. 'That's mine, Fagin.'

'No, no, my dear,' said the Jew. 'Mine, Bill, mine, You shall have the books.'

'If that ain't mine!' said Bill Sikes, putting on his hat with a determined air; 'mine and Nancy's, that is; I'll take the boy back again.'

The Jew started. Oliver started too, though from a very different cause; for he hoped that the dispute might really end in his being taken back.

'Come! Hand over, will you?' said Sikes.

'This is hardly fair, Bill; hardly fair, is it, Nancy?' enquired the Jew.

'Fair, or not fair,' retorted Sikes, 'hand over, I tell you! Do you think Nancy and me has got nothing else to do with our precious time but to spend it in scouting arter, and kidnapping, every young boy as gets grabbed through you? Give it here, you avaricious old skeleton; give it here!'

With this gentle remonstrance, Mr Sikes plucked the note from between the Jew's finger and thumb; and looking the old man coolly in the face, folded it up small, and tied it in his neckerchief.

'That's for our share of the trouble,' said Sikes; 'and not half enough, neither. You may keep the books, if you're fond of reading. If you a'n't, sell 'em.'

'They're very pretty,' said Charley Bates: who, with sundry grimaces, had been affecting to read one of the volumes in question: 'beautiful writing, isn't it, Oliver?' At sight of the dismayed look with which Oliver regarded his tormentors, Master Bates, who was blessed with a lively sense of the ludicrous, fell into another ecstasy, more boisterous than the first.

'They belong to the old gentleman,' said Oliver, wringing his hands; 'to the good, kind, old gentleman who took me into his house, and had me nursed, when I was near dying of the fever. Oh, pray send them back; send him back the books and money. Keep me here all my life long; but pray, pray send them back. He'll think I stole them; the old lady: all of them who were so kind to me: will think I stole them. Oh, do have mercy upon me, and send them back!'

With these words, which were uttered with all the energy of passionate grief, Oliver fell upon his knees at the Jew's feet; and beat his hands together, in perfect desperation.

'The boy's right,' remarked Fagin, looking covertly round, and knitting his shaggy eyebrows into a hard knot. 'You're right, Oliver, you're right; they *will* think you have stolen 'em. Ha! ha!' chuckled the Jew, rubbing his hands; 'it couldn't have happened better, if we had chosen our time!'

'Of course it couldn't,' replied Sikes; 'I know'd that,

directly I see him coming through Clerkenwell, with
the books under his arm. It's all right enough. They're
soft-hearted psalm-singers, or they wouldn't have
taken him in at all; and they'll ask no questions after
him, fear they should be obliged to prosecute, and so
get him lagged. He's safe enough.'

Oliver had looked from one to the other, while these
words were being spoken, as if he were bewildered,
and could scarcely understand what passed; but when
Bill Sikes concluded, he jumped suddenly to his feet,
and tore wildly from the room: uttering shrieks for
help, which made the bare old house echo to the roof.

'Keep back the dog, Bill!' cried Nancy, springing
before the door, and closing it, as the Jew and his two
pupils darted out in pursuit. 'Keep back the dog; he'll
tear the boy to pieces.'

'Serve him right!' cried Sikes, struggling to disen-
gage himself from the girl's grasp. 'Stand off from me,
or I'll split your head against the wall.'

'I don't care for that, Bill, I don't care for that,'
screamed the girl, struggling violently with the man:
'the child shan't be torn down by the dog, unless you
kill me first.'

'Shan't he!' said Sikes, setting his teeth. 'I'll soon do
that, if you don't keep off.'

The housebreaker flung the girl from him to the
further end of the room, just as the Jew and the two
boys returned, dragging Oliver among them.

'What's the matter here?' said Fagin, looking round.

'The girl's gone mad, I think,' replied Sikes, savagely.

'No, she hasn't,' said Nancy, pale and breathless
from the scuffle; 'no, she hasn't, Fagin; don't think it.'

'Then keep quiet, will you?' said the Jew, with a
threatening look.

'No, I won't do that, neither,' replied Nancy, speaking very loud. 'Come! What do you think of that?'

Mr Fagin was sufficiently well acquainted with the manners and customs of that particular species of humanity to which Nancy belonged, to feel tolerably certain that it would be rather unsafe to prolong any conversation with her, at present. With the view of diverting the attention of the company, he turned to Oliver.

'So you wanted to get away, my dear, did you?' said the Jew, taking up a jagged and knotted club which lay in a corner of the fireplace; 'eh?'

Oliver made no reply. But he watched the Jew's motions, and breathed quickly.

'Wanted to get assistance; called for the police; did you?' sneered the Jew, catching the boy by the arm. 'We'll cure you of that, my young master.'

The Jew inflicted a smart blow on Oliver's shoulders with the club; and was raising it for a second, when the girl, rushing forward, wrested it from his hand. She flung it into the fire, with a force that brought some of the glowing coals whirling out into the room.

'I won't stand by and see it done, Fagin,' cried the girl. 'You've got the boy, and what more would you have? – Let him be – let him be – or I shall put that mark on some of you, that will bring me to the gallows before my time.'

The girl stamped her foot violently on the floor as she vented this threat; and with her lips compressed, and her hands clenched, looked alternately at the Jew and the other robber: her face quite colourless from the passion of rage into which she had gradually worked herself.

'Why, Nancy!' said the Jew, in a soothing tone; after

a pause, during which he and Mr Sikes had stared at one another in a disconcerted manner; 'you – you're more clever than ever tonight. Ha! ha! my dear, you are acting beautifully.'

'Am I!' said the girl. 'Take care I don't overdo it. You will be the worse for it, Fagin, if I do; and so I tell you in good time to keep clear of me.'

There is something about a roused woman: especially if she add to all her other strong passions, the fierce impulses of recklessness and despair: which few men like to provoke. The Jew saw that it would be hopeless to affect any further mistake regarding the reality of Miss Nancy's rage; and, shrinking involuntarily back a few paces, cast a glance, half imploring and half cowardly, at Sikes: as if to hint that he was the fittest person to pursue the dialogue.

Mr Sikes, thus mutely appealed to; and possibly feeling his personal pride and influence interested in the immediate reduction of Miss Nancy to reason; gave utterance to about a couple of score of curses and threats, the rapid production of which reflected great credit on the fertility of his invention. As they produced no visible effect on the object against whom they were discharged, however, he resorted to more tangible arguments.

'What do you mean by this?' said Sikes; backing the enquiry with a very common imprecation concerning the most beautiful of human features: which, if it were heard above, only once out of every fifty thousand times that it is uttered below, would render blindness as common a disorder as measles: 'what do you mean by it? Burn my body! Do you know who you are, and what you are?'

'Oh, yes, I know all about it,' replied the girl,

laughing hysterically; and shaking her head from side to side, with a poor assumption of indifference.

'Well, then, keep quiet,' rejoined Sikes, with a growl like that he was accustomed to use when addressing his dog, 'or I'll quiet you for a good long time to come.'

The girl laughed again: even less composedly than before; and, darting a hasty look at Sikes, turned her face aside, and bit her lip till the blood came.

'You're a nice one,' added Sikes, as he surveyed her with a contemptuous air, 'to take up the humane and gen-teel side! A pretty subject for the child, as you call him, to make a friend of!'

'God Almighty help me, I am!' cried the girl passionately; 'and I wish I had been struck dead in the street, or had changed places with them we passed so near tonight, before I had lent a hand in bringing him here. He's a thief, a liar, a devil, all that's bad, from this night forth. Isn't that enough for the old wretch, without blows?'

'Come, come, Sikes,' said the Jew, appealing to him in a remonstratory tone, and motioning towards the boys, who were eagerly attentive to all that passed; 'we must have civil words; civil words, Bill.'

'Civil words!' cried the girl, whose passion was frightful to see. 'Civil words, you villain! Yes, you deserve 'em from me. I thieved for you when I was a child not half as old as this!' pointing to Oliver. 'I have been in the same trade, and in the same service, for twelve years since. Don't you know it? Speak out! Don't you know it?'

'Well, well,' replied the Jew, with an attempt at pacification; 'and, if you have, it's your living!'

'Aye, it is!' returned the girl; not speaking, but pouring out the words in one continuous and vehement scream. 'It is my living; and the cold, wet, dirty streets are my home; and you're the wretch that drove me to them long ago, and that'll keep me there, day and night, day and night, till I die!'

'I shall do you a mischief!' interposed the Jew, goaded by these reproaches; 'a mischief worse than that, if you say much more!'

The girl said nothing more; but, tearing her hair and dress in a transport of passion, made such a rush at the Jew as would probably have left signal marks of her revenge upon him, had not her wrists been seized by Sikes at the right moment; upon which, she made a few ineffectual struggles, and fainted.

'She's all right now,' said Sikes, laying her down in a corner. 'She's uncommon strong in the arms, when she's up in this way.'

The Jew wiped his forehead: and smiled, as if it were a relief to have the disturbance over; but neither he, nor Sikes, nor the dog, nor the boys, seemed to consider it in any other light than a common occurrence incidental to business.

'It's the worst of having to do with women,' said the Jew, replacing his club; 'but they're clever, and we can't get on, in our line, without 'em. Charley, show Oliver to bed.'

'I suppose he'd better not wear his best clothes tomorrow, Fagin, had he?' enquired Charley Bates.

'Certainly not,' replied the Jew, reciprocating the grin with which Charley put the question.

Master Bates, apparently much delighted with his commission, took the cleft stick: and led Oliver into an adjacent kitchen, where there were two or three of the beds on which he had slept before; and here, with many uncontrollable bursts of laughter, he produced the identical old suit of clothes which Oliver had so much congratulated himself upon leaving off at Mr Brownlow's; and the accidental display of which, to Fagin, by the Jew who purchased them, had been the very first clue received, of his whereabout.

'Pull off the smart ones,' said Charley, 'and I'll give 'em to Fagin to take care of. What fun it is!'

Poor Oliver unwillingly complied. Master Bates rolling up the new clothes under his arm, departed from the room, leaving Oliver in the dark, and locking the door behind him.

The noise of Charley's laughter, and the voice of Miss Betsy, who opportunely arrived to throw water over her friend, and perform other feminine offices for the promotion of her recovery, might have kept many people awake under more happy circumstances than those in which Oliver was placed. But he was sick and weary; and he soon fell sound asleep.

CHAPTER 17

Oliver's destiny continuing unpropitious, brings a great man to London to injure his reputation

It is the custom on the stage, in all good murderous melodramas, to present the tragic and the comic scenes, in as regular alternation, as the layers of red and white in a side of streaky bacon. The hero sinks upon his straw bed, weighed down by fetters and misfortunes; in the next scene, his faithful but unconscious squire regales the audience with a comic song. We behold, with throbbing bosoms, the heroine in the grasp of a proud and ruthless baron: her virtue and her life alike in danger, drawing forth her dagger to preserve the one at the cost of the other; and just as our expectations are wrought up to the highest pitch, a whistle is heard, and we are straightway transported to the great hall of the castle: where a grey-headed seneschal sings a funny chorus with a funnier body of vassals, who are free of all sorts of places, from church vaults to palaces, and roam about in company, carolling perpetually.

Such changes appear absurd; but they are not so unnatural as they would seem at first sight. The transitions in real life from well-spread boards to deathbeds, and from mourning-weeds to holiday garments, are not a whit less startling; only, there, we are busy actors, instead of passive lookers-on, which makes a vast difference. The actors in the mimic life of the theatre, are blind to violent transitions and abrupt impulses of passion or feeling, which, presented before the eyes of mere spectators, are at once condemned as outrageous and preposterous.

As sudden shiftings of the scene, and rapid changes of time and place, are not only sanctioned in books by long usage, but are by many considered as the great art of authorship: an author's skill in his craft being, by such critics, chiefly estimated with relation to the dilemmas in which he leaves his characters at the end of every chapter: this brief introduction to the present one may perhaps be deemed unnecessary. If so, let it be considered a delicate intimation on the part of the historian that he is going back to the town in which Oliver Twist was born; the reader taking it for granted that there are good and substantial reasons for making the journey, or he would not be invited to proceed upon such an expedition.

Mr Bumble emerged at early morning from the workhouse-gate, and walked with portly carriage and commanding steps, up the High Street. He was in the full bloom and pride of beadlehood; his cocked hat and coat were dazzling in the morning sun; he clutched his cane with the vigorous tenacity of health and power. Mr Bumble always carried his head high; but this morning it was higher than usual. There was an abstraction in his eye, an elevation in his air, which might have warned an observant stranger that thoughts were passing in the beadle's mind, too great for utterance.

Mr Bumble stopped not to converse with the small shopkeepers and others who spoke to him, deferentially, as he passed along. He merely returned their salutations with a wave of his hand, and relaxed not in his dignified pace, until he reached the farm where Mrs Mann tended the infant paupers with parochial care.

'Drat that beadle!' said Mrs Mann, hearing the well-known shaking at the garden-gate. 'If it isn't him at this time in the morning! Lauk, Mr Bumble, only think of its being you! Well, dear me, it *is* a pleasure, this is! Come into the parlour, sir, please.'

The first sentence was addressed to Susan; and the exclamations of delight were uttered to Mr Bumble: as the good lady unlocked the garden-gate: and showed him, with great attention and respect, into the house.

'Mrs Mann,' said Mr Bumble; not sitting upon, or dropping himself into a seat, as any common jackanapes would: but letting himself gradually and slowly down into a chair; 'Mrs Mann, ma'am, good-morning.'

'Well, and good-morning to *you*, sir,' replied Mrs Mann, with many smiles; 'and hoping you find yourself well, sir!'

'So-so, Mrs Mann,' replied the beadle. 'A porochial life is not a bed of roses, Mrs Mann.'

'Ah, that it isn't indeed, Mr Bumble,' rejoined the lady. And all the infant paupers might have chorused the rejoinder with great propriety, if they had heard it.

'A porochial life, ma'am,' continued Mr Bumble, striking the table with his cane, 'is a life of worrit, and vexation, and hardihood; but all public characters, as I may say, must suffer prosecution.'

Mrs Mann, not very well knowing what the beadle meant, raised her hands with a look of sympathy, and sighed.

'Ah! You may well sigh, Mrs Mann!' said the beadle.

Finding she had done right, Mrs Mann sighed again: evidently to the satisfaction of the public character: who, repressing a complacent smile by looking sternly at his cocked hat, said, 'Mrs Mann, I am a-going to London.'

'Lauk, Mr Bumble!' cried Mrs Mann, starting back.

'To London, ma'am,' resumed the inflexible beadle, 'by coach. I and two paupers, Mrs Mann! A legal action is a-coming on, about a settlement; and the board has appointed me – me, Mrs Mann – to depose to the matter before the quarter-sessions at Clerkinwell. And I very much question,' added Mr Bumble, drawing himself up, 'whether the Clerkinwell Sessions will not find themselves in the wrong box before they have done with me.'

'Oh! you mustn't be too hard upon them, sir,' said Mrs Mann, coaxingly.

'The Clerkinwell Sessions have brought it upon themselves, ma'am,' replied Mr Bumble; 'and if the Clerkinwell Sessions find that they come off rather worse than they expected, the Clerkinwell Sessions have only themselves to thank.'

There was so much determination and depth of purpose about the menacing manner in which Mr Bumble delivered himself of these words, that Mrs Mann appeared quite awed by them. At length she said, 'You're going by coach, sir? I thought it was always usual to send them paupers in carts.'

'That's when they're ill, Mrs Mann,' said the beadle. 'We put the sick paupers into open carts in the rainy weather, to prevent their taking cold.'

'Oh!' said Mrs Mann.

'The opposition coach contracts for these two; and takes them cheap,' said Mr Bumble. 'They are both in a very low state, and we find it would come two pound cheaper to move 'em than to bury 'em – that is, if we can throw 'em upon another parish, which I think we shall be able to do, if they don't die upon the road to spite us. Ha! ha! ha!'

When Mr Bumble had laughed a little while, his eyes again encountered the cocked hat; and he became grave.

'We are forgetting business, ma'am,' said the beadle; 'here is your porochial stipend for the month.'

Mr Bumble produced some silver money rolled up in paper, from his pocketbook; and requested a receipt: which Mrs, Mann wrote.

'It's very much blotted, sir,' said the farmer of infants; 'but it's formal enough, I dare say. Thank you, Mr Bumble, sir, I am very much obliged to you, I'm sure.'

Mr Bumble nodded, blandly, in acknowledgement of Mrs Mann's curtsey; and enquired how the children were.

'Bless their dear little hearts!' said Mrs Mann with emotion, 'they're as well as can be, the dears! Of course, except the two that died last week. And little Dick.'

'Isn't that boy no better?' enquired Mr Bumble.

Mrs Mann shook her head.

'He's a ill-conditioned, wicious, bad-disposed porochial child that,' said Mr Bumble angrily. 'Where is he?'

'I'll bring him to you in one minute, sir,' replied Mrs Mann. 'Here, you Dick!'

After some calling, Dick was discovered. Having had his face put under the pump, and dried upon Mrs Mann's gown, he was led into the awful presence of Mr Bumble, the beadle.

The child was pale and thin; his cheeks were sunken; and his eyes large and bright. The scanty parish dress, the livery of his misery, hung loosely on his feeble body; and his young limbs had wasted away, like those of an old man.

Such was the little being who stood trembling beneath Mr Bumble's glance; not daring to lift his eyes from the floor; and dreading even to hear the beadle's voice.

'Can't you look at the gentleman, you obstinate boy?' said Mrs Mann.

The child meekly raised his eyes, and encountered those of Mr Bumble.

'What's the matter with you, porochial Dick?' enquired Mr Bumble, with well-timed jocularity.

'Nothing, sir,' replied the child faintly.

'I should think not,' said Mrs Mann, who had of course laughed very much at Mr Bumble's humour. 'You want for nothing, I'm sure.'

'I should like – ' faltered the child.

'Heyday!' interposed Mrs Mann, 'I suppose you're going to say that you *do* want for something, now? Why, you little wretch – '

Stop, Mrs Mann, stop!' said the beadle, raising his hand with a show of authority. 'Like what, sir, eh?'

'I should like,' faltered the child, 'if somebody that can write, would put a few words down for me on a piece of paper, and fold it up and seal it, and keep it for me, after I am laid in the ground.'

'Why, what does the boy mean?' exclaimed Mr Bumble, on whom the earnest manner and wan aspect of the child had made some impression: accustomed as he was to such things. 'What do you mean, sir?'

'I should like,' said the child, 'to leave my dear love to poor Oliver Twist; and to let him know how often I have sat by myself and cried to think of his wandering about in the dark nights with nobody to help him. And I should like to tell him,' said the child, pressing his small hands together, and speaking with great fervour, 'that I was glad to die when I was very young; for, perhaps if I had lived to be a man, and had grown old, my little sister who is in Heaven, might forget me, or be unlike me; and it would be so much happier if we were both children there together.'

Mr Bumble surveyed the little speaker, from head to foot, with indescribable astonishment; and, turning to his companion, said, 'They're all in one story, Mrs Mann. That out-dacious Oliver has demogalised them all!'

'I couldn't have believed it, sir!' said Mrs Mann,

holding up her hands, and looking malignantly at Dick. 'I never see such a hardened little wretch!'

'Take him away, ma'am!' said Mr Bumble imperiously. 'This must be stated to the board, Mrs Mann.'

'I hope the gentlemen will understand that it isn't my fault, sir?' said Mrs Mann, whimpering pathetically.

'They shall understand that, ma'am; they shall be acquainted with the true state of the case,' said Mr Bumble. 'There; take him away, I can't bear the sight on him.'

Dick was immediately taken away, and locked up in the coal-cellar. Mr Bumble shortly afterwards took himself off, to prepare for his journey.

At six o'clock next morning, Mr Bumble: having exchanged his cocked hat for a round one, and encased his person in a blue greatcoat with a cape to it: took his place on the outside of the coach, accompanied by the criminals whose settlement was disputed; with whom, in due course of time, he arrived in London. He experienced no other crosses on the way, than those which originated in the perverse behaviour of the two paupers, who persisted in shivering, and complaining of the cold, in a manner which, Mr Bumble declared, caused his teeth to chatter in his head, and made him feel quite uncomfortable; although he had a greatcoat on.

Having disposed of these evil-minded persons for the night, Mr Bumble sat himself down in the house at which the coach stopped; and took a temperate dinner of steaks, oyster sauce, and porter. Putting a glass of hot gin-and-water on the chimney-piece, he drew his chair to the fire; and, with sundry moral reflections on the too-prevalent sin of discontent and complaining, composed himself to read the paper.

The very first paragraph upon which Mr Bumble's eye rested, was the following advertisement.

FIVE GUINEAS REWARD

Whereas a young boy, named Oliver Twist, absconded, or was enticed, on Thursday evening last, from his home at Pentonville; and has not since been heard of. The above reward will be paid to any person who will give such information as will lead to the discovery of the said Oliver Twist, or tend to throw any light upon his previous history, in which the advertiser is, for many reasons, warmly interested.

And then followed a full description of Oliver's dress, person, appearance, and disappearance: with the name and address of Mr Brownlow at full length.

Mr Bumble opened his eyes; read the advertisement, slowly and carefully, three several times; and in something more than five minutes was on his way to Pentonville: having actually, in his excitement, left the glass of hot gin-and-water, untasted.

'Is Mr Brownlow at home?' enquired Mr Bumble of the girl who opened the door.

To this enquiry the girl returned the not uncommon, but rather evasive reply of 'I don't know; where do you come from?'

Mr Bumble no sooner uttered Oliver's name, in explanation of his errand, than Mrs Bedwin, who had been listening at the parlour door, hastened into the passage in a breathless state.

'Come in, come in,' said the old lady: 'I knew we should hear of him. Poor dear! I knew we should! I was certain of it. Bless his heart! I said so, all along.'

Having said this, the worthy old lady hurried back into the parlour again; and seating herself on a sofa, burst into tears. The girl, who was not quite so susceptible, had run upstairs meanwhile; and now returned with a request that Mr Bumble would follow her immediately: which he did.

He was shown into the little back study, where sat Mr Brownlow and his friend Mr Grimwig, with decanters and glasses before them. The latter gentleman at once burst into the exclamation: 'A beadle! A parish beadle, or I'll eat my head.'

'Pray don't interrupt just now,' said Mr Brownlow. 'Take a seat, will you?'

Mr Bumble sat himself down: quite confounded by the oddity of Mr Grimwig's manner. Mr Brownlow moved the lamp, so as to obtain an uninterrupted view of the Beadle's countenance; and said, with a little impatience, 'Now, sir, you come in consequence of having seen the advertisement?'

'Yes, sir,' said Mr Bumble.

'And you *are* a beadle, are you not?' enquired Mr Grimwig.

'I am a porochial beadle, gentlemen,' rejoined Mr Bumble, proudly.

'Of course,' observed Mr Grimwig aside to his friend, 'I knew he was. A beadle all over!'

Mr Brownlow gently shook his head to impose silence on his friend, and resumed: 'Do you know where this poor boy is now?'

'No more than nobody,' replied Mr Bumble.

'Well, what *do* you know of him?' enquired the old gentleman. 'Speak out, my friend, if you have anything to say. What *do* you know of him?'

'You don't happen to know any good of him, do

you?' said Mr Grimwig, caustically; after an attentive perusal of Mr Bumble's features.

Mr Bumble, catching at the enquiry very quickly, shook his head with portentous solemnity.

'You see?' said Mr Grimwig, looking triumphantly at Mr Brownlow.

Mr Brownlow looked apprehensively at Mr Bumble's pursed-up countenance; and requested him to communicate what he knew regarding Oliver, in as few words as possible.

Mr Bumble put down his hat; unbuttoned his coat; folded his arms; inclined his head in a retrospective manner; and, after a few moments' reflection, commenced his story.

It would be tedious if given in the beadle's words: occupying, as it did, some twenty minutes in the telling; but the sum and substance of it was, That Oliver was a foundling, born of low and vicious parents. That he had, from his birth, displayed no better qualities than treachery, ingratitude, and malice. That he had terminated his brief career in the place of his birth, by making a sanguinary and cowardly attack on an unoffending lad, and running away in the night-time from his master's house. In proof of his really being the person he represented himself, Mr Bumble laid upon the table the papers he had brought to town. Folding his arms again, he then awaited Mr Brownlow's observations.

'I fear it is all too true,' said the old gentleman sorrowfully, after looking over the papers. 'This is not much for your intelligence; but I would gladly have given you treble the money, if it had been favourable to the boy.'

It is not improbable that if Mr Bumble had been

possessed of this information at an earlier period of the interview, he might have imparted a very different colouring to his little history. It was too late to do it now, however; so he shook his head gravely, and, pocketing the five guineas, withdrew.

Mr Brownlow paced the room to and fro for some minutes; evidently so much disturbed by the beadle's tale, that even Mr Grimwig forbore to vex him further.

At length he stopped, and rang the bell violently.

'Mrs Bedwin,' said Mr Brownlow, when the house-keeper appeared; 'that boy, Oliver, is an imposter.'

'It can't be, sir. It cannot be,' said the old lady energetically.

'I tell you he is,' retorted the old gentleman. 'What do you mean by can't be? We have just heard a full account of him from his birth; and he has been a thorough-paced little villain, all his life.'

'I never will believe it, sir,' replied the old lady, firmly. 'Never!'

'You old women never believe anything but quack-doctors, and lying storybooks,' growled Mr Grimwig. 'I knew it all along. Why didn't you take my advice in the beginning; you would, if he hadn't had a fever, I suppose, eh? He was interesting, wasn't he? Interesting! Bah!' And Mr Grimwig poked the fire with a flourish.

'He was a dear, grateful, gentle child, sir,' retorted Mrs Bedwin, indignantly. 'I know what children are, sir; and have done these forty years; and people who can't say the same, shouldn't say anything about them. That's my opinion!'

This was a hard hit at Mr Grimwig, who was a bachelor. As it extorted nothing from that gentleman but a smile, the old lady tossed her head, and smoothed down her apron preparatory to another speech, when she was stopped by Mr Brownlow.

'Silence!' said the old gentleman, feigning an anger he was far from feeling. 'Never let me hear the boy's name again. I rang to tell you that. Never. Never, on any pretence, mind! You may leave the room, Mrs Bedwin. Remember! I am in earnest.'

There were sad hearts at Mr Brownlow's that night.

Oliver's heart sank within him, when he thought of his good kind friends; it was well for him that he could not know what they had heard, or it might have broken outright.

CHAPTER 18

How Oliver passed his time in the improving society of his reputable friends

About noon next day, when the Dodger and Master Bates had gone out to pursue their customary avocations, Mr Fagin took the opportunity of reading Oliver a long lecture on the crying sin of ingratitude: of which he clearly demonstrated he had been guilty, to no ordinary extent, in wilfully absenting himself from the society of his anxious friends; and, still more, in endeavouring to escape from them after so much trouble and expense had been incurred in his recovery. Mr Fagin laid great stress on the fact of his having taken Oliver in, and cherished him, when, without his timely aid, he might have perished with hunger; and he related the dismal and affecting history of a young lad whom, in his philanthropy, he had succoured under parallel circumstances, but who, proving unworthy of his confidence and evincing a desire to communicate with the police, had unfortunately come to be hanged at the Old Bailey one morning. Mr Fagin did not seek to conceal his share in the catastrophe, but lamented with tears in his eyes that the wrong-headed and treacherous behaviour of the young person in question, had rendered it necessary that he should become the victim of certain evidence for the crown: which, if it were not precisely true, was indispensably necessary for the safety of him (Mr Fagin) and a few select friends. Mr Fagin concluded by drawing a rather disagreeable picture of the discomforts of hanging; and, with great friendliness and politeness of manner, expressed his anxious hopes that he might never be obliged to submit Oliver Twist to that unpleasant operation.

Little Oliver's blood ran cold, as he listened to the Jew's words, and imperfectly comprehended the dark threats conveyed in them. That it was possible even for justice itself to confound the innocent with the guilty when they were in accidental companionship, he knew already; and that deeply-laid plans for the destruction of inconveniently knowing or over-communicative persons, had been really devised and carried out by the old Jew on more occasions than one, he thought by no means unlikely, when he recollected the general nature of the altercations between that gentleman and Mr Sikes: which seemed to bear reference to some foregone conspiracy of the kind. As he glanced timidly up, and met the Jew's searching look, he felt that his pale face and trembling limbs were neither unnoticed nor unrelished by that wary old gentleman.

The Jew, smiling hideously, patted Oliver on the head, and said, that if he kept himself quiet, and applied himself to business, he saw they would be very good friends yet. Then, taking his hat, and covering himself with an old patched greatcoat, he went out, and locked the room-door behind him.

And so Oliver remained all that day, and for the greater part of many subsequent days, seeing nobody, between early morning and midnight, and left during the long hours to commune with his own thoughts. Which, never failing to revert to his kind friends, and the opinion they must long ago have formed of him, were sad indeed.

After the lapse of a week or so, the Jew left the room-door unlocked; and he was at liberty to wander about the house.

It was a very dirty place. The rooms upstairs had great high wooden chimney-pieces and large doors, with panelled walls and cornices to the ceilings; which, although they were black with neglect and dust, were ornamented in various ways. From all of these tokens Oliver concluded that a long time ago, before the old Jew was born, it had belonged to better people, and had perhaps been quite gay and handsome: dismal and dreary as it looked now.

Spiders had built their webs in the angles of the walls and ceilings; and sometimes, when Oliver walked softly into a room, the mice would scamper across the floor, and run back terrified to their holes. With these exceptions, there was neither sight nor sound of any living thing; and often, when it grew dark, and he was tired of wandering from room to room, he would crouch in the corner of the passage by the street-door, to be as near living people as he could; and would remain there, listening and counting the hours, until the Jew or the boys returned.

In all the rooms, the mouldering shutters were fast closed: the bars which held them were screwed tight into the wood; the only light which was admitted, stealing its way through round holes at the top: which made the rooms more gloomy, and filled them with strange shadows. There was a back-garret window with rusty bars outside, which had no shutter; and out of this, Oliver often gazed with a melancholy face for hours together; but nothing was to be descried from it but a confused and crowded mass of house-tops, blackened chimneys, and gable-ends. Sometimes, indeed, a grizzly head might be seen, peering over the parapet-wall of a distant house: but it was quickly withdrawn again; and as the window of Oliver's observatory was nailed down, and dimmed with the rain and smoke of years, it was as much as he could do to make out the forms of the different objects beyond, without making any attempt to be seen or heard – which he had as much chance of being, as if he had lived inside the ball of St Paul's Cathedral.

One afternoon, the Dodger and Master Bates being engaged out that evening, the first-named young gentleman took it into his head to evince some anxiety regarding the decoration of his person (to do him justice, this was by no means an habitual weakness with him); and, with this end and aim, he condescendingly commanded Oliver to assist him in his toilet, straightway.

Oliver was but too glad to make himself useful; too happy to have some faces, however bad, to look upon; too desirous to conciliate those about him when he could honestly do so; to throw any objection in the way of this proposal. So he at once expressed his readiness; and, kneeling on the floor, while the

Dodger sat upon the table so that he could take his foot in his lap, he applied himself to a process which Mr Dawkins designated as 'japanning his trotter-cases'. The phrase, rendered into plain English, signifieth, cleaning his boots.

Whether it was the sense of freedom and independence which a rational animal may be supposed to feel when he sits on a table in an easy attitude smoking a pipe, swinging one leg carelessly to and fro, and having his boots cleaned all the time, without even the past trouble of having taken them off, or the prospective misery of putting them on, to disturb his reflections; or whether it was the goodness of the tobacco that soothed the feelings of the Dodger, or the mildness of the beer that mollified his thoughts; he was evidently tinctured, for the nonce, with a spice of romance and enthusiasm, foreign to his general nature. He looked down on Oliver, with a thoughtful countenance, for a brief space; and then, raising his head, and heaving a gentle sigh, said, half in abstraction, and half to Master Bates: 'What a pity it is he isn't a prig!'

'Ah!' said Master Charles Bates; 'he don't know what's good for him.'

The Dodger sighed again, and resumed his pipe: as did Charley Bates. They both smoked, for some seconds, in silence.

'I suppose you don't even know what a prig is?' said the Dodger mournfully.

'I think I know that,' replied Oliver, looking up. 'It's a th — ; you're one, are you not?' enquired Oliver, checking himself.

'I am,' replied the Dodger. 'I'd scorn to be anything else.' Mr Dawkins gave his hat a ferocious cock, after delivering this sentiment, and looked at Master Bates, as if to denote that he would feel obliged by his saying anything to the contrary.

'I am,' repeated the Dodger. 'So's Charley. So's Fagin. So's Sikes. So's Nancy. So's Bet. So we all are, down to the dog. And he's the downiest one of the lot!'

'And the least given to peaching,' added Charley Bates.

'He wouldn't so much as bark in a witness-box, for fear of committing himself; no, not if you tied him up in one, and left him there without wittles for a fortnight,' said the Dodger.

'Not a bit of it,' observed Charley.

'He's a rum dog. Don't he look fierce at any strange cove that laughs or sings when he's in company!' pursued the Dodger. 'Won't he growl at all, when he hears a fiddle playing! And don't he hate other dogs as ain't of his breed! Oh, no!'

'He's an out-and-out Christian,' said Charley.

This was merely intended as a tribute to the animal's abilities, but it was an appropriate remark in another sense, if Master Bates had only known it; for there are a good many ladies and gentlemen, claiming to be out-and-out Christians, between whom, and Mr Sikes' dog, there exist strong and singular points of resemblance.

'Well, well,' said the Dodger, recurring to the point from which they had strayed: with that mindfulness of his profession which influenced all his proceedings.

'This hasn't got anything to do with young Green here.'

'No more it has,' said Charley. 'Why don't you put yourself under Fagin, Oliver?'

'And make your fortun' out of hand?' added the Dodger, with a grin.

'And so be able to retire on your property, and do the gen–teel: as I mean to, in the very next leap-year but four that ever comes, and the forty-second Tuesday in Trinity-week,' said Charley Bates.

'I don't like it,' rejoined Oliver, timidly; 'I wish they would let me go. I – I – would rather go.'

'And Fagin would *rather* not!' rejoined Charley.

Oliver knew this too well; but thinking it might be dangerous to express his feelings more openly, he only sighed, and went on with his boot-cleaning.

'Go!' exclaimed the Dodger. 'Why, where's your spirit? Don't you take any pride out of yourself? Would you go and be dependent on your friends?'

'Oh, blow that!' said Master Bates: drawing two or three silk handkerchiefs from his pocket, and tossing them into a cupboard, 'that's too mean, that is.'

'*I* couldn't do it,' said the Dodger, with an air of haughty disgust.

'You can leave your friends, though,' said Oliver with a half smile; 'and let them be punished for what you did.'

'That,' rejoined the Dodger, with a wave of his pipe, 'that was all out of consideration for Fagin, 'cause the traps know that we work together, and he might have got into trouble if we hadn't made out lucky; that was the move, wasn't it, Charley?'

Master Bates nodded assent, and would have spoken; but the recollection of Oliver's flight came so suddenly upon him, that the smoke he was inhaling got entangled with a laugh, and went up into his head, and down into his throat: and brought on a fit of coughing and stamping, about five minutes long.

'Look here!' said the Dodger, drawing forth a handful of shillings and halfpence. 'Here's a jolly life!

What's the odds where it comes from? Here, catch hold; there's plenty more where they were took from. You won't, won't you? Oh, you precious flat!'

'It's naughty, ain't it, Oliver?' enquired Charley Bates. 'He'll come to be scragged, won't he?'

'I don't know what that means,' replied Oliver.

'Something in this way, old feller,' said Charley. As he said it, Master Bates caught up an end of his neckerchief: and, holding it erect in the air, dropped his head on his shoulder, and jerked a curious sound through his teeth: thereby indicating, by a lively panto-mimic representation, that scragging and hanging were one and the same thing.

'That's what it means,' said Charley. 'Look how he stares, Jack! I never did see such prime company as that 'ere boy; he'll be the death of me, I know he will.' Master Charles Bates, having laughed heartily again, resumed his pipe with tears in his eyes.

'You've been brought up bad,' said the Dodger, surveying his boots with much satisfaction when Oliver had polished them. 'Fagin will make something of you, though, or you'll be the first he ever had that turned out unprofitable. You'd better begin at once; for you'll come to the trade long before you think of it; and you're only losing time, Oliver.'

Master Bates backed this advice with sundry moral admonitions of his own: which, being exhausted, he and his friend Mr Dawkins launched into a glowing description of the numerous pleasures incidental to the life they led, interspersed with a variety of hints to Oliver that the best thing he could do, would be to secure Fagin's favour without more delay, by the means which they themselves had employed to gain it.

'And always put this in your pipe, Nolly,' said the

Master Bates explains a professional technicality

Dodger, as the Jew was heard unlocking the door above, 'if you don't take fogles and tickers – '

'What's the good of talking in that way?' interposed Master Bates: 'he don't know what you mean.'

'If you don't take pocket-handkechers and watches,' said the Dodger, reducing his conversation to the level of Oliver's capacity, 'some other cove will; so that the coves that lose 'em will be all the worse, and you'll be all the worse too, and nobody half a ha'p'orth the better, except the chaps wot gets them – and you've just as good a right to them as they have.'

'To be sure, to be sure!' said the Jew, who had entered, unseen by Oliver. 'It all lies in a nutshell, my dear; in a nutshell, take the Dodger's word for it. Ha! ha! ha! He understands the catechism of his trade.'

The old man rubbed his hands gleefully together, as he corroborated the Dodger's reasoning in these terms; and chuckled with delight at his pupil's proficiency.

The conversation proceeded no farther at this time, for the Jew had returned home accompanied by Miss Betsy, and a gentleman whom Oliver had never seen before, but who was accosted by the Dodger as Tom Chitling; and who, having lingered on the stairs to exchange a few gallantries with the lady, now made his appearance.

Mr Chitling was older in years than the Dodger: having perhaps numbered eighteen winters; but there was a degree of deference in his deportment towards that young gentleman which seemed to indicate that he felt himself conscious of a slight inferiority in point of genius and professional acquirements. He had small twinkling eyes, and a pock-marked face; wore a fur cap, a dark corduroy jacket, greasy fustian trousers, and an apron. His wardrobe was, in truth, rather out of

repair; but he excused himself to the company by
stating that his 'time' was only out an hour before; and
that, in consequence of having worn the regimentals
for six weeks past, he had not been able to bestow any
attention on his private clothes. Mr Chitling added,
with strong marks of irritation, that the new way of
fumigating clothes up yonder was infernal unconsti-
tutional, for it burnt holes in them, and there was no
remedy against the County. The same remark he
considered to apply to the regulation mode of cutting
the hair: which he held to be decidedly unlawful.
Mr Chitling wound up his observations by stating
that he had not touched a drop of anything for forty-
two mortal long hard-working days; and that he
'wished he might be busted if he warn't as dry as
a lime-basket'.

'Where do you think this gentleman has come from,
Oliver?' enquired the Jew, with a grin, as the other
boys put a bottle of spirits on the table.

'I – I – don't know, sir,' replied Oliver.

'Who's that?' enquired Tom Chitling, casting a
contemptuous look at Oliver.

'A young friend of mine, my dear,' replied the Jew.

'He's in luck, then,' said the young man, with a
meaning look at Fagin. 'Never mind where I came
from, young 'un; you'll find your way there, soon
enough, I'll bet a crown!'

At this sally, the boys laughed. After some more
jokes on the same subject, they exchanged a few short
whispers with Fagin; and withdrew.

After some words apart between the last comer and
Fagin, they drew their chairs towards the fire; and the
Jew, telling Oliver to come and sit by him, led the
conversation to the topics most calculated to interest

his hearers. These were, the great advantages of the trade, the proficiency of the Dodger, the amiability of Charley Bates, and the liberality of the Jew himself. At length these subjects displayed signs of being thoroughly exhausted; and Mr Chitling did the same: for the house of correction becomes fatiguing after a week or two. Miss Betsy accordingly withdrew; and left the party to their repose.

From this day, Oliver was seldom left alone; but was placed in almost constant communication with the two boys, who played the old game with the Jew every day: whether for their own improvement or Oliver's, Mr Fagin best knew. At other times the old man would tell them stories of robberies he had committed in his younger days: mixed up with so much that was droll and curious, that Oliver could not help laughing heartily, and showing that he was amused in spite of all his better feelings.

In short, the wily old Jew had the boy in his toils. Having prepared his mind, by solitude and gloom, to prefer any society to the companionship of his own sad thoughts in such a dreary place, he was now slowly instilling into his soul the poison which he hoped would blacken it, and change its hue for ever.

CHAPTER 19

In which a notable plan is discussed and determined on

It was a chill, damp, windy night, when the Jew: buttoning his greatcoat tight round his shrivelled body, and pulling the collar up over his ears so as completely to obscure the lower part of his face:

emerged from his den. He paused on the step as the door was locked and chained behind him; and having listened while the boys made all secure, and until their retreating footsteps were no longer audible, slunk down the street as quickly as he could.

The house to which Oliver had been conveyed, was in the neighbourhood of Whitechapel. The Jew stopped for an instant at the corner of the street; and, glancing suspiciously round, crossed the road, and struck off in the direction of Spitalfields.

The mud lay thick upon the stones, and a black mist hung over the streets; the rain fell sluggishly down, and everything felt cold and clammy to the touch. It seemed just the night when it befitted such a being as the Jew to be abroad. As he glided stealthily along, creeping beneath the shelter of the walls and doorways, the hideous old man seemed like some loathsome reptile, engendered in the slime and darkness through which he moved: crawling forth by night, in search of some rich offal for a meal.

He kept on his course, through many winding and narrow ways, until he reached Bethnal Green; then, turning suddenly off to the left, he soon became involved in a maze of the mean and dirty streets which abound in that close and densely-populated quarter.

The Jew was evidently too familiar with the ground he traversed to be at all bewildered, either by the darkness of the night, or the intricacies of the way. He hurried through several alleys and streets, and at length turned into one, lighted only by a single lamp at the farther end. At the door of a house in this street, he knocked; having exchanged a few muttered words with the person who opened it, he walked upstairs.

A dog growled as he touched the handle of a

room-door; and a man's voice demanded who was there.

'Only me, Bill; only me, my dear,' said the Jew, looking in.

'Bring in your body then,' said Sikes. 'Lie down, you stupid brute! Don't you know the devil when he's got a greatcoat on?'

Apparently, the dog had been somewhat deceived by Mr Fagin's outer garment; for as the Jew unbuttoned it, and threw it over the back of a chair, he retired to the corner from which he had risen: wagging his tail as he went, to show that he was as well satisfied as it was in his nature to be.

'Well!' said Sikes.

'Well, my dear,' replied the Jew. 'Ah! Nancy.'

The latter recognition was uttered with just enough of embarrassment to imply a doubt of its reception; for Mr Fagin and his young friend had not met, since she had interfered in behalf of Oliver. All doubts upon the subject, if he had any, were speedily removed by the young lady's behaviour. She took her feet off the fender, pushed back her chair, and bade Fagin draw up his, without saying more about it: for it was a cold night, and no mistake.

'It *is* cold, Nancy dear,' said the Jew, as he warmed his skinny hands over the fire. 'It seems to go right through one,' added the old man, touching his side.

'It must be a piercer, if it finds its way through *your* heart,' said Mr Sikes. 'Give him something to drink, Nancy. Burn my body, make haste! It's enough to turn a man ill, to see his lean old carcase shivering in that way, like a ugly ghost just rose from the grave.'

Nancy quickly brought a bottle from a cupboard, in which there were many: which, to judge from the diversity of their appearance, were filled with several kinds of liquids. Sikes, pouring out a glass of brandy, bade the Jew drink it off.

'Quite enough, quite, thankye, Bill,' replied the Jew, putting down the glass, after just setting his lips to it.

'What! You're afraid of our getting the better of you, are you?' enquired Sikes, fixing his eyes on the Jew. 'Ugh!'

With a hoarse grunt of contempt, Mr Sikes seized the glass, and threw the remainder of its contents into the ashes: as a preparatory ceremony to filling it again for himself: which he did at once.

The Jew glanced round the room, as his companion tossed down the second glassful; not in curiosity, for he had seen it often before; but in a restless and suspicious manner habitual to him. It was a meanly-furnished apartment, with nothing but the contents of the closet to induce the belief that its occupier was anything but a working man; and with no more suspicious articles displayed to view than two or three heavy bludgeons which stood in a corner, and a 'life-preserver' that hung over the chimney-piece.

'There,' said Sikes, smacking his lips. 'Now I'm ready.'

'For business?' enquired the Jew.

'For business,' replied Sikes; 'so say what you've got to say.'

'About the crib at Chertsey, Bill?' said the Jew, drawing his chair forward, and speaking in a very low voice.

'Yes. Wot about it?' enquired Sikes.

'Ah! you know what I mean, my dear,' said the Jew. 'He knows what I mean, Nancy, don't he?'

'No, he don't,' sneered Mr Sikes. 'Or he won't,

and that's the same thing. Speak out, and call things by their right names; don't sit there, winking and blinking, and talking to me in hints, as if you warn't the very first that thought about the robbery. Wot d'ye mean?'

'Hush, Bill, hush!' said the Jew who had in vain attempted to stop this burst of indignation; 'somebody will hear us, my dear. Somebody will hear us.'

'Let 'em hear!' said Sikes; 'I don't care.' But as Mr Sikes *did* care, on reflection, he dropped his voice as he said the words, and grew calmer.

'There, there,' said the Jew, coaxingly. 'It was only my caution, nothing more. Now, my dear, about that crib at Chertsey; when is it to be done, Bill, eh? When is it to be done? Such plate, my dear, such plate!' said the Jew: rubbing his hands, and elevating his eyebrows in a rapture of anticipation.

'Not at all,' replied Sikes coldly.

'Not to be done at all!' echoed the Jew, leaning back in his chair.

'No, not at all,' rejoined Sikes. 'At least it can't be a put-up job, as we expected.'

'Then it hasn't been properly gone about,' said the Jew, turning pale with anger. 'Don't tell me!'

'But I will tell you,' retorted Sikes. 'Who are you that's not to be told? I tell you that Toby Crackit has been hanging about the place for a fortnight, and he can't get one of the servants into a line.'

'Do you mean to tell me, Bill,' said the Jew: softening as the other grew heated: 'that neither of the two men in the house can be got over?'

'Yes, I do mean to tell you so,' replied Sikes. 'The old lady has had 'em these twenty year; and if you were to give 'em five hundred pound, they wouldn't be in it.'

'But do you mean to say, my dear,' remonstrated the Jew, 'that the women can't be got over?'

'Not a bit of it,' replied Sikes.

'Not by flash Toby Crackit?' said the Jew incredulously. 'Think what women are, Bill.'

'No; not even by flash Toby Crackit,' replied Sikes. 'He says he's worn sham whiskers, and a canary waistcoat, the whole blessed time he's been loitering down there, and it's all of no use.'

'He should have tried mustachios and a pair of military trousers, my dear,' said the Jew.

'So he did,' rejoined Sikes, 'and they warn't of no more use than the other plant.'

The Jew looked blank at this information. After ruminating for some minutes with his chin sunk on his breast, he raised his head and said, with a deep sigh, that if flash Toby Crackit reported aright, he feared the game was up.

'And yet,' said the old man, dropping his hands on his knees, 'it's a sad thing, my dear, to lose so much when we had set our hearts upon it.'

'So it is,' said Mr Sikes. 'Worse luck!'

A long silence ensued; during which the Jew was plunged in deep thought, with his face wrinkled into an expression of villainy perfectly demoniacal. Sikes eyed him furtively from time to time. Nancy, apparently fearful of irritating the housebreaker, sat with her eyes fixed upon the fire, as if she had been deaf to all that passed.

'Fagin,' said Sikes, abruptly breaking the stillness that prevailed; 'is it worth fifty shiners extra, if it's safely done from the outside?'

'Yes,' said the Jew, as suddenly rousing himself.

'Is it a bargain?' enquired Sikes.

'Yes, my dear, yes,' rejoined the Jew; his eyes glistening, and every muscle in his face working, with the excitement that the enquiry had awakened.

'Then,' said Sikes, thrusting aside the Jew's hand, with some disdain, 'let it come off as soon as you like. Toby and me were over the garden-wall the night afore last, sounding the panels of the door and shutters. The crib's barred up at night like a jail; but there's one part we can crack, safe and softly.'

'Which is that, Bill?' asked the Jew, eagerly.

'Why,' whispered Sikes, 'as you cross the lawn – '

'Yes?' said the Jew, bending his head forward, with his eyes almost starting out of it.

'Umph!' cried Sikes, stopping short, as the girl, scarcely moving her head, looked suddenly round, and pointed for an instant to the Jew's face. 'Never mind which part it is. You can't do it without me, I know; but it's best to be on the safe side when one deals with you.'

'As you like, my dear, as you like,' replied the Jew. 'Is there no help wanted, but yours and Toby's?'

'None,' said Sikes. ' 'Cept a centre-bit and a boy. The first we've both got; the second you must find us.'

'A boy!' exclaimed the Jew. 'Oh! then it's a panel, eh?'

'Never mind wot it is!' replied Sikes. 'I want a boy, and he mustn't be a big 'un. Lord!' said Mr Sikes, reflectively, 'if I'd only got that young boy of Ned, the chimbley-sweeper's! He kept him small on purpose, and let him out by the job. But the father gets lagged; and then the Juvenile Delinquent Society comes, and takes the boy away from a trade where he was arning money, teaches him to read and write, and in time makes a 'prentice of him. And so they go on,' said Mr

Sikes, his wrath rising with the recollection of his wrongs, 'so they go on; and, if they'd got money enough (which it's a Providence they haven't), we shouldn't have half a dozen boys left in the whole trade, in a year or two.'

'No more we should,' acquiesced the Jew, who had been considering during this speech, and had only caught the last sentence. 'Bill!'

'What now?' enquired Sikes.

The Jew nodded his head towards Nancy, who was still gazing at the fire; and intimated, by a sign, that he would have her told to leave the room. Sikes shrugged his shoulders impatiently, as if he thought the precaution unnecessary; but complied, nevertheless, by requesting Miss Nancy to fetch him a jug of beer.

'You don't want any beer,' said Nancy, folding her arms, and retaining her seat very composedly.

'I tell you I do!' replied Sikes.

'Nonsense,' rejoined the girl coolly. 'Go on, Fagin. I know what he's going to say, Bill; he needn't mind me.'

The Jew still hesitated. Sikes looked from one to the other in some surprise.

'Why, you don't mind the old girl, do you, Fagin?' he asked at length. 'You've known her long enough to trust her, or the Devil's in it. She ain't one to blab. Are you, Nancy?'

'*I* should think not!' replied the young lady: drawing her chair up to the table, and putting her elbows upon it.

'No, no, my dear, I know you're not,' said the Jew; 'but – ' and again the old man paused.

'But wot?' enquired Sikes.

'I didn't know whether she mightn't p'r'aps be out of sorts, you know, my dear, as she was the other night,' replied the Jew.

At this confession, Miss Nancy burst into a loud laugh; and, swallowing a glass of brandy, shook her head with an air of defiance, and burst into sundry exclamations of 'Keep the game a-going!' 'Never say die!' and the like. These seemed to have the effect of reassuring both gentlemen; for the Jew nodded his head with a satisfied air, and resumed his seat; as did Mr Sikes likewise.

'Now, Fagin,' said Nancy with a laugh. 'Tell Bill at once, about Oliver!'

'Ha! you're a clever one, my dear; the sharpest girl I ever saw!' said the Jew, patting her on the neck. 'It *was* about Oliver I was going to speak, sure enough. Ha! ha! ha!'

'What about him?' demanded Sikes.

'He's the boy for you, my dear,' replied the Jew in a hoarse whisper; laying his finger on the side of his nose, and grinning frightfully.

'He!' exclaimed Sikes.

'Have him, Bill!' said Nancy. 'I would, if I was in your place. He mayn't be so much up, as any of the others; but that's not what you want, if he's only to open a door for you. Depend upon it he's a safe one, Bill.'

'I know he is,' rejoined Fagin. 'He's been in good training these last few weeks, and it's time he began to work for his bread. Besides, the others are all too big.'

'Well, he is just the size I want,' said Mr Sikes, ruminating.

'And will do everything you want, Bill, my dear,' interposed the Jew; 'he can't help himself. That is, if you frighten him enough.'

'Frighten him!' echoed Sikes. 'It'll be no sham frightening, mind you. If there's anything queer about him when we once get into work; in for a penny, in for a pound. You won't see him alive again, Fagin. Think of that, before you send him. Mark my words!' said the robber, poising a crowbar, which he had drawn from under the bedstead.

'I've thought of it all,' said the Jew with energy. 'I've – I've had my eye upon him, my dears, close – close. Once let him feel that he is one of us; once fill his mind with the idea that he has been a thief; and he's ours! Ours for his life. Oho! It couldn't have come about better!' The old man crossed his arms upon his breast; and, drawing his head and shoulders into a heap, literally hugged himself for joy.

'Ours!' said Sikes. 'Yours, you mean.'

'Perhaps I do, my dear,' said the Jew, with a shrill chuckle. 'Mine, if you like, Bill.'

'And wot,' said Sikes, scowling fiercely on his agreeable friend, 'wot makes you take so much pains about one chalk-faced kid, when you know there are fifty boys snoozing about Common Garden every night, as you might pick and choose from?'

'Because they're of no use to me, my dear,' replied the Jew, with some confusion, 'not worth the taking. Their looks convict 'em when they get into trouble, and I lose 'em all. With this boy, properly managed, my dears, I could do what I couldn't with twenty of them. Besides,' said the Jew, recovering his self-possession, 'he has us now if he could only give us leg-bail again; and he *must* be in the same boat with us. Never mind how he came there; it's quite enough for my power over him that he was in a robbery; that's all I want. Now, how much better this is, than being obliged to put the poor leetle boy out of the way – which would be dangerous, and we should lose by it besides.'

'When is it to be done?' asked Nancy, stopping some turbulent exclamation on the part of Mr Sikes, expressive of the disgust with which he received Fagin's affectation of humanity.

'Ah, to be sure,' said the Jew; 'when is it to be done, Bill?'

'I planned with Toby, the night arter tomorrow,' rejoined Sikes in a surly voice, 'if he heerd nothing from me to the contrary.'

'Good,' said the Jew; 'there's no moon.'

'No,' rejoined Sikes.

'It's all arranged about bringing off the swag, is it?' asked the Jew.

Sikes nodded.

'And about – '

'Oh, ah, it's all planned,' rejoined Sikes, interrupting him. 'Never mind particulars. You'd better bring the boy here tomorrow night. I shall get off the stones an hour arter daybreak. Then you hold your tongue, and keep the melting-pot ready, and that's all you'll have to do.'

After some discussion, in which all three took an active part, it was decided that Nancy should repair to the Jew's next evening when the night had set in, and bring Oliver away with her; Fagin craftily observing, that, if he evinced any disinclination to the task, he would be more willing to accompany the girl who had so recently interfered in his behalf, than anybody else. It was also solemnly arranged that poor Oliver should, for the purposes of the contemplated expedition, be unreservedly consigned to the care and custody of

Mr William Sikes; and further, that the said Sikes should deal with him as he thought fit; and should not be held responsible by the Jew for any mischance or evil that might befall him, or any punishment with which it might be necessary to visit him: it being understood that, to render the compact in this respect binding, any representations made by Mr Sikes on his return should be required to be confirmed and corroborated, in all important particulars, by the testimony of flash Toby Crackit.

These preliminaries adjusted, Mr Sikes proceeded to drink brandy at a furious rate, and to flourish the crowbar in an alarming manner; yelling forth, at the same time, most unmusical snatches of song, mingled with wild execrations. At length, in a fit of professional enthusiasm, he insisted upon producing his box of housebreaking tools: which he had no sooner stumbled in with, and opened for the purpose of explaining the nature and properties of the various implements it contained, and the peculiar beauties of their construction, than he fell over the box upon the floor, and went to sleep where he fell.

'Good-night, Nancy,' said the Jew, muffling himself up as before.

'Good-night.'

Their eyes met, and the Jew scrutinised her narrowly. There was no flinching about the girl. She was as true and earnest in the matter as Toby Crackit himself could be.

The Jew again bade her good-night, and bestowing a sly kick upon the prostrate form of Mr Sikes while her back was turned, groped downstairs.

'Always the way!' muttered the Jew to himself as he turned homeward. 'The worst of these women is, that a very little thing serves to call up some long-forgotten feeling; and the best of them is, that it never lasts. Ha! ha! The man against the child, for a bag of gold!'

Beguiling the time with these pleasant reflections, Mr Fagin wended his way, through mud and mire, to his gloomy abode: where the Dodger was sitting up, impatiently awaiting his return.

'Is Oliver a-bed? I want to speak to him,' was his first remark as they descended the stairs.

'Hours ago,' replied the Dodger, throwing open a door. 'Here he is!'

The boy was lying, fast asleep, on a rude bed upon the floor; so pale with anxiety, and sadness, and the closeness of his prison, that he looked like death; not death as it shows in shroud and coffin, but in the guise it wears when life has just departed; when a young and gentle spirit has, but an instant, fled to Heaven, and the gross air of the world has not had time to breathe upon the changing dust it hallowed.

'Not now,' said the Jew, turning softly away. 'Tomorrow. Tomorrow.'

CHAPTER 20

Wherein Oliver is delivered over to Mr William Sikes

When Oliver awoke in the morning, he was a good deal surprised to find that a new pair of shoes, with strong thick soles, had been placed at his bedside; and that his old shoes had been removed. At first, he was pleased with the discovery: hoping that it might be the forerunner of his release; but such thoughts were quickly dispelled, on his sitting down to breakfast along with the Jew, who told him, in a tone and manner which increased his alarm, that he was to be taken to the residence of Bill Sikes that night.

'To – to – stop there, sir?' asked Oliver, anxiously.

'No, no, my dear. Not to stop there,' replied the Jew. 'We shouldn't like to lose you. Don't be afraid, Oliver, you shall come back to us again. Ha! ha! ha! We won't be so cruel as to send you away, my dear. Oh no, no!'

The old man, who was stooping over the fire toasting a piece of bread, looked round as he bantered Oliver thus; and chuckled as if to show that he knew he would still be very glad to get away if he could.

'I suppose,' said the Jew, fixing his eyes on Oliver, 'you want to know what you're going to Bill's for – eh, my dear?'

Oliver coloured, involuntarily, to find that the old thief had been reading his thoughts; but boldly said, Yes, he did want to know.

'Why, do you think?' enquired Fagin, parrying the question.

'Indeed I don't know, sir,' replied Oliver.

'Bah!' said the Jew, turning away with a disappointed countenance from a close perusal of the boy's face. 'Wait till Bill tells you, then.'

The Jew seemed much vexed by Oliver's not expressing any greater curiosity on the subject; but the truth is, that, although Oliver felt very anxious, he was too much confused by the earnest cunning of Fagin's looks, and his own speculations, to make any further enquiries just then. He had no other opportunity; for the Jew remained very surly and silent till night: when he prepared to go abroad.

'You may burn a candle,' said the Jew, putting one

upon the table. 'And here's a book for you to read, till
they come to fetch you. Good-night!'

'Good-night!' replied Oliver, softly.

The Jew walked to the door: looking over his
shoulder at the boy as he went. Suddenly stopping, he
called him by his name.

Oliver looked up; the Jew, pointing to the candle,
motioned him to light it. He did so; and, as he placed
the candlestick upon the table, saw that the Jew was
gazing fixedly at him, with lowering and contracted
brows, from the dark end of the room.

'Take heed, Oliver! take heed!' said the old man,
shaking his right hand before him in a warning manner.
'He's a rough man, and thinks nothing of blood when
his own is up. Whatever falls out, say nothing; and do
what he bids you. Mind!' Placing a strong emphasis on
the last word, he suffered his features gradually to
resolve themselves into a ghastly grin, and, nodding his
head, left the room.

Oliver leaned his head upon his hand when the old
man disappeared, and pondered, with a trembling
heart, on the words he had just heard. The more he
thought of the Jew's admonition, the more he was at a
loss to divine its real purpose and meaning. He could
think of no bad object to be attained by sending him to
Sikes, which would not be equally well answered by
his remaining with Fagin; and after meditating for a
long time, concluded that he had been selected to
perform some ordinary menial offices for the housebreaker, until another boy, better suited for his
purpose, could be engaged. He was too well accustomed to suffering, and had suffered too much where
he was, to bewail the prospect of change very severely.
He remained lost in thought for some minutes;

and then, with a heavy sigh, snuffed the candle, and taking up the book which the Jew had left with him, began to read.

He turned over the leaves. Carelessly at first; but, lighting on a passage which attracted his attention, he soon became intent upon the volume. It was a history of the lives and trials of great criminals; and the pages were soiled and thumbed with use. Here, he read of dreadful crimes that made the blood run cold; of secret murders that had been committed by the lonely wayside; of bodies hidden from the eye of man in deep pits and wells; which would not keep them down, deep as they were, but had yielded them up at last, after many years, and so maddened the murderers with their sight, that in their horror they had confessed their guilt, and yelled for the gibbet to end their agony. Here, too, he read of men who, lying in their beds at dead of night, had been tempted (so they said) and led on, by their own bad thoughts, to such dreadful bloodshed as it made the flesh creep, and the limbs quail, to think of. The terrible descriptions were so real and vivid, that the sallow pages seemed to turn red with gore; and the words upon them, to be sounded in his ears, as if they were whispered, in hollow murmurs, by the spirits of the dead.

In a paroxysm of fear, the boy closed the book, and thrust it from him. Then, falling upon his knees, he prayed Heaven to spare him from such deeds; and rather to will that he should die at once, than be reserved for crimes, so fearful and appalling. By degrees, he grew more calm, and besought, in a low and broken voice, that he might be rescued from his present dangers; and that if any aid were to be raised up for a poor outcast boy who had never known the love of friends or kindred, it might come to him now, when, desolate and deserted, he stood alone in the midst of wickedness and guilt.

He had concluded his prayer, but still remained with his head buried in his hands, when a rustling noise aroused him.

'What's that!' he cried, starting up, and catching sight of a figure standing by the door. 'Who's there?'

'Me. Only me,' replied a tremulous voice.

Oliver raised the candle above his head: and looked towards the door. It was Nancy.

'Put down the light,' said the girl, turning away her head. 'It hurts my eyes.'

Oliver saw that she was very pale, and gently enquired if she were ill. The girl threw herself into a chair, with her back towards him: and wrung her hands; but made no reply.

'God forgive me!' she cried after a while. 'I never thought of this.'

'Has anything happened?' asked Oliver. 'Can I help you? I will if I can. I will, indeed.'

She rocked herself to and fro; caught her throat; and, uttering a gurgling sound, gasped for breath.

'Nancy!' cried Oliver, 'What is it?'

The girl beat her hands upon her knees, and her feet upon the ground; and, suddenly stopping, drew her shawl close round her: and shivered with cold.

Oliver stirred the fire. Drawing her chair close to it, she sat there, for a little time, without speaking; but at length she raised her head, and looked round.

'I don't know what comes over me sometimes,' said she, affecting to busy herself in arranging her dress; 'it's this damp, dirty room, I think. Now, Nolly, dear, are you ready?'

'Am I to go with you?' asked Oliver.

'Yes; I have come from Bill,' replied the girl. 'You are to go with me.'

'What for?' asked Oliver, recoiling.

'What for?' echoed the girl, raising her eyes, and averting them again, the moment they encountered the boy's face. 'Oh! For no harm.'

'I don't believe it,' said Oliver: who had watched her closely.

'Have it your own way,' rejoined the girl, affecting to laugh. 'For no good, then.'

Oliver could see that he had some power over the girl's better feelings, and, for an instant, thought of appealing to her compassion for his helpless state. But, then, the thought darted across his mind that it was barely eleven o'clock; and that many people were still in the streets: of whom surely some might be found to give credence to his tale. As the reflection occurred to him, he stepped forward: and said, somewhat hastily, that he was ready.

Neither his brief consideration, nor its purport, was lost on his companion. She eyed him narrowly, while he spoke; and cast upon him a look of intelligence which sufficiently showed that she guessed what had been passing in his thoughts.

'Hush!' said the girl, stooping over him, and pointing to the door as she looked cautiously round. 'You can't help yourself. I have tried hard for you, but all to no purpose. You are hedged round and round. If ever you are to get loose from here, this is not the time.'

Struck by the energy of her manner, Oliver looked up in her face with great surprise. She seemed to speak the truth; her countenance was white and agitated; and she trembled with very earnestness.

'I have saved you from being ill-used once, and I will again, and I do now,' continued the girl aloud; 'for those who would have fetched you, if I had not, would have been far more rough than me. I have promised for your being quiet and silent; if you are not, you will only do harm to yourself and me too, and perhaps be my death. See here! I have borne all this for you already, as true as God sees me show it.'

She pointed, hastily, to some livid bruises on her neck and arms; and continued, with great rapidity: 'Remember this! And don't let me suffer more for you, just now. If I could help you, I would; but I have not the power. They don't mean to harm you; whatever they make you do, is no fault of yours. Hush! Every word from you is a blow for me. Give me your hand. Make haste! Your hand!'

She caught the hand which Oliver instinctively placed in hers, and, blowing out the light, drew him after her up the stairs. The door was opened, quickly, by someone shrouded in the darkness, and was as quickly closed, when they had passed out. A hackney-cabriolet was in waiting; with the same vehemence which she had exhibited in addressing Oliver, the girl pulled him in with her, and drew the curtains close. The driver wanted no directions, but lashed his horse into full speed, without the delay of an instant.

The girl still held Oliver fast by the hand, and continued to pour into his ear, the warnings and assurances she had already imparted. All was so quick and hurried, that he had scarcely time to recollect where he was, or how he came there, when the carriage stopped at the house to which the Jew's steps had been directed on the previous evening.

For one brief moment, Oliver cast a hurried glance

along the empty street, and a cry for help hung upon his lips. But the girl's voice was in his ear, beseeching him in such tones of agony to remember her, that he had not the heart to utter it. While he hesitated, the opportunity was gone; he was already in the house, and the door was shut.

'This way,' said the girl, releasing her hold for the first time. 'Bill!'

'Hallo!' replied Sikes: appearing at the head of the stairs, with a candle. 'Oh! That's the time of day. Come on!'

This was a very strong expression of approbation, an uncommonly hearty welcome from a person of Mr Sikes' temperament. Nancy, appearing much gratified thereby, saluted him cordially.

'Bull's-eye's gone home with Tom,' observed Sikes, as he lighted them up. 'He'd have been in the way.'

'That's right,' rejoined Nancy.

'So you've got the kid,' said Sikes, when they had all reached the room: closing the door as he spoke.

'Yes, here he is,' replied Nancy.

'Did he come quiet?' enquired Sikes.

'Like a lamb,' rejoined Nancy.

'I'm glad to hear it,' said Sikes, looking grimly at Oliver; 'for the sake of his young carcase: as would other-ways have suffered for it. Come here, young un; and let me read you a lectur', which is as well got over at once.'

Thus addressing his new pupil, Mr Sikes pulled off Oliver's cap and threw it into a corner; and then, taking him by the shoulder, sat himself down by the table, and stood the boy in front of him.

'Now, first: do you know wot this is?' enquired Sikes, taking up a pocket-pistol which lay on the table.

Oliver replied in the affirmative.

'Well, then, look here,' continued Sikes. 'This is powder; that 'ere's a bullet; and this is a little bit of a old hat for waddin'.'

Oliver murmured his comprehension of the different bodies referred to; and Mr Sikes proceeded to load the pistol, with great nicety and deliberation.

'Now it's loaded,' said Mr Sikes, when he had finished.

'Yes, I see it is, sir,' replied Oliver.

'Well,' said the robber, grasping Oliver's wrist, and putting the barrel so close to his temple that they touched; at which moment the boy could not repress a start; 'if you speak a word when you're out o' doors with me, except when I speak to you, that loading will be in your head without notice. So, if you *do* make up your mind to speak without leave, say your prayers first.'

Having bestowed a scowl upon the object of this warning, to increase its effect, Mr Sikes continued.

'As near as I know, there isn't anybody as would be asking very partickler arter you, if you *was* disposed of; so I needn't take this devil-and-all of trouble to explain matters to you, if it warn't for your own good. D'ye hear me?'

'The short and the long of what you mean,' said Nancy: speaking very emphatically, and slightly frowning at Oliver as if to bespeak his serious attention to her words: 'is, that if you're crossed by him in this job you have on hand, you'll prevent his ever telling tales afterwards, by shooting him through the head, and will take your chance of swinging for it, as you do for a great many other things in the way of business, every month of your life.'

'That's it!' observed Mr Sikes, approvingly; 'women can always put things in fewest words. – Except when it's blowing up; and then they lengthens it out. And now that he's thoroughly up to it, let's have some supper, and get a snooze before starting.'

In pursuance of this request, Nancy quickly laid the cloth; disappearing for a few minutes, she presently returned with a pot of porter and a dish of sheep's heads: which gave occasion to several pleasant witticisms on the part of Mr Sikes, founded upon the singular coincidence of 'jemmies' being a cant name, common to them, and also to an ingenious implement much used in his profession. Indeed, the worthy gentleman, stimulated perhaps by the immediate prospect of being on active service, was in great spirits and good humour; in proof whereof, it may be here remarked, that he humorously drank all the beer at a draught, and did not utter, on a rough calculation, more than fourscore oaths during the whole progress of the meal.

Supper being ended – it may be easily conceived that Oliver had no great appetite for it – Mr Sikes disposed of a couple of glasses of spirits and water, and threw himself on the bed; ordering Nancy, with many imprecations in case of failure, to call him at five precisely. Oliver stretched himself in his clothes, by command of the same authority, on a mattress upon the floor; and the girl, mending the fire, sat before it, in readiness to rouse them at the appointed time.

For a long time Oliver lay awake, thinking it not impossible that Nancy might seek that opportunity of whispering some further advice; but the girl sat brooding over the fire, without moving, save now and then to trim the light. Weary with watching and anxiety, he at length fell asleep.

When he awoke, the table was covered with tea-things, and Sikes was thrusting various articles into the pockets of his greatcoat, which hung over the back of a chair. Nancy was busily engaged in preparing breakfast. It was not yet daylight; for the candle was still burning, and it was quite dark outside. A sharp rain, too, was beating against the windowpanes; and the sky looked black and cloudy.

'Now, then!' growled Sikes, as Oliver started up; 'half-past five! Look sharp, or you'll get no breakfast; for it's late as it is.'

Oliver was not long in making his toilet; having taken some breakfast, he replied to a surly enquiry from Sikes, by saying that he was quite ready.

Nancy, scarcely looking at the boy, threw him a handkerchief to tie round his throat; Sikes gave him a large rough cape to button over his shoulders. Thus attired, he gave his hand to the robber, who, merely pausing to show him with a menacing gesture, that he had that same pistol in a side-pocket of his greatcoat, clasped it firmly in his, and, exchanging a farewell with Nancy, led him away.

Oliver turned, for an instant, when they reached the door, in the hope of meeting a look from the girl. But she had resumed her old seat in front of the fire, and sat, perfectly motionless, before it.

CHAPTER 21

The Expedition

It was a cheerless morning when they got into the street; blowing and raining hard; and the clouds looking dull and stormy. The night had been very wet: large pools of water had collected in the road: and the kennels were overflowing. There was a faint glimmering of the coming day in the sky; but it rather aggravated than relieved the gloom of the scene: the sombre light only serving to pale that which the street lamps afforded, without shedding any warmer or brighter tints upon the wet house-tops, and dreary streets. There appeared to be nobody stirring in that quarter of the town; the windows of the houses were all closely shut; and the streets through which they passed, were noiseless and empty.

By the time they had turned into the Bethnal Green Road, the day had fairly begun to break. Many of the lamps were already extinguished: a few country waggons were slowly toiling on, towards London; now and then, a stagecoach, covered with mud, rattled briskly by: the driver bestowing, as he passed, an admonitory lash upon the heavy waggoner who, by keeping on the wrong side of the road, had endangered his arriving at the office, a quarter of a minute after his time. The public houses, with gas-lights burning inside, were already open. By degrees, other shops began to be unclosed, and a few scattered people were met with. Then, came straggling groups of labourers going to their work; then, men and women with fish-baskets on their heads; donkey-carts laden with vegetables; chaise-carts filled with live-stock or whole carcasses of meat; milk-women with pails; an unbroken concourse of people, trudging out with various supplies to the eastern suburbs of the town. As they approached the City, the noise and traffic gradually increased; when they threaded the streets between Shoreditch and Smithfield, it had swelled into a roar of sound and bustle. It was as light as it was likely to be, till night came on again, and the busy morning of half the London population had begun.

Turning down Sun Street and Crown Street, and crossing Finsbury Square, Mr Sikes struck, by way of Chiswell Street, into Barbican: thence into Long Lane, and so into Smithfield; from which latter place arose a tumult of discordant sounds that filled Oliver Twist with amazement.

It was market-morning. The ground was covered, nearly ankle-deep, with filth and mire; a thick steam, perpetually rising from the reeking bodies of the cattle, and mingling with the fog, which seemed to rest upon the chimney-tops, hung heavily above. All the pens in the centre of the large area, and as many temporary pens as could be crowded into the vacant space, were filled with sheep; tied up to posts by the gutter side were long lines of beasts and oxen, three or four deep. Countrymen, butchers, drovers, hawkers, boys, thieves, idlers, and vagabonds of every low grade, were mingled together in a mass; the whistling of drovers, the barking of dogs, the bellowing and plunging of oxen, the bleating of sheep, the grunting and squeaking of pigs, the cries of hawkers, the shouts, oaths, and quarrelling on all sides; the ringing of bells and roar of voices, that issued from every public house; the crowding, pushing, driving, beating, whooping, and yelling; the hideous and discordant din that resounded from every corner of the market; and the unwashed, unshaven, squalid, and dirty figures constantly running to and fro, and bursting in and out of the throng; rendered it a stunning and bewildering scene, which quite confounded the senses.

Mr Sikes, dragging Oliver after him, elbowed his way through the thickest of the crowd, and bestowed very little attention on the numerous sights and sounds, which so astonished the boy. He nodded, twice or thrice, to a passing friend; and, resisting as many invitations to take a morning dram, pressed steadily onward, until they were clear of the turmoil, and had made their way through Hosier Lane into Holborn.

'Now, young un!' said Sikes, looking up at the clock of St Andrew's Church, 'hard upon seven! you must step out. Come, don't lag behind already, Lazy-legs!'

Mr Sikes accompanied this speech with a jerk at his little companion's wrist; Oliver, quickening his pace into a kind of trot, between a fast walk and a run, kept up with the rapid strides of the housebreaker as well as he could.

They held their course at this rate, until they had passed Hyde Park corner, and were on their way to Kensington: when Sikes relaxed his pace, until an empty cart, which was at some little distance behind, came up. Seeing 'Hounslow' written on it, he asked the driver with as much civility as he could assume, if he would give them a lift as far as Isleworth.

'Jump up,' said the man. 'Is that your boy?'

'Yes; he's my boy,' replied Sikes, looking hard at Oliver, and putting his hand abstractedly into the pocket where the pistol was.

'Your father walks rather too quick for you, don't he, my man?' enquired the driver: seeing that Oliver was out of breath.

'Not a bit of it,' replied Sikes, interposing. 'He's used to it. Here, take hold of my hand, Ned. In with you!'

Thus addressing Oliver, he helped him into the cart; and the driver, pointing to a heap of sacks, told him to lie down there, and rest himself.

As they passed the different milestones, Oliver wondered, more and more, where his companion meant to take him. Kensington, Hammersmith, Chiswick, Kew Bridge, Brentford, were all passed; and yet they went on as steadily as if they had only just begun their journey. At length, they came to a public house called the Coach and Horses: a little way beyond which, another road appeared to turn off. And here, the cart stopped.

Sikes dismounted with great precipitation, holding Oliver by the hand all the while; and lifting him down directly, bestowed a furious look upon him, and rapped the side-pocket with his fist, in a significant manner.

'Goodbye, boy,' said the man.

'He's sulky,' replied Sikes, giving him a shake; 'he's sulky. A young dog! Don't mind him.'

'Not I!' rejoined the other, getting into his cart. 'It's a fine day, after all.' And he drove away.

Sikes waited until he had fairly gone; and then, telling Oliver he might look about him if he wanted, once again led him onward on his journey.

They turned round to the left, a short way past the public house; and then, taking a right-hand road, walked on for a long time: passing many large gardens and gentlemen's houses on both sides of the way, and stopping for nothing but a little beer, until they reached a town. Here against the wall of a house, Oliver saw written up in pretty large letters, 'Hampton.' They lingered about, in the fields, for some hours. At length, they came back into the town; and, turning into an old public house with a defaced signboard, ordered some dinner by the kitchen fire.

The kitchen was an old, low-roofed room; with a great beam across the middle of the ceiling, and benches, with high backs to them, by the fire; on which were seated several rough men in smock-frocks, drinking and smoking. They took no notice of Oliver; and very little of Sikes; and, as Sikes took very little notice of them, he and his young comrade sat in a corner by themselves, without being much troubled by their company.

They had some cold meat for dinner, and sat so long after it, while Mr Sikes indulged himself with three or four pipes, that Oliver began to feel quite certain they were not going any further. Being much tired with the walk, and getting up so early, he dozed a little at first; then, quite overpowered by fatigue and the fumes of the tobacco, fell asleep.

It was quite dark when he was awakened by a push from Sikes. Rousing himself sufficiently to sit up and look about him, he found that worthy in close fellowship and communication with a labouring man, over a pint of ale.

'So, you're going on to Lower Halliford, are you?' enquired Sikes.

'Yes, I am,' replied the man, who seemed a little the worse – or better, as the case might be – for drinking; 'and not slow about it neither. My horse hasn't got a load behind him going back, as he had coming up in the mornin'; and he won't be long a-doing of it. Here's luck to him! Ecod! he's a good un!'

'Could you give my boy and me a lift as far as there?' demanded Sikes, pushing the ale towards his new friend.

'If you're going directly, I can,' replied the man, looking out of the pot. 'Are you going to Halliford?'

'Going on to Shepperton,' replied Sikes.

'I'm your man, as far as I go,' replied the other. 'Is all paid, Becky?'

'Yes, the other gentleman's paid,' replied the girl.

'I say!' said the man, with tipsy gravity; 'that won't do, you know.'

'Why not?' rejoined Sikes. 'You're a-going to accommodate us, and wot's to prevent my standing treat for a pint or so, in return?'

The stranger reflected upon this argument, with a very profound face; having done so, he seized Sikes by the hand: and declared he was a real good fellow. To which Mr Sikes replied, he was joking; as, if he had been sober, there would have been strong reason to suppose he was.

After the exchange of a few more compliments, they bade the company good-night, and went out; the girl gathering up the pots and glasses as they did so, and lounging out to the door, with her hands full, to see the party start.

The horse, whose health had been drunk in his absence, was standing outside: ready harnessed to the cart. Oliver and Sikes got in without any further ceremony; and the man to whom he belonged, having lingered for a minute or two 'to bear him up', and to defy the hostler and the world to produce his equal, mounted also. Then, the hostler was told to give the horse his head: and, his head being given him, he made a very unpleasant use of it: tossing it into the air with great disdain, and running into the parlour windows over the way; after performing those feats, and supporting himself for a short time on his hind-legs, he started off at great speed, and rattled out of the town right gallantly.

The night was very dark. A damp mist rose from the river, and the marshy ground about; and spread itself over the dreary fields. It was piercing cold, too; all was gloomy and black. Not a word was spoken; for the driver had grown sleepy; and Sikes was in no mood to lead him into conversation. Oliver sat huddled together, in a corner of the cart; bewildered with alarm and apprehension; and figuring strange objects in the gaunt trees, whose branches waved grimly to and fro, as if in some fantastic joy at the desolation of the scene.

As they passed Sunbury Church, the clock struck seven. There was a light in the ferry-house window opposite: which streamed across the road, and threw into more sombre shadow a dark yew tree with graves beneath it. There was a dull sound of falling water not far off; and the leaves of the old tree stirred gently in the night wind. It seemed like quiet music for the repose of the dead.

Sunbury was passed through, and they came again into the lonely road. Two or three miles more, and the cart stopped. Sikes alighted, took Oliver by the hand, and they once again walked on.

They turned into no house at Shepperton, as the weary boy had expected; but still kept walking on, in mud and darkness, through gloomy lanes and over cold open wastes, until they came within sight of the lights of a town at no great distance. On looking intently forward, Oliver saw that the water was just below them, and that they were coming to the foot of a bridge.

Sikes kept straight on, until they were close upon the bridge; then turned suddenly down a bank upon the left.

'The water!' thought Oliver, turning sick with fear. 'He has brought me to this lonely place to murder me!'

He was about to throw himself on the ground, and make one struggle for his young life, when he saw that they stood before a solitary house: all ruinous and decayed. There was a window on each side of the dilapidated entrance; and one story above; but no light was visible. The house was dark, dismantled: and, to all appearance, uninhabited.

Sikes, with Oliver's hand still in his, softly approached the low porch, and raised the latch. The door yielded to the pressure, and they passed in together.

CHAPTER 22

The Burglary

'Hallo!' cried a loud, hoarse voice, as soon as they set foot in the passage.

'Don't make such a row,' said Sikes, bolting the door. 'Show a glim, Toby.'

'Aha! my pal!' cried the same voice. 'A glim, Barney, a glim! Show the gentleman in, Barney; wake up first, if convenient.'

The speaker appeared to throw a boot-jack, or some such article, at the person he addressed, to rouse him from his slumbers: for the noise of a wooden body, falling violently, was heard; and then an indistinct muttering, as of a man between asleep and awake.

'Do you hear?' cried the same voice. 'There's Bill Sikes in the passage with nobody to do the civil to him; and you sleeping there, as if you took laudanum with your meals, and nothing stronger. Are you any fresher now, or do you want the iron candlestick to wake you thoroughly?'

A pair of slipshod feet shuffled, hastily, across the bare floor of the room, as this interrogatory was put; and there issued, from a door on the right hand: first, a feeble candle: and next, the form of the same individual who has been heretofore described as labouring under the infirmity of speaking through his nose, and officiating as waiter at the public house on Saffron Hill.

'Bister Sikes!' exclaimed Barney, with real or counterfeit joy; 'cub id, sir; cub id.'

233

'Here! you get on first,' said Sikes, putting Oliver in front of him. 'Quicker! or I shall tread upon your heels.'

Muttering a curse upon his tardiness, Sikes pushed Oliver before him; and they entered a low dark room with a smoky fire, two or three broken chairs, a table, and a very old couch: on which, with his legs much higher than his head, a man was reposing at full length, smoking a long clay pipe. He was dressed in a smartly-cut snuff-coloured coat, with large brass buttons; an orange neckerchief; a coarse, staring, shawl-pattern waistcoat; and drab breeches. Mr Crackit (for he it was) had no very great quantity of hair, either upon his head or face; but what he had, was of a reddish dye, and tortured into long corkscrew curls, through which he occasionally thrust some very dirty fingers, ornamented with large common rings. He was a trifle above the middle size, and apparently rather weak in the legs; but this circumstance by no means detracted from his own admiration of his top-boots, which he contemplated, in their elevated situation, with lively satisfaction.

'Bill, my boy!' said this figure, turning his head towards the door, 'I'm glad to see you. I was almost afraid you'd given it up: in which case I should have made a personal wentur. Hallo!'

Uttering this exclamation in a tone of great surprise, as his eye rested on Oliver, Mr Toby Crackit brought himself into a sitting posture, and demanded who that was.

'The boy. Only the boy!' replied Sikes, drawing a chair towards the fire.

'Wud of Bister Fagid's lads,' exclaimed Barney, with a grin.

'Fagin's, eh!' exclaimed Toby, looking at Oliver. 'Wot an inwalable boy that'll make, for the old ladies' pockets in chapels! His mug is a fortun' to him.'

'There – there's enough of that,' interposed Sikes, impatiently; and stooping over his recumbent friend, he whispered a few words in his ear: at which Mr Crackit laughed immensely. and honoured Oliver with a long stare of astonishment.

'Now,' said Sikes, as he resumed his seat, 'if you'll give us something to eat and drink while we're waiting, you'll put some heart in us; or in me, at all events. Sit down by the fire, younker, and rest yourself; for you'll have to go out with us again tonight, though not very far off.'

Oliver looked at Sikes, in mute and timid wonder; and drawing a stool to the fire, sat with his aching head upon his hands, scarcely knowing where he was, or what was passing around him.

'Here,' said Toby, as the young Jew placed some fragments of food, and a bottle, upon the table, 'Success to the crack!' He rose to honour the toast; and, carefully depositing his empty pipe in a corner, advanced to the table, filled a glass with spirits, and drank off its contents. Mr Sikes did the same.

'A drain for the boy,' said Toby, half-filling a wine glass. 'Down with it, innocence.'

'Indeed,' said Oliver, looking piteously up into the man's face; 'indeed, I –'

'Down with it!' echoed Toby. 'Do you think I don't know what's good for you? Tell him to drink it, Bill.'

'He had better!' said Sikes, clapping his hand upon his pocket. 'Burn my body, if he isn't more trouble than a whole family of Dodgers. Drink it, you perwerse imp; drink it!'

Frightened by the menacing gestures of the two men, Oliver hastily swallowed the contents of the glass, and immediately fell into a violent fit of coughing: which delighted Toby Crackit and Barney, and even drew a smile from the surly Mr Sikes.

This done, and Sikes having satisfied his appetite (Oliver could eat nothing but a small crust of bread which they made him swallow), the two men laid themselves down on chairs for a short nap. Oliver retained his stool by the fire; Barney, wrapped in a blanket, stretched himself on the floor: close outside the fender.

They slept, or appeared to sleep, for some time; nobody stirring but Barney, who rose once or twice to throw coals upon the fire. Oliver fell into a heavy doze: imagining himself straying along the gloomy lanes, or wandering about the dark churchyard, or retracing some one or other of the scenes of the past day: when he was roused by Toby Crackit jumping up and declaring it was half-past one.

In an instant, the other two were on their legs, and all were actively engaged in busy preparation. Sikes and his companion enveloped their necks and chins in large dark shawls, and drew on their great-coats; Barney, opening a cupboard, brought forth several articles, which he hastily crammed into the pockets.

'Barkers for me, Barney,' said Toby Crackit.

'Here they are,' replied Barney, producing a pair of pistols. 'You loaded them yourself.'

'All right!' replied Toby, stowing them away. 'The persuaders?'

'I've got 'em,' replied Sikes.

'Crape, keys, centre-bits, darkies – nothing forgotten?'

enquired Toby: fastening a small crowbar to a loop inside the skirt of his coat.

'All right,' rejoined his companion. 'Bring them bits of timber, Barney. That's the time of day.'

With these words, he took a thick stick from Barney's hands, who, having delivered another to Toby, busied himself in fastening on Oliver's cape.

'Now then!' said Sikes, holding out his hand.

Oliver: who was completely stupefied by the un-wonted exercise, and the air, and the drink which had been forced upon him: put his hand mechanically into that which Sikes extended for the purpose.

'Take his other hand, Toby.' said Sikes. 'Look out, Barney.'

The man went to the door, and returned to an-nounce that all was quiet. The two robbers issued forth with Oliver between them. Barney, having made all fast, rolled himself up as before, and was soon asleep again.

It was now intensely dark. The fog was much heavier than it had been in the early part of the night; and the atmosphere was so damp, that, although no rain fell, Oliver's hair and eyebrows, within a few minutes after leaving the house, had become stiff with the half-frozen moisture that was floating about. They crossed the bridge, and kept on towards the lights which he had seen before. They were at no great distance off; and, as they walked pretty briskly, they soon arrived at Chertsey.

'Slap through the town,' whispered Sikes; 'there'll be nobody in the way, tonight, to see us.'

Toby acquiesced; and they hurried through the main street of the little town, which at that late hour was wholly deserted. A dim light shone at intervals from some bedroom window; and the hoarse barking of dogs occasionally broke the silence of the night. But there was nobody abroad. They had cleared the town, as the church-bell struck two.

Quickening their pace, they turned up a road upon the left hand. After walking about a quarter of a mile, they stopped before a detached house surrounded by a wall: to the top of which, Toby Crackit, scarcely pausing to take breath, climbed in a twinkling.

'The boy next,' said Toby. 'Hoist him up; I'll catch hold of him.'

Before Oliver had time to look round, Sikes had caught him under the arms; and in three or four seconds he and Toby were lying on the grass on the other side. Sikes followed directly. And they stole cautiously towards the house.

And now, for the first time, Oliver, well-nigh mad with grief and terror, saw that housebreaking and robbery, if not murder, were the objects of the expedition. He clasped his hands together, and involuntarily uttered a subdued exclamation of horror. A mist came before his eyes; the cold sweat stood upon his ashy face; his limbs failed him; and he sank upon his knees.

'Get up!' murmured Sikes, trembling with rage, and drawing the pistol from his pocket; 'Get up, or I'll strew your brains upon the grass.'

'Oh! for God's sake let me go!' cried Oliver; 'let me run away and die in the fields. I will never come near London; never, never! Oh! pray have mercy on me, and do not make me steal. For the love of all the bright angels that rest in Heaven, have mercy upon me!'

The man to whom this appeal was made, swore a dreadful oath, and had cocked the pistol, when Toby, striking it from his grasp, placed his hand upon the boy's mouth, and dragged him to the house.

'Hush!' cried the man; 'it won't answer here. Say another word, and I'll do your business myself with a crack on the head. That makes no noise, and is quite as certain, and more genteel. Here, Bill, wrench the shutter open. He's game enough now, I'll engage. I've seen older hands of his age took the same way. for a minute or two, on a cold night.'

Sikes, invoking terrific imprecations upon Fagin's head for sending Oliver on such an errand, plied the crowbar vigorously, but with little noise. After some delay, and some assistance from Toby, the shutter to which he had referred, swung open on its hinges.

It was a little lattice window, about five feet and a half above the ground, at the back of the house: which belonged to a scullery, or small brewing-place, at the end of the passage. The aperture was so small, that the inmates had probably not thought it worth while to defend it more securely; but it was large enough to admit a boy of Oliver's size, nevertheless. A very brief exercise of Mr Sikes's art, sufficed to overcome the fastening of the lattice; and it soon stood wide open also.

'Now listen, you young limb,' whispered Sikes, drawing a dark lantern from his pocket, and throwing the glare full on Oliver's face; 'I'm a-going to put you through there. Take this light; go softly up the steps straight afore you, and along the little hall, to the street door; unfasten it, and let us in.'

'There's a bolt at the top, you won't be able to reach,' interposed Toby. 'Stand upon one of the hall chairs. There are three there, Bill, with a jolly large blue unicorn and gold pitchfork on 'em: which is the old lady's arms.'

'Keep quiet, can't you?' replied Sikes, with a threatening look. 'The room-door is open, is it?'

'Wide,' replied Toby, after peeping in to satisfy himself. 'The game of that is, that they always leave it open with a catch, so that the dog, who's got a bed in here, may walk up and down the passage when he feels wakeful. Ha! ha! Barney 'ticed him away tonight. So neat!'

Although Mr Crackit spoke in a scarcely audible whisper, and laughed without noise, Sikes imperiously commanded him to be silent, and to get to work. Toby complied, by first producing his lantern, and placing it on the ground; then by planting himself firmly with his head against the wall beneath the window, and his hands upon his knees, so as to make a step of his back. This was no sooner done, than Sikes, mounting upon him, put Oliver gently through the window with his feet first; and, without leaving hold of his collar, planted him safely on the floor inside.

'Take this lantern,' said Sikes, looking into the room. 'You see the stairs afore you?'

Oliver, more dead than alive, gasped out, 'Yes.' Sikes, pointing to the street-door with the pistol-barrel, briefly advised him to take notice that he was within shot all the way; and that if he faltered, he would fall dead that instant.

'It's done in a minute,' said Sikes, in the same low whisper. 'Directly I leave go of you, do your work. Hark!'

'What's that?' whispered the other man.

They listened intently.

'Nothing,' said Sikes, releasing his hold of Oliver. 'Now!'

In the short time he had had to collect his senses,

The burglary

the boy had firmly resolved that, whether he died in the attempt or not, he would make one effort to dart upstairs from the hall, and alarm the family. Filled with this idea, he advanced at once, but stealthily.

'Come back!' suddenly cried Sikes aloud. 'Back! back!'

Scared by the sudden breaking of the dead stillness of the place, and by a loud cry which followed it, Oliver let his lantern fall, and knew not whether to advance or fly.

The cry was repeated – a light appeared – a vision of two terrified half-dressed men at the top of the stairs swam before his eyes – a flash – a loud noise – a smoke – a crash somewhere, but where he knew not – and he staggered back.

Sikes had disappeared for an instant; but he was up again, and had him by the collar before the smoke had cleared away. He fired his own pistol after the men, who were already retreating; and dragged the boy up.

'Clasp your arm tighter,' said Sikes, as he drew him through the window. 'Give me a shawl here. They've hit him. Quick! How the boy bleeds!'

Then came the loud ringing of a bell, mingled with the noise of firearms, and the shouts of men, and the sensation of being carried over uneven ground at a rapid pace. And then, the noises grew confused in the distance; and a cold deadly feeling crept over the boy's heart; and he saw or heard no more.

CHAPTER 23

*Which contains the substance of a pleasant
conversation between Mr Bumble and a lady;
and shows that even a beadle may be
susceptible on some points*

The night was bitter cold. The snow lay on the ground, frozen into a hard thick crust, so that only the heaps that had drifted into byways and corners were affected by the sharp wind that howled abroad: which, as if expending increased fury on such prey as it found, caught it savagely up in clouds, and, whirling it into a thousand misty eddies, scattered it in air. Bleak, dark, and piercing cold, it was a night for the well-housed and fed to draw round the bright fire and thank God they were at home; and for the homeless, starving wretch to lay him down and die. Many hunger-worn outcasts close their eyes in our bare streets, at such times, who, let their crimes have been what they may, can hardly open them in a more bitter world.

Such was the aspect of out-of-doors affairs, when Mrs Corney, the matron of the workhouse to which our readers have been already introduced as the birthplace of Oliver Twist, sat herself down before a cheerful fire in her own little room, and glanced, with no small degree of complacency, at a small round table: on which stood a tray of corresponding size, furnished with all necessary materials for the most grateful meal that matrons enjoy. In fact, Mrs Corney was about to solace herself with a cup of tea. As she glanced from the table to the fireplace, where the smallest of all possible kettles was singing a small song in a small voice, her inward satisfaction evidently increased – so much so, indeed, that Mrs Corney smiled.

'Well!' said the matron, leaning her elbow on the table, and looking reflectively at the fire; 'I'm sure we have all on us a great deal to be grateful for! A great deal, if we did but know it. Ah!'

Mrs Corney shook her head mournfully, as if deploring the mental blindness of those paupers who did not know it; and thrusting a silver spoon (private property) into the inmost recesses of a two-ounce tin tea-caddy, proceeded to make the tea.

How slight a thing will disturb the equanimity of our frail minds! The black teapot, being very small and easily filled, ran over while Mrs Corney was moralising; and the water slightly scalded Mrs Corney's hand.

'Drat the pot!' said the worthy matron, setting it down very hastily on the hob; 'a little stupid thing, that only holds a couple of cups! What use is it of, to anybody! Except,' said Mrs Corney, pausing, 'except to a poor desolate creature like me. Oh dear!'

With these words, the matron dropped into her chair, and, once more resting her elbow on the table, thought of her solitary fate. The small teapot, and the single cup, had awakened in her mind sad recollections of Mr Corney (who had not been dead more than five-and-twenty years); and she was over-powered.

'I shall never get another!' said Mrs Corney, pettishly; 'I shall never get another – like him.'

Whether this remark bore reference to the husband,

or the teapot, is uncertain. It might have been the latter; for Mrs Corney looked at it as she spoke; and took it up afterwards. She had just tasted her first cup, when she was disturbed by a soft tap at the room-door.

'Oh, come in with you!' said Mrs Corney, sharply. 'Some of the old women dying, I suppose. They always die when I'm at meals. Don't stand there, letting the cold air in, don't. What's amiss now, eh?'

'Nothing, ma'am, nothing,' replied a man's voice.

'Dear me!' exclaimed the matron, in a much sweeter tone, 'is that Mr Bumble?'

'At your service, ma'am,' said Mr Bumble, who had been stopping outside to rub his shoes clean, and to shake the snow off his coat; and who now made his appearance, bearing the cocked-hat in one hand, and a bundle in the other. 'Shall I shut the door, ma'am?'

The lady modestly hesitated to reply, lest there should be any impropriety in holding an interview with Mr Bumble, with closed doors. Mr Bumble taking advantage of the hesitation, and being very cold himself, shut it without permission.

'Hard weather, Mr Bumble,' said the matron.

'Hard, indeed, ma'am,' replied the beadle. 'Anti-porochial weather this, ma'am. We have given away, Mrs Corney, we have given away a matter of twenty quartern loaves and a cheese and a half, this very blessed afternoon; and yet them paupers are not contented.'

'Of course not. When would they be, Mr Bumble?' said the matron, sipping her tea.

'When, indeed, ma'am!' rejoined Mr Bumble. 'Why here's one man that, in consideration of his wife and large family, has a quartern loaf and a good pound of cheese, full weight. Is he grateful, ma'am? Is he grateful? Not a copper farthing's worth of it! What does he do, ma'am, but ask for a few coals; if it's only a pocket handkerchief full, he says! Coals! What would he do with coals? Toast his cheese with 'em, and then come back for more. That's the way with these people, ma'am; give 'em a apron full of coals today, and they'll come back for another, the day after tomorrow, as brazen as alabaster.'

The matron expressed her entire concurrence in this intelligible simile; and the beadle went on.

'I never,' said Mr Bumble, 'see anything like the pitch it's got to. The day afore yesterday, a man – you have been a married woman, ma'am, and I may mention it to you – a man, with hardly a rag upon his back (here Mrs Corney looked at the floor), goes to our overseer's door when he has got company coming to dinner; and says, he must be relieved, Mrs Corney. As he wouldn't go away, and shocked the company very much, our overseer sent him out a pound of potatoes and half a pint of oatmeal. "My heart!" says the ungrateful villain, "what's the use of *this* to me? You might as well give me a pair of iron spectacles!" "Very good," says our overseer, taking 'em away again, "you won't get anything else here." "Then I'll die in the streets!" says the vagrant. "Oh no, you won't," says our overseer.'

'Ha! ha! That was very good! So like Mr Grannett, wasn't it?' interposed the matron. 'Well, Mr Bumble?'

'Well, ma'am,' rejoined the beadle, 'he went away; and he *did* die in the streets. There's a obstinate pauper for you!'

'It beats anything I could have believed,' observed the matron emphatically. 'But don't you think out-of-door relief a very bad thing, anyway, Mr Bumble? You're a gentleman of experience, and ought to know. Come.'

'Mrs Corney,' said the beadle, smiling as men smile who are conscious of superior information, 'out-of-door relief, properly managed: properly managed, ma'am: is the porochial safeguard. The great principle of out-of-door relief is, to give the paupers exactly what they don't want; and then they get tired of coming.'

'Dear me!' exclaimed Mrs Corney. 'Well, that is a good one, too!'

'Yes. Betwixt you and me, ma'am,' returned Mr Bumble, 'that's the great principle; and that's the reason why, if you look at any cases that get into them owdacious newspapers, you'll always observe that sick families have been relieved with slices of cheese. That's the rule now, Mrs Corney, all over the country. But, however,' said the beadle, stopping to unpack his bundle, 'these are official secrets, ma'am; not to be spoken of; except, as I may say, among the porochial officers, such as ourselves. This is the port wine, ma'am, that the board ordered for the infirmary; real, fresh, genuine port wine; only out of the cask this forenoon; clear as a bell; and no sediment!'

Having held the first bottle up to the light, and shaken it well to test its excellence. Mr Bumble placed them both on the top of a chest of drawers; folded the handkerchief in which they had been wrapped; put it carefully in his pocket; and took up his hat, as if to go.

'You'll have a very cold walk, Mr Bumble,' said the matron.

'It blows, ma'am,' replied Mr Bumble, turning up his coat-collar, 'enough to cut one's ears off.'

The matron looked, from the little kettle, to the

OLIVER TWIST

beadle, who was moving towards the door; and as the beadle coughed, preparatory to bidding her good-night, bashfully enquired whether – whether he wouldn't take a cup of tea?

Mr Bumble instantaneously turned back his collar again; laid his hat and stick upon a chair; and drew another chair up to the table. As he slowly seated himself, he looked at the lady. She fixed her eyes upon the little teapot. Mr Bumble coughed again, and slightly smiled.

Mrs Corney rose to get another cup and saucer from the closet. As she sat down, her eyes once again encountered those of the gallant beadle; she coloured, and applied herself to the task of making his tea. Again Mr Bumble coughed – louder this time than he had coughed yet.

'Sweet, Mr Bumble?' enquired the matron, taking up the sugar-basin.

'Very sweet, indeed, ma'am,' replied Mr Bumble. He fixed his eyes on Mrs Corney as he said this; and if ever a beadle looked tender, Mr Bumble was that beadle at that moment.

The tea was made, and handed in silence. Mr Bumble, having spread a handkerchief over his knees to prevent the crumbs from sullying the splendour of his shorts, began to eat and drink; varying these amusements, occasionally, by fetching a deep sigh; which, however, had no injurious effect upon his appetite, but, on the contrary, rather seemed to facilitate his operations in the tea and toast department.

'You have a cat, ma'am, I see,' said Mr Bumble, glancing at one who, in the centre of her family, was basking before the fire; 'and kittens too, I declare!'

'I am so fond of them, Mr Bumble, you can't think,'

Mr Bumble and Mrs Corney taking tea

replied the matron. 'They're *so* happy, *so* frolicsome, and *so* cheerful, that they are quite companions for me.'

'Very nice animals, ma'am,' replied Mr Bumble, approvingly; 'so very domestic.'

'Oh, yes!' rejoined the matron with enthusiasm; 'so fond of their home too, that it's quite a pleasure, I'm sure.'

'Mrs Corney, ma'am,' said Mr Bumble, slowly, and marking the time with his teaspoon, 'I mean to say this, ma'am; that any cat, or kitten, that could live with you, ma'am, and *not* be fond of its home, must be a ass, ma'am.'

'Oh, Mr Bumble!' remonstrated Mrs Corney.

'It's of no use disguising facts, ma'am,' said Mr Bumble, slowly flourishing the teaspoon with a kind of amorous dignity which made him doubly impressive; 'I would drown it myself, with pleasure.'

'Then you're a cruel man,' said the matron vivaciously, as she held out her hand for the beadle's cup; 'and a very hard-hearted man besides.'

'Hard-hearted, ma'am?' said Mr Bumble. 'Hard?' Mr Bumble resigned his cup without another word; squeezed Mrs Corney's little finger as she took it; and inflicting two open-handed slaps upon his laced waistcoat, gave a mighty sigh, and hitched his chair a very little morsel farther from the fire.

It was a round table; and as Mrs Corney and Mr Bumble had been sitting opposite each other, with no great space between them, and fronting the fire, it will be seen that Mr Bumble, in receding from the fire, and still keeping at the table, increased the distance between himself and Mrs Corney; which proceeding, some prudent readers will doubtless be disposed to

admire, and to consider an act of great heroism on Mr
Bumble's part: he being in some sort tempted by time,
place, and opportunity, to give utterance to certain
soft nothings, which however well they may become
the lips of the light and thoughtless, do seem immeas-
urably beneath the dignity of judges of the land,
members of parliament, ministers of state, lord
mayors, and other great public functionaries, but
more particularly beneath the stateliness and gravity
of a beadle: who (as is well known) should be the
sternest and most inflexible among them all.

Whatever were Mr Bumble's intentions, however
(and no doubt they were of the best): it unfortunately
happened, as has been twice before remarked, that the
table was a round one; consequently Mr Bumble,
moving his chair by little and little, soon began to
diminish the distance between himself and the matron;
and, continuing to travel round the outer edge of the
circle, brought his chair, in time, close to that in which
the matron was seated. Indeed, the two chairs touched;
and when they did so, Mr Bumble stopped.

Now, if the matron had moved her chair to the right,
she would have been scorched by the fire; and if to the
left, she must have fallen into Mr Bumble's arms; so
(being a discreet matron, and no doubt foreseeing
these consequences at a glance) she remained where
she was, and handed Mr Bumble another cup of tea.

'Hard-hearted, Mrs Corney?' said Mr Bumble,
stirring his tea, and looking up into the matron's face;
'are *you* hard-hearted, Mrs Corney?'

'Dear me!' exclaimed the matron, 'what a very
curious question from a single man. What can you
want to know for, Mr Bumble?'

The beadle drank his tea to the last drop; finished a

piece of toast; whisked the crumbs off his knees; wiped his lips; and deliberately kissed the matron.

'Mr Bumble!' cried that discreet lady in a whisper; for the fright was so great, that she had quite lost her voice, 'Mr Bumble, I shall scream!' Mr Bumble made no reply; but, in a slow and dignified manner, put his arm round the matron's waist.

As the lady had stated her intention of screaming, of course she would have screamed at this additional boldness, but that the exertion was rendered unnecessary by a hasty knocking at the door: which was no sooner heard, than Mr Bumble darted, with much agility, to the wine bottles, and began dusting them with great violence: while the matron sharply demanded who was there. It is worthy of remark, as a curious physical instance of the efficacy of a sudden surprise in counteracting the effects of extreme fear, that her voice had quite recovered all its official asperity.

'If you please, mistress,' said a withered old female pauper, hideously ugly: putting her head in at the door, 'Old Sally is a-going fast.'

'Well, what's that to me?' angrily demanded the matron. 'I can't keep her alive, can I?'

'No, no, mistress,' replied the old woman, 'nobody can; she's far beyond the reach of help. I've seen a many people die; little babes and great strong men; and I know when death's a-coming, well enough. But she's troubled in her mind: and when the fits are not on her – and that's not often, for she is dying very hard – she says she has got something to tell, which you must hear. She'll never die quiet till you come, mistress.'

At this intelligence, the worthy Mrs Corney muttered a variety of invectives against old women

who couldn't even die without purposely annoying
their betters; and, muffling herself in a thick shawl
which she hastily caught up, briefly requested Mr
Bumble to stay till she came back, lest anything
particular should occur. Bidding the messenger walk
fast, and not be all night hobbling up the stairs, she
followed her from the room with a very ill grace,
scolding all the way.

Mr Bumble's conduct on being left to himself was
rather inexplicable. He opened the closet, counted
the teaspoons, weighed the sugar-tongs, closely
inspected a silver milk-pot to ascertain that it was of
the genuine metal, and, having satisfied his curiosity
on these points, put on his cocked-hat corner-wise,
and danced with much gravity four distinct times
round the table. Having gone through this very
extraordinary performance, he took off his cocked-
hat again, and, spreading himself before the fire with
his back towards it, seemed to be mentally engaged in
taking an exact inventory of the furniture.

CHAPTER 24

Treats of a very poor subject. But it is a short one,
and may be found of importance in this history

It was no unfit messenger of death, who had disturbed
the quiet of the matron's room. Her body was bent by
age; her limbs trembled with palsy; her face, distorted
into a mumbling leer, resembled more the grotesque
shaping of some wild pencil, than the work of Nature's
hand.

Alas! How few of Nature's faces are left alone to

gladden us with their beauty! The cares, and sorrows, and hungerings, of the world, change them as they change hearts; and it is only when those passions sleep, and have lost their hold for ever, that the troubled clouds pass off, and leave Heaven's surface clear. It is a common thing for the countenances of the dead, even in that fixed and rigid state, to subside into the long-forgotten expression of sleeping infancy, and settle into the very look of early life; so calm, so peaceful, do they grow again, that those who knew them in their happy childhood, kneel by the coffin's side in awe, and see the Angel even upon earth.

The old crone tottered along the passages, and up the stairs, muttering some indistinct answers to the chidings of her companion; being at length compelled to pause for breath, she gave the light into her hand, and remained behind to follow as she might: while the more nimble superior made her way to the room where the sick woman lay.

It was a bare garret-room, with a dim light burning at the farther end. There was another old woman watching by the bed; the parish apothecary's apprentice was standing by the fire, making a toothpick out of a quill.

'Cold night, Mrs Corney,' said this young gentleman, as the matron entered.

'Very cold, indeed, sir,' replied the mistress, in her most civil tones, and dropping a curtsey as she spoke.

'You should get better coals out of your contractors,' said the apothecary's deputy, breaking a lump on the top of the fire with the rusty poker; 'these are not at all the sort of thing for a cold night.'

'They're the board's choosing, sir,' returned the

matron. 'The least they could do, would be to keep us pretty warm: for our places are hard enough.'

The conversation was here interrupted by a moan from the sick woman.

'Oh!' said the young man, turning his face towards the bed, as if he had previously quite forgotten the patient, 'it's all U.P. there, Mrs Corney.'

'It is, is it, sir?' asked the matron.

'If she lasts a couple of hours, I shall be surprised,' said the apothecary's apprentice, intent upon the tooth-pick's point. 'It's a break-up of the system altogether. Is she dozing, old lady?'

The attendant stooped over the bed, to ascertain; and nodded in the affirmative.

'Then perhaps she'll go off in that way, if you don't make a row,' said the young man. 'Put the light on the floor. She won't see it there.'

The attendant did as she was told: shaking her head meanwhile, to intimate that the woman would not die so easily; having done so, she resumed her seat by the side of the other nurse, who had by this time returned. The mistress, with an expression of impatience, wrapped herself in her shawl, and sat at the foot of the bed.

The apothecary's apprentice, having completed the manufacture of the toothpick, planted himself in front of the fire, and made good use of it for ten minutes or so: when apparently growing rather dull, he wished Mrs Corney joy of her job, and took himself off on tiptoe.

When they had sat in silence for some time, the two old women rose from the bed, and crouching over the fire, held out their withered hands to catch the heat. The flame threw a ghastly lock on their shrivelled faces, and made their ugliness appear terrible, as, in this position, they began to converse in a low voice.

'Did she say any more, Anny dear, while I was gone?' enquired the messenger.

'Not a word,' replied the other. 'She plucked and tore at her arms for a little time; but I held her hands, and she soon dropped off. She hasn't much strength in her, so I easily kept her quiet. I ain't so weak for an old woman, although I am on parish allowance; no, no!'

'Did she drink the hot wine the doctor said she was to have?' demanded the first.

'I tried to get it down,' rejoined the other. 'But her teeth were tight set, and she clenched the mug so hard that it was as much as I could do to get it back again. So I drank it; and it did me good!'

Looking cautiously round, to ascertain that they were not overheard, the two hags cowered nearer to the fire, and chuckled heartily.

'I mind the time,' said the first speaker, 'when she would have done the same, and made rare fun of it afterwards.'

'Ay, that she would,' rejoined the other; 'she had a merry heart. A many, many, beautiful corpses she laid out, as nice and neat as waxwork. My old eyes have seen them – ay, and those old hands touched them too; for I have helped her, scores of times.'

Stretching forth her trembling fingers as she spoke, the old creature shook them exultingly before her face, and fumbling in her pocket, brought out an old time-discoloured tin snuffbox, from which she shook a few grains into the outstretched palm of her companion, and a few more into her own. While they were thus employed, the matron, who had been impatiently watching until the dying woman should awaken from her stupor, joined them by the fire, and sharply asked how long she was to wait.

'Not long, mistress,' replied the second woman, looking up into her face. 'We have none of us long to wait for Death. Patience, patience! He'll be here soon enough for us all.'

'Hold your tongue, you doting idiot!' said the matron, sternly. 'You, Martha, tell me; has she been in this way before?'

'Often,' answered the first woman.

'But will never be again,' added the second one; 'that is, she'll never wake again but once – and mind, mistress, that won't be for long!'

'Long or short,' said the matron, snappishly, 'she won't find me here when she does wake; take care, both of you, how you worry me again for nothing. It's no part of my duty to see all the old women in the house die, and I won't – that's more. Mind that, you impudent old harridans. If you make a fool of me again, I'll soon cure you, I warrant you!'

She was bouncing away, when a cry from the two women, who had turned towards the bed, caused her to look round. The patient had raised herself upright, and was stretching her arms towards them.

'Who's that?' she cried, in a hollow voice.

'Hush, hush!' said one of the women, stooping over her. 'Lie down, lie down!'

'I'll never lie down again alive!' said the woman, struggling. 'I *will* tell her! Come here! Nearer! Let me whisper in your ear.'

She clutched the matron by the arm, and forcing her into a chair by the bedside, was about to speak, when looking round, she caught sight of the two old women bending forward in the attitude of eager listeners.

'Turn them away,' said the woman, drowsily; 'make haste! make haste!'

The two old crones, chiming in together, began pouring out many piteous lamentations that the poor dear was too far gone to know her best friends; and were uttering sundry protestations that they would never leave her, when the superior pushed them from the room, closed the door, and returned to the bed-side. On being excluded, the old ladies changed their tone, and cried through the keyhole that old Sally was drunk; which, indeed, was not unlikely; since, in addition to a moderate dose of opium prescribed by the apothecary, she was labouring under the effects of a final taste of gin-and-water which had been privily administered, in the openness of their hearts, by the worthy old ladies themselves.

'Now listen to me,' said the dying woman aloud, as if making a great effort to revive one latent spark of energy. 'In this very room – in this very bed – I once nursed a pretty young creetur', that was brought into the house with her feet cut and bruised with walking, and all soiled with dust and blood. She gave birth to a boy, and died. Let me think – what was the year again?'

'Never mind the year,' said the impatient auditor; 'what about her?'

'Ay,' murmured the sick woman, relapsing into her former drowsy state, 'what about her? – what about – I know!' she cried, jumping fiercely up: her face flushed, and her eyes starting from her head – 'I robbed her, so I did! She wasn't cold – I tell you she wasn't cold, when I stole it!'